HOME GAME

Waiting for the Next Generation

by USA TODAY bestselling author
GINGER SCOTT

Home Game

The Waiting Series Next Generation

Ginger Scott

Y'all can thank Autumn for this one. She's persistent. As are the voices in my head.

Chapter One

Peyton Johnson

It's pretty much dead inside Jack's tonight. There's the old couple—the Denizens—in the corner booth, and two guys at the end of the counter who just got off from their shift at the prison. And me—the only seventeen-year-old in this town who isn't celebrating the last week of summer—because her mom insists she works a summer job.

"It builds character." She used those exact words. I think they were plucked straight from a parenting book Grammy gave her.

Know what builds character? Being the daughter of a retired NFL quarterback who found his second calling as the new head coach—at my high school. I'm filled to the brim with character. I ooze it. And it's not that I'm against working. I don't take our fortune for granted one bit. I lived through the sacrifices that came with it, like all the times my mom's stoic features cracked into painful shards when my dad was flattened on his back and taken off the field on a cart.

I know more about brain scans than a normal teenager should. I get the risks that come along with competitive sports. I have nightmares about them thanks to the loss of my uncle Trig, whose brain was so badly injured from his years on the gridiron that it started to lie to him.

As hokey as the sentiment sounds, I believe working as a server at Jack's Pancake House does teach me valuable lessons. I just didn't want to have to learn them this summer—*this week*, at the very least.

My phone buzzes by the register with more notifications. I shouldn't look, but the pull to see what everyone else is doing while I'm here is too strong. Social media is the devil, luring people in and twisting their minds with its bag of negative tricks. I wonder how I'll feel when I look this time—jealous or excluded? Perhaps both.

It's a short video of Lexi and Tasha jumping from some jagged rocks into the pooled water at the springs. My mom would hate it. It looks so fun, though. It's still light out in the video, so they're probably catching up on their posts now at the campsite. Half of our senior class is there, baking in the desert sun all day then cooling off in the clear water of the springs. It's a two-hour drive from Jack's. If I left right now, I could maybe make it there in time to join the party before everyone passes out for the night.

Of course, I won't. Because I have to open tomorrow. At least the breakfast shift earns great tips.

I turn my screen off and flip my phone over, avoiding

the other posts begging to taunt me. The soft *ding* sounds over my shoulder, alerting me of a new customer walking through the main door. My hand automatically grabs a couple of menus from underneath the counter as I turn around. The first thing I'm struck by are his dark blue eyes. Not far behind is the chin-length wavy brown hair that he's running his hand through before placing the gray ball cap back on his head. He's wearing a plain white T-shirt and fitted jeans. He's alone, and he's . . . young. As in not a prison worker in his forties or a senior citizen taking advantage of the specials. He's my age, I'm guessing, and I don't recognize him.

His gaze latches on to mine as he approaches and takes the stool directly across the counter from me. I hand him two menus, my brain not quite catching up.

"Welcome to Jack's," I say, my pulse racing more than it should. I'm acting like I've never seen a cute boy before. In my life. Let alone the fact I'm sort of dating a very cute boy right now. Kind of. We might be on a break. Or maybe we're done this time. I don't know what our status is exactly, but I do know that Bryce does not have hair like this guy. And he's shorter. And he's leaving next year. Not that this guy is staying. Or even part of the picture.

Stop it, Peyton!

"Are these . . . different?" He's holding both menus side-by-side, his eyes scanning to compare them. I snag one and return it to the stack behind me.

"No, sorry about that. I'm used to people coming in here in pairs. Would you like some coffee?" I turn over the mug that's placed on the napkin in front of him and reach toward the coffee pot. He stares at the mug and scrunches one side of his face.

"You don't have to say yes, you know."

His features relax, and he lets out a short, breathy laugh.

"Yeah, sorry. No, I hate coffee. I'll take a water." His gaze hits mine again, and it feels like a punch in the heart. There's something familiar in his eyes, though I'm certain we don't know each other.

I fill a glass with ice water and set it in place of the coffee mug, then toss a straw down next to it.

"I have to warn you, it's a paper straw. You have about two minutes to drink before it turns into a spitball."

He chuckles and flicks the wrapped straw toward me before picking up the glass and drinking.

"Need a minute with the menu?" I glance from the stranger toward the kitchen window. It's empty and quiet. Neil, the evening cook, is probably sitting in the back placing online bets on sports. Neil's home for the summer from college and his family owns this place. He's been working at Jack's since it opened my freshman year of high school.

"What's good here . . . Peyton?" I snap back to face my new friend, catching him sitting up high and leaning over the counter to get a clear view of my name badge. I smirk, the pull of flirting hard to resist.

"You like pancakes?" I lean on my elbow on the counter and lift a brow. "It's kind of our thing. I'm not big on fruit, but people say the pineapple ones are really good."

He sucks in his bottom lip, still somehow smiling through it. Not a big smile, though. More of a private one. Like he has a secret. *I'm in trouble.*

His eyes flit up from the menu to meet mine from under his dark lashes.

"What do *you* like?"

I swallow slowly and tuck the inside of my cheek between my teeth for a beat. *I can do this.*

"I'm kind of old school. I like the plain ones with maple syrup and a ton of butter."

He nods and pushes the menu toward me.

"Well, all right, then." He winks.

Who winks? And why do I like it?

"Coming right up," I say as I tap the edge of the menu on the countertop. That is a phrase I have never said. Not once. Ever. And Neil, who was *not* far enough away from the window when I uttered it, is quick to poke fun of me the second I push through the kitchen door.

"And would you like anything . . . *on the side?*" He pretends to fluff his hair as he does an impression of what I think is supposed to be me. I shove the ticket flat against the center of his chest and he coughs out a laugh.

"What? It's cute to see you get all flustered. It's rare to see you off your game," he teases.

"I'm not flustered. Just, he wants pancakes. Shouldn't you—" I flit my hand toward the griddle, but he's still busy laughing at me.

"Is that why you came all the way in here instead of hanging the ticket on the clip and ringing the bell?" He quirks a brow. I flit my hand toward the griddle again, then turn my back to him.

"I came in here because we're out of coffee filters up front," I throw over my shoulder. It's a lie, but Neil doesn't leave the kitchen. He has no idea where the coffee filters are. Hell, he might not even know *what* they are.

I get to the back where the stock of paper supplies is piled neatly in boxes, all labeled. I pat my back pocket in search of my phone so I can text for advice as I sink against the wall of cardboard. *Shit.* I left it by the register. Not that I'd know what to say to my best friends. Or that I really want to scroll through more of their fun while I'm stuck here "building character." But the need for a distraction right this second is making me itchy. Which means . . . I'd probably end up texting Bryce. Comfortable, familiar Bryce.

This is how we always end up back together. He goes away for some quarterback camp or college visit, and the reality of things hits me, so I tell him we should take a break. Sometimes he's the one to suggest it, like this time. He's been gone the entire summer. And I haven't really missed *him*, per se. But I have missed his company.

Maybe I've simply missed company, period.

I have no desire to follow Bryce to college. I don't really care much for any of the places he's looking to play. To be honest, sometimes I feel as though I go out with him to make my dad happy, which is hilarious considering my father wanted to throttle him the first time they met. He sure loves him now, though. The great Reed Johnson has two daughters. I think Bryce is the surrogate son he never had. He definitely plays like my father.

Glancing up, I spot the open box of coffee filters and grab a fresh stack to carry back as my excuse. I don't make eye contact with Neil as I pass by, but I swear I feel him smirking at me.

My new friend's eyes dart up from his phone screen when I enter the dining room, and his mouth ticks up on one side like he overheard me and Neil a minute ago. Maybe I'm projecting. Either way, the heat is taking over my neck and cheeks. I wish I wasn't wearing an apron over this Kelly green polo shirt. I could not possibly be wearing a less flattering color.

"You should check your phone," he says. I glance at him over my shoulder as he points toward the register. "It was buzzing like crazy while you were gone."

I nod with a soft smile.

"Thanks."

I tuck the filters on top of the stack that already exists, then snag my phone to see what excitement I'm missing. There are a dozen more notifications, which I skip because I'm sure they're more posts of my friends having a great time without me. But then there's the missed call from Bryce. My thumb hovers over his name for a second but instead moves to check my voicemail. He didn't leave a message, but why would he? We aren't together. His choice this time. Maybe it was mutual. I don't even know anymore.

The sharp ping of the bell makes me jump a little, so I shove my phone in my back pocket and move to the window where Neil has slid the plate of fresh pancakes. We make eye contact, his smirk still firmly in place, along with a tittering laugh.

"Shut it," I snap, pinching the air at him as if I'm stapling his lips shut with my fingers. If I could, I think I would.

I plate the dish with a carafe of warm syrup and several fresh pats of butter, then deliver the hotcakes along with a set of silverware to my new friend. Or enemy. Or . . .

"So, are you new here?" I blurt out after letting go of his plate.

His gaze hovers on my face for a few seconds as he twists his plate around, the faint smile never having left. I don't think it's dimmed since he walked in.

"Yeah, we just moved in over the weekend—the new development on Canyon Road. We were waiting for the build to get done. It should have been ready three months ago." He drops his attention to his food, soaking the cakes in syrup then dropping slices of butter in various spots. I'm internally amused because it's exactly the way I go at these things when I'm hungry.

"You'll be going to the new school, then, huh?" I lean against the counter again, trying to find the comfort I barely grasped before. He takes a massive bite and nods as he looks up at me.

"Too bad. I can't give you any tips." I shrug and do my best to ignore the sudden drop in serotonin as my stomach tightens. *Yeah, yeah, so I wanted him to go to Coolidge High. It's fine. Whatever. So, fine. Why should I care?*

"All high schools are basically the same, though, aren't they?" he says, quickly stuffing more pancake into his mouth.

We both laugh softly.

"I guess so," I say. Though, I'm not sure my high school experience has ever truly been typical. This place still has a small-town vibe, but growth is swallowing it up. And it's impossible to escape my dad's legacy, especially now. I do my best to focus on my cheer competitions and the stunt team. And when I'm not working, I try to appreciate the real friendships I've made. Lexi and Tasha don't care that my family owns half the land within the town limits, or that my dad is on ESPN every other week. Don't get me wrong, they love the perks that come along with our ranch and our vacations, but it's not why we're friends. Bryce, however? I don't know. I've never felt like it was something real between us. Even when he was trying hard to be every-thing I thought I wanted him to be. The letters, which he hasn't written since last summer, feel forced when I look back on them now.

The chime for the entrance breaks me out of my thoughts, and it takes my mind a few extra seconds to realize it's Bryce walking through the door. My new friend spins his stool halfway around to follow my gaze, probably because my eyes have popped out.

"Fuck, seriously?" he mutters, his voice low but loud enough that I catch his words. My mind swirls a million miles per second trying to make sense of them.

"Hey, you are here!" Bryce steps behind the counter with open arms that I fall into—mostly out of habit, partly out of panic.

"You're home early," I say, inching my palms between us so I can push against his chest enough to break our hold.

"I am," he says, leaning his head to the side, his green eyes all sorts of suspicious. He's so used to me just falling back into our routine. Maybe I'm used to it, too. I scratch nervously at the back of my neck as Bryce pivots his gaze toward my new friend.

"Oh, shit! What are the odds?" Bryce crosses his arms over his chest and takes a half step back, his eyelids heavy and his stare sharp and full of contempt.

I glance at the new guy as he chuckles under his breath for a second before stuffing one last bite in his mouth. Leaning to one side, he pulls his wallet from his pocket and fishes out a twenty that he drops on the counter.

"Peyton," he says with a nod as he gets to his feet. I don't even know his name, so all I can do is suck in my lips and lift my brow. I'm pretty sure I don't want the two of them filling me in on how they know each other. The vibe is chilly enough as it is.

"Good call on the plain ones. Delicious," he says as his eyes meet mine. He makes the chef's kiss gesture then shifts his focus to Bryce. And for the first time since he walked in, his smile drops completely.

I busy myself clearing his plate as he leaves the restaurant.

"You friends with that guy? Or are you—"

I sense that possessive, jealous tone and decide to nip it right out of the gate.

"Stop it, Bryce. He just came in for the first time tonight. He read my name badge. I have no idea who the hell he is." I glance to my left while I wipe down the counter space he just vacated and manage to catch him stepping into an older blue pickup.

"Peyt, that's Wyatt Stone," he laughs, his tone incredulous. *How could I not know all the important quarterbacks in the state by face?*

"Really?" I look back to the window just as the pickup's headlights flicker on and blind my view.

"Uh, yeah. Really," Bryce says, sliding up to sit on the counter. I roll my eyes at him, and he gets down. The managers hate it when he does that. I hate it when he does that.

"Huh, well, he was nice." I give Bryce a shrug as I carry the bin of dirty dishes into the back. I feel the heat of his stare on my back, but thankfully, he doesn't follow me. Neil has moved to the chair by the office and is busy on his phone, *thank God.*

I might not have recognized his face, but yeah . . . Wyatt Stone. I know the name. It's been plastered on my dad's scouting board in his office at school for the last two years. And when he got word that Wyatt's family was moving to Vista High's boundaries last spring, my dad started uttering his name a lot more—at the dinner table, during family vacations, in the car everywhere we went.

So that's Wyatt Stone. The guy getting half of my dad's starting offense thanks to strict district boundaries and a statewide crackdown on illegal recruiting.

Bryce has helped himself to a Coke by the time I return to the counter area, and he's sitting on Wyatt's stool.

"You off soon?" he asks before sipping a drink through his paper straw. It makes a slurping sound that sends unpleasant shivers up my spine.

"Thirty minutes. Why?"

I could probably talk Neil into leaving early, but I'm not interested in spending time with Bryce right now.

"Ah, too bad. I'm heading to the springs. Thought maybe you'd like to come with." He inches his head to one side in invitation. This move usually works. Normally, I'd be waiting for it. Maybe I've grown up.

"Yeah, I wish I could. But I open tomorrow too. So . . ." I lift a palm and shrug, then let my hand drop back to my side.

Bryce lets out a sharp but quiet laugh.

"Okay, then. Well, I guess I'll see you . . . I don't know. Later?" He eyes me as he pulls the straw from his glass, drops it on the counter I just cleaned, then takes a huge gulp of soda before leaving the half-filled glass for me to clear.

"Yeah. I'll see you later," I say, fighting against two years of bad habits and nodding with a smile instead of leaning over the counter to kiss him. He looks . . . shocked. And that makes me feel almost as good as I did when Wyatt winked at me.

Chapter Two

Wyatt Stone

The soothing rumble of my father's old seventy-four Camaro tickles my ears. I smile at the bucket full of suds and wring out the hand towel before lifting my head in time to see my mom scratch the undercarriage on the massive dip in the driveway to the Quick Mart.

I wince.

A heavy elbow plunks down on my shoulder, and the lineman we all call Whiskey because his name is Jack, gargles out a laugh.

"Your mom need anyone to help her learn to drive that thing? Because I'm up for the—" I elbow his ribs before he finishes that last word.

"Dude, that's my dad's old car. Chill," I say with a slight shrug and a look of disgust.

"Fuck. Sorry, man. I was just being clever and shit." His mouth squiggles into a guilty semi-straight line, but I don't let him off the hook. I scowl as I shake my head and leave him to finish washing the massive F-350 that pulled in for our fundraiser.

My mom rolls the window down as I approach, and it sticks about halfway. Dad was supposed to fix that. He was always fixing something. Our eyes meet over the rim of the glass pane and share a fond smirk.

"I know she's not *street-ready,* as your dad would say, but I figured she could use a wash." I nod and guide my mom to move the car into an open spot where some of my teammates are waiting to get moving on the next vehicle. A soppy rag flings soapy water across the hood within seconds and my mom gets out of the car, handing me a small cooler.

"Is this what I hope it is?" A tempered smile tugs up one side of my mouth as I peek inside and see the frozen watermelon balls. "Yes!" I whisper.

"You know, most boys your age would prefer something like hot wings or beer," she says as we walk over to a nearby tree for shade.

"Yeah, well, I'd prefer those too if it weren't a hundred-seventy degrees out with four hours of this fucking car wash left to go," I laugh out. She grimaces at my F-bomb, and I whisper a quick apology before diving into the cool, sweet treat I have loved since I was a kid.

My mom crosses her arms with ease as she steps back and lets a soft smile settle in. I know what her reaction means without her having to voice it. For most of my life, I shared this snack with my dad. After long practices. During road trips. While helping him clean the garage. I'm not sure if it's my favorite because I love the taste or because of the memories that come with it.

"I should probably get back to work." I tip the cooler above my mouth and slurp up the slushy juice left behind before leaving the cooler with my mom. I kiss her cheek and jog back to the main driveway where Whiskey and Jody are now waving their shirts over their heads in an attempt to garner more traffic.

"You trying to repel people?" I tease Whiskey. He swings his twisted T-shirt around his neck and holds on to both ends while grinding his hips in the air. It's vulgar and not even remotely sexy, but it is funny as shit. And somehow, it earns him a honk from an SUV full of girls.

"Yeah! There are my people. Come on, ladies. Get a wash!" He shimmies the now stretched-out shirt along his back as he approaches their vehicle. One of them rolls down the back window and waves a twenty at him, and he leans in so she can kiss his cheek. How he's such a ladies man baffles me.

"Thanks, ladies!" He waves the cash in the air as he marches back toward Jody and me.

"We didn't even have to wash that thing," Jody mumbles to my side.

"Dude oozes charm. I don't get it," I say, high-fiving Whiskey when he reaches us. He beams with pride before announcing he's going on break. *I don't think going on break this early is a thing, but whatever.* He heads to our booster table to deposit the cash, then ducks inside the small store to cool off.

"So, that car. You said it's your dad's?" Jody brings my attention back to him. I nod, then glance to the right, where a dozen guys are towel-drying the Camaro, and my mom is handing over more money than we can probably afford. She knows how important it is to cultivate a leadership image in this community, especially with the booster families. It was always easy when we lived in the city. My dad was a firefighter, which comes with a level of built-in respect. Add to that the fact he volunteered to help coach on his off days, and our family was always held in high regard.

"I'm sorry," Jody says, snapping me out of my haze.

I shake my head and give him a quick, tight smile. I haven't talked about my dad much with any of the guys. I still feel out of place, even though we got to know each other better at camp. And bringing up your dad's sudden cancer diagnosis and rapid decline isn't really team-building material.

"Thanks. I'm good." We nod at each other and turn our attention back to the busy traffic.

For the next hour, Jody and I manage to shmooze another two hundred bucks from idle traffic, people stuck at the nearby stoplight on their way to lunch or a weekend errand. I'm about to tap out for a short break and a water run when I spot a familiar face stopped in a beat-up Jeep about a dozen cars back. She was cute at the diner, but driving around in a bright-red bikini top, her dirty-blonde hair twisted up on her head, and shades resting on her sun-kissed cheeks? Yeah, she's not cute—she's fucking hot.

"Hey, I'll be right back," I say almost dismissively to Jody as I jog down the sidewalk toward her rumbling vehicle. Her pink lips tick up on one side as I approach.

I rest my arms on the edge of her passenger window and glance toward the light to make sure it's still red. I'm relieved that it is.

"You know, I've been thinking about those pancakes all day." I squint as I tilt my head, the sun bright as hell and my cheeks raw from taking in too much of it all morning.

"You should probably eat at a few more places because our pancakes aren't *that* good," she says, the quirk in her lip remaining. It's good to know we're still flirting after that asshole Bryce showed up and ruined the vibe. I got the distinct impression from Peyton's reaction to him that they weren't together, but I wasn't about to jump to conclusions.

"Maybe you should show me what's good," I say, laying it on thicker than I wanted to, but hell, that light will go green any second now.

She laughs and wraps her hands around the top of the steering wheel before stretching her arms straight.

"Maybe," she hums, her mouth pulling into a tight, shy smirk. I want to kiss it.

I grip the edge of the door and lean back, glancing toward my teammates, several of them watching me shoot my shot. I laugh nervously as Jody leans his elbow on Whiskey's thick shoulder and nods toward me. The hot breeze is cooking my skin, my ripped-sleeve T-shirt flapping against my muscles.

"You need a car wash? This thing looks pretty dirty," I say, glancing down at the caked—on mud on the tire rims.

"This thing is *always* dirty," she laughs out.

"It's your lucky day, then," I say, tilting my head in the direction of the mini-mart. "Don't let those guys fool you. They actually do a good job. Plus, I'd personally see that you get the absolute best customer service."

I quirk a brow and hold my bottom lip in my teeth to temper my hopeful grin. She chews at the inside of her mouth, her gaze taking in the ragtag crew over my shoulder before dipping down toward her purse.

"I only have a ten," she says, slightly wincing.

"That's ten bucks more than we have now," I say, patting the window sill. "Come on. I'll direct you in."

I back away before she can change her mind. She shakes her head and laughs but puts her blinker on and slips into the right turn lane as the traffic begins to move. I jog to meet her as she pulls into one of the open spots, but I don't get there in time to help her out of the Jeep. Maybe that's a good thing, because as she hops out in short, tattered jean shorts, her tight stomach bronze from plenty of desert sun, my compression shorts get all kinds of tight and uncomfortable.

A few of the guys hold fists to their mouths as she passes by, and I glare at them with a warning expression. I swear to God, if one of them whistles or says some degrading shit right now, I will pop them in the jaw.

Peyton tugs her leather bag up her shoulder, reaches into it, and pulls out a ten. She pushes her sunglasses up on her head, the pink on her cheeks more pronounced now. Her eyes are golden brown, a new fact I add to the growing mental file I seem to be keeping on her.

"You guys really don't have to do much more than spray the mud off," she says over her hiked shoulder. Maybe she feels bad about only having ten bucks. I wasn't actually kidding, though, when I said ten bucks is ten more than we've got.

"No, we'll do it up right," I say, taking the cash from her and handing it to one of the volunteer moms.

There's an odd pause when the mom takes it from me, and her eyes shift to Peyton for a quick second before she mouths out a drawn-out, "Oh-kay."

My stomach lurches a bit; I don't want Peyton to think we're thumbing our noses at her money. It's not like we haven't had a ton of people only donate five or ten bucks all day. I don't get this lady's reaction. Or the way the guys are still pacing around the Jeep like they're admiring some museum exhibit.

"Take a seat in the shade. We'll get you all set in a few minutes," I say, sighing as I rush over to the hose and turn the spray on full blast.

I start to rinse off the back tires and nod at Jody to get off his ass and help. I'm closest to him and Whiskey so far, so I feel as though I can order them around more than I can the other guys. But seriously, most of them look like lazy fucks right now, standing around and gawking. I get it —Peyton's hot. But we've also got a fucking car wash to run.

After a minute, more of the guys pitch in, and pretty soon, we've gotten all the mud from the undercarriage and rims, and a thick layer of suds is going on the body. I drop the hose and sink my hand into one of the buckets near Whiskey to help scrub the passenger door, and he chuckles at me as he kneels down next to me.

"I can't believe you got her to donate money to our program, dude. You're a fucking legend."

I pull my brow in as I continue to scrub.

"Why? Because she goes to the old campus? I met her the other night, and she seemed pretty cool, so—"

His hand covers the top of mine mid-swipe, halting me. My head swivels until I take in his hung-open mouth and tilted head. I must look really confused because he puffs out a short laugh and moves his fist to his mouth to cover his escalating laughter.

"Holy shit, you . . . bro . . . you don't know?" His voice hushes quickly as he leans in. I'm starting to get really fucking irritated.

I shake my head with widened eyes.

"Know what, *bro*?" I hold his stare for a beat, then lean back on my heels and toss my rag into a nearby bucket.

"Wyatt, that's Peyton Johnson. As in, her dad is *Reed* Johnson. As in, *the man.* And now the most famous high school football coach in America, for the school that is our—"

"Fuuuuuuuuuuck," I breathe out, this time falling to my ass. I rest my palms on my kneecaps and push my hand through my dirty, sweaty hair. I blink a few times before turning my attention to the Jeep, then I pinch the bridge of my nose.

"This is his Jeep, isn't it?" My eyes are squeezed shut, the pounding headache almost instant. And it's not because I'm dehydrated. It's because I'm a dumbass.

"Pretty sure with a plate like QB14EVA, yeah. This is the Jeep," he says.

I let my hand smear down my face as my head falls forward.

"Dude, I *saw* that Jeep in the *Sports Illustrated* story last year," I utter.

"You mean *this* Jeep," he corrects, landing a heavy hand on my back. "And we all saw it."

"That's why everyone was so weird," I breathe, bringing my face out of hiding. I'm covered in dirt, and suds, and car wash stink. My shirt is half-soaked, and my shorts are stuck to my thighs from the puddle I'm sitting in. I hop up to my feet but stay crouched as I hold a palm on my chin.

"I guess we better make this thing look nice," I finally say.

Whiskey coughs out one of his unhealthy-sounding, raspy laughs, then struggles his way to a stand before holding a palm out to help me up. I get to my feet and spot Peyton through the Jeep windows. She's standing alone under the same tree my mom and I were an hour ago looking at her phone, probably posting on social about how she got the pathetic new Vista High quarterback to wash her dad's Jeep for ten bucks.

"You know what? Actually, nah. Let's kill it. We're done

here. Everyone? Drop your rags," I say, holding my hands out as I step back. There are a dozen guys scrubbing around the Jeep, and within seconds, they've all stood up and backed away. I feel their confusion as they glance at one another, and I know this is a moment I need to seize. If I'm going to lead them and earn their respect, I can't fawn over some celebrity quarterback who probably couldn't give a shit about our team. Especially when he's our rival.

So what if his daughter is the hottest girl I've ever seen?

Making my way through the pooled suds on the concrete, I step up to the booster table and shake my head at the volunteer mom, who clearly knew the details I was missing.

"Dude, I made a mistake. I need her ten back."

The woman's mouth curves into a knowing smirk, and she slips the bill from the metal cashier's box and hands it to me.

"You're getting it now, kiddo." She reaches forward and pats my cheek with her other hand. I catch the name on her jersey as I walk around the table—Arenas. She's Jody's mom.

"Hey, so there's been a mistake," I announce while still several paces away from Peyton. My voice is loud enough to get the attention of the few people waiting around for their cars to be finished. Peyton's eyes flash from her phone screen to me, and for a second, I consider backing off because of the way her eyes widen, and her cheeks flush even more. I hold firm, though. I won't be a dick, but I can't start my season off like this.

I hand her ten back to her, and she takes it timidly, her head cocked to the side a smidge.

"We gave it the rinse you asked for. Sorry for the soapy film left on it, but I didn't realize you don't just go to Coolidge. You're the enemy's queen. No hard feelings?"

She holds my stare for a few solid seconds, and it's somehow quiet enough around us that I hear her breathe. The air draws in sharp, and she holds it in her chest while realization shifts her eyes from stunned circles into jaded, resentful slits. She wads up the ten spot in her palm and then throws it at my chest.

"I bet you thought you were better than Bryce, but it turns out . . . you're *just* like him." Her eyes burn into me for about half a second before she brushes past me, her bare shoulder scorching against mine on her way back to her Jeep.

She climbs in with ease, her arm flexing some pretty impressive muscle tone as she swings herself up. The Jeep rumbles to life, and she pivots to look me in the eyes before dropping her sunglasses back down and driving over the concrete barrier along with a half dozen bushes in the median separating the Quick Mart lot from the rest of the shopping center. She roars down the street seconds later.

"Man, fuck that. You're nothing like that pussy Hampton," Whiskey says about Bryce. "You'll prove that in a couple of months, though. And it won't be in their fancy-ass stadium, either. It'll be on *our* shitty turf."

He slaps my back and coughs out a laugh with his joke. The disparity between our two schools is pretty massive.

Sure, Vista's new. Our buildings are nice, the carpet's clean, and the desks are a lot more comfortable than the old ones I was used to at my last school. But the money Reed Johnson has poured into the Coolidge football program is renowned. As is his affection for his senior quarterback, which is *exactly* the reason my mom moved us to the north side of town. Am I better than Bryce Hampton on the field? Yeah, I'm pretty sure I am. But proving that to a coach who is locked in with all sorts of bias is hard, and me and Mom have had enough hard shit for a lifetime.

Clearly, Peyton didn't intend for her words to rile up anyone but me, but within minutes, I already feel the push from the rest of the guys to take the throne for our team. They're with me even more than they were after camp—after I had to go head-to-head with that sheltered little prick Bryce in drill after drill this summer.

I'm also pretty sure Peyton wasn't talking about our football skills with that sharp diss she left behind. And while her mini-speech did me wonders in terms of my QB reputation, it made me feel pretty hollow inside.

It also made me like her a little bit more.

Chapter Three

Peyton

I know I should live for football season. It's part of the family, as in football basically has its own seat at our Thanksgiving table. But honestly? I hate when we get pulled out of the gym from our stunting work so we can whip up some cheesy dance for Friday nights.

When I was a freshman, I was more into the hype of it all. Game night. Practicing on the track while the guys ran through their plays. That was when Bryce was my first crush. My first kiss, first boyfriend. All my firsts. Maybe I've changed—grown faster than he has. Not physically, but emotionally. I'm less enamored with the glory of the game. Perhaps I'm jaded, having grown up with so many stories. My parents are the football fairytale. My dad, a literal football legend. I guess I'm just over it.

"Okay, let's take it from the top one more time," Coach Nelson shouts through her bullhorn before pressing play on her phone's music app. The song pipes through the crackling speakers on the field and our school principal scurries up the bleachers to the press box to see what's wrong with our AV system. *Nothing but the best for Coolidge High.*

My family basically rebuilt this entire stadium—from the sprinklers to the scoreboard. Well, we didn't actually *build* anything. We wrote a check. But still, my grandpa's name is on the field. And as embarrassing as the opulence feels to me sometimes, I do like that my grandpa's name will live on for years out here—at home. *Our* home.

The music cuts out about ten seconds in and our coach groans.

"He has to fix that now? Ugh. Fine, let's break for the day. I'm sure we're fine for the scrimmage game. Bring it in. Peyt? You got this?"

I nod to Coach and usher the squad in.

"Ladies and Jordan!" It's the first year we've had a guy on the squad, and Jordan has been a game changer for our stunts.

Everyone gathers around me and I do my best to psych everyone up for a Friday night game that doesn't matter except in the minds of the local football purists who eat, live, and breathe for their Coolidge Bears.

"Look, we do our jobs out here and they will show up for us when we need them. And I don't mean in the stands at competition, but with their credit cards and spare cash when we need to fund our trip to nationals. So, let's say it loud and proud, guys, and we can tumble inside this weekend. Ready?" I meet my friend Lexi's stare across from me in our tight circle. She nods and counts us down.

"One, two, three—"

"Bear Down!" we all shout.

The whistles from the football team come about a half second later, and some of our younger members blush and giggle. I don't even bother glancing over my shoulder. I know Bryce was the loudest of them all. He wants my attention, for me to melt that he's noticing me. Last year, I melted. And just like that we were back together again. I spent the season right by his side, feeling his ups and downs, especially when our football team was knocked out in the first round of the playoffs thanks to his last-minute interception. I lost myself in him, and I didn't even flinch when he flirted with other girls in front of me. I was used to it. I bought in to the easy excuses—date the most popular guy in southern Arizona and deal with the attention he gets . . . *needs.*

Somehow, I don't find him as attractive as I used to. Sure, he's good looking. But that feeling I once got in my stomach when he smiled at me or slung his arm over my shoulder has morphed into a different kind entirely. I think my mom was right when I talked to her about it. Bryce and I have grown apart. At least, I've grown apart from him. My dad, however, still sees us as together. And that's half my battle—shedding my dad's expectations for who I date. Funny how hard I fought to get him to approve of Bryce in the first place when we were freshmen.

"Hey," Lexi says, bumping her hip into mine. I glance at her and avoid looking anywhere beyond her. "We're thinking of heading into the city for the night. Tasha's mom said she'd get us a suite in Scottsdale so we can maybe go to a salon. You know, do the hair and nails thing before school officially starts. You in?"

I chew at the inside of my cheek. I haven't had a lot of friends' time this summer, so maybe my mom will be on board. I'm almost eighteen; a week shy. She has to trust me at some point.

"Yeah, let me run it by my dad," I say, knowing he'll be the easier one to sell the idea on.

"Awesome. I'll swing by your house to pick you up in an hour. Tasha will make our appointments for the morning." My friend holds out her pinky and we shake, a ritual the three of us have done since first grade. We're inseparable—Lexi, Tasha, and me—and the pinky promise carries a lot of weight. We use it for everything from silent goodbyes to secret promises.

"Hi, Mr. Johnson," Lexi says as her eyes peer over my shoulder. She bats her lashes, an annoying thing she's done to my dad since we started getting into boys in sixth grade. I suppose to many females my dad is handsome. But he's my dad, and Lexi is eighteen. And my parents are so in love it's nauseating. And gross. I don't want to even think beyond that.

"Lex, good to see you. Say hi to your dad for me," he says, careful to use that parental tone he reserves for when he wants to be taken seriously. Or when he wants my friend to stop flirting with him.

"Will do. See you later," Lexi adds, giving one last batt of her lashes before skipping off toward the parking lot.

I shake my head and roll my eyes.

"You need a lift tonight, old man?" I poke my elbow into my dad's side, then turn to lift up on my toes so he can kiss the top of my head.

"I'm not sure when exactly my Jeep became *your* Jeep, but yeah, I'm gonna need a ride home," he says, chuckling.

"Okay, just let me pack this stuff up and we can go." I take our team prop bag from the bench and unzip it wide to stuff in our pompoms and the foldable CHS letters we use for dance routines. I turn to scoop up the few remaining pompoms at my other side and halt when I'm met by a bare-chested Bryce, who kindly picked the stragglers up for me.

"Thanks," I say, trying not to sound annoyed. I hold the bag open and he drops the pompoms inside, then quickly takes the bag straps from my hand. He zips it closed and slings the bag over his arm. I think he assumes he'll be walking me to my car.

"Oh, I got it. Dad and I drove together, so—"

"I thought maybe we could get a bite?" Bryce shrugs, an innocent-looking gesture that I know he's rehearsed. *That* used to work on me too.

"Uh, I . . ."

"I can take the Jeep home. You go on. I'll let your mom know you'll miss dinner," Dad says. I know the two of them didn't plot this together, but it still feels that way. I almost give in, then remember Lexi—my savior.

"Wait, no. I can't!" I grip my dad's wrist before he has a

chance to walk away. His face scrunches up as his eyes draw in.

"I told Lexi and Tasha I would hang out with them. Tasha's mom paid for a hotel suite in the city, and—"

"Whoa, whoa. I'm sorry, but what? No. You are not going to party in the city and shack up in some hotel. Did you run this by your mom yet? Because I'm sure she's not on board." He's shaking his head at me and my shoulders deflate. He wouldn't have cared if I didn't have an alternative set of plans with his ideal match for me.

"Right, I know. I was going to ask Mom when I got home, but it's just that Tasha's mom already paid," I say, having no clue whether that's true or not. "And school starts in a few days. I've spent the summer working and haven't really seen the girls much."

"They're at our house almost every night," my dad responds.

I sigh.

"Yeah, I know. But that's not the same. I come home tired from a long day of work, and all we do is stream some show and fall asleep." I stop to let my dad finish his sudden fit of laughter.

"I'm sorry, but you come home after a hard day's work? You . . . are exhausted?" My dad holds his gut as he laughs out hard, then holds his side as if it's given him a cramp. I cross my arms over my chest and purse my lips.

"Jack's is hard work. Stop making a joke out of it. And I've taken my responsibilities very seriously. Remember? Building character?" I blink a few times and hold my frown firm. My dad stifles his laughter and finally composes himself, clearing his throat enough to utter a short, "Sorry."

"I mean, she did have to serve pancakes to Wyatt Stone," Bryce pipes in.

My stomach instantly tightens. Why? I have no clue. Maybe because of the way Bryce is trying to redirect my conversation with my dad. Or perhaps it's because of the interaction I had with Wyatt yesterday at the car wash. Or possibly it's the fact I have not stopped thinking about the way the ripped T-shirt stuck to his chest and stomach while he washed cars.

My dad's quick stare washes all of those thoughts away. I'm about to be grilled. I can feel it. I shoot an annoyed look Bryce's way, then roll my head back to face my father.

"He came in once for pancakes. I didn't even know who he was. Bryce had to tell me. I swear you both have a crush on the guy, though. Now, I'd like to get home and ask Mom what she thinks about me spending the night with my friends in the city. If you don't mind?" I'm pushing it with the attitude, but I refuse to be bullied into a date I don't want to go on. And now I have leverage. My dad wants to ask me questions about Wyatt—questions I could not possibly answer but that he will ask anyway. Because *he's obsessed!*

"Fine. If your mom agrees you can go. Bryce, you looked great out there today," my dad says, patting my ex-boyfriend on the chest twice to placate his need for constant praise.

"Thanks, Coach. Just doing my job," Bryce says, stepping into my path after my dad's back is turned. His breath is hot against my bare shoulder as his chin lifts and his eyes meet mine. More moves that would have affected me differently a year ago.

"Text me later. Maybe I'll drive up too," he suggests, his eyes lingering on mine, waiting. I hold his stare for a full second before a sharp laugh slips out and my mouth hangs open.

"Yeah, okay."

Bryce backs away with a careful smirk on his face, his tongue caught in his front teeth. It's cute—he's cute. He's also arrogant and annoying. And has zero sense of sarcasm. There's no chance I'm texting him anything.

I get to the Jeep before my father, who gets caught talking with a few of his players on the sideline. I turn the engine on so I can blast the air at my face. This area is an inferno until well into October. I shoot my mom a text to prep her for my request to go into the city with my friends.

ME: *Dad is trying to push me into a date with Bryce tonight. Lexi and Tasha are going into the city. Tasha's mom got a suite. I said I would ask you if I could go. Please, Mom. I'm begging.*

I can tell she sees my message right away, but the dots that indicate she's answering disappear and reappear about a dozen times before my dad gets to the Jeep and ushers me out of the driver's seat so he can drive. My phone vibrates with my mom's response as soon as I climb into the passenger side.

MOM: *You can go. But be responsible. You know that you get attention, and you don't want the wrong kind.*

I sink back into my seat with relief and turn to my dad.

"Mom said yes," I say, holding up my phone screen to face him for proof. My dad shakes his head and blinks rapidly, no doubt shocked that I got her permission. He doesn't know about my conversations with Mom about Bryce, though. At least, I don't think my mom has shared them with him yet. I am certain that's the only reason she's loosening her rules. My mom might be strict, but she is also incredibly sympathetic to the plight of her teenage daughter.

"And she knows it's Tasha?" My dad is throwing out a Hail Mary. Tasha is a lot like my Aunt Sarah, always up for a party, and definitely attracted to the wild side.

I nod, leaving my dad to huff out a short laugh in disbelief. His eyebrows rise as he shakes his head.

"Huh. Didn't see that coming, but okay," he says, shifting the gear into reverse and peeling us backward in the school lot.

I grab the handle as the Jeep jerks forward and the familiar smile inches up my face. My dad flies from the parking lot and crosses the paved road to take to the small stretch of open desert next to campus. I howl with laughter as the tires kick up dust and spit bits of rock in our wake while my dad twists and turns over the rugged land. It's a silly joy ride he's been taking me on since I was a kid, a lot safer than the off-roading he does with Uncle Jason and some of their friends. It's a good thrill though, and he ends it the same way he always does, with a perfectly timed fish-tail that adds dirt to the berm he's been creating on this open land for years. We own it, and I doubt anything will ever be built here as long as my dad can drive this Jeep.

I brush the stray hairs from my face as my dad and I idle amidst brush-covered mounds. We laugh like kids until my dad shifts back into drive and weaves us toward the main road home. He doesn't broach the topic of Wyatt until we're halfway there. But I am ready. I knew it was coming.

"So . . . you know Wyatt."

I laugh at his poor attempt to segue.

"I have to ask, Peyt. I mean, you didn't tell me you met him. Did he slide into your DMs or—"

"Ugh! Dad, no! And don't say things like that. It's . . . creepy. People don't say that anymore." Heat crawls up my neck and into my cheeks. This conversation is going to kill me.

"Hey, I see the memes. I know sliding into DMs is a thing," he argues.

I flatten my palms over my face and growl.

"It's not *really* a thing you say—*except in memes!*" I drop my palms to my lap and glare at him.

He holds up a palm.

"Okay, fine. I get it. So he didn't hit you up on social media. Then, how did you meet?" My dad's hands grip the steering wheel. Of all people for the universe to literally *throw* into my life this week, it had to be Wyatt Stone.

"It's like Bryce said, Dad. He came in for pancakes.

Once. A couple nights ago. He said something about finishing moving into his family's house. I didn't even know who he was until Bryce walked in and told me. That's it."

And really, that is. Of course, then there was the car wash altercation, when apparently Wyatt figured out who *I* was. After which I drove through a median, taking out a lot of nice landscaping just to get away. *Peyton Johnson, always up for a grand exit.* I think I'll leave that part out.

"Okay, so they moved in. They have an address, then," my dad says, chewing at the inside of his cheek as he rests his wrists on the top of the steering wheel. It's pretty much a straight shot the rest of the way home.

"I'm afraid so, Dad. Looks like you're going to have to actually beat the amazing Wyatt Stone on the field instead of through bylaws and loopholes in the state's high school athletic association code."

My tone is a bit snarky, but it's warranted. My dad has been cooking up ways to not have to deal with Wyatt ever since the new boundaries were drawn. He wore his welcome out with the state office by trying to keep his offense intact. Honestly? I think they might have grandfathered a lot of the guys in on our team if my dad weren't so damn hot-headed about insisting they do it.

"Oh, trust me, Peyt. We're ready for him. The passes your boy Bryce was dealing today are hands down the best in the state. Maybe the Southwest region. Kid has a cannon." My dad beams with pride.

"He's not my boy, Dad."

He blows out and flaps his lips, waving his hand.

"Whatever. You know what I mean. I can't keep up with you guys. One day you want to follow Bryce to college, the next you don't even want to have dinner with him. So much drama."

I cringe at the *drama* word.

"It's not drama, Dad. We broke up when he went to camp, and I'm kinda over it all." I shrug when my dad glances my way.

"Over Bryce? Ha! Nah. I give it two weeks."

"Gah!" I groan, immediately turning my attention to the view out my passenger window. Resting my elbow on the ledge, I pinch the bridge of my nose and wonder if my dad was this relentless with my mom when they were in high school. I know they broke up a few times. And I know it was basically always my dad's fault. But my dad? He owned it all. Every fuckup he ever made. And that's the difference between him and Bryce. My dad grew up. He evolved. Bryce . . . he is stuck in patterns.

Our wheels hit the driveway just as the sun is starting to set. My friends will be here any minute, and I really want to get a shower in before we leave. I grab my gym bag from the Jeep and race into the mudroom where I kick off my shoes and toss my bag on the laundry counter. I'm almost free and clear, stopping to give my mom a kiss on the cheek before mouthing a silent thank you to her, when my dad hits me with one more question.

"So, this Wyatt kid . . ." he starts. My eyes shut and I hold my breath for a beat.

"What about him?" I brace myself for my dad to

butcher another thing from my generation. I open my eyes to catch my mom's puzzled brow. I didn't mention any of the Wyatt stuff to her because there wasn't anything to it. Until . . . right . . . now.

"What's he look like? I mean, in real life." My eyes scan the expanse of our kitchen as my lips part in search of words.

"I have no idea, Dad. He looks like your basic eighteen-year-old guy who throws a football." I shift my gaze to my dad's and hold my open-eyed glare on his.

"Peyt. Throw me a bone. I need every inch I can get this season. Is he big? Is he as tall as they report in the stat book? How does he stack up against Bryce? Come on, kiddo. You know how this works. Give me the rundown." My dad slides into a stool next to my mom, who is now amused as well as slightly confused.

I take a deep breath and let my shoulders drop on my exhale.

"Fine. He's tall. Definitely taller than Bryce. Not as bulky. He was in jeans so it's hard to say for sure, but he seems pretty solid head to toe. His arms looked strong. He has those forearm veins like you. And he held his fork like a caveman when he ate his pancakes. That's all I've got."

My lips tingle while I maintain my dad's stare. I win the bluff, though, and am dismissed to rush up the stairs and into the safety of my bathroom. I pull the tie and pins from my hair while my mind mentally flashes through visions of Wyatt Stone standing in this room with me. I focus on my own eyes in my reflection, slowly peeling away pieces of clothing and imagining that it's Wyatt's fingertips grazing my bare shoulder instead of my own. And when I finally step under the stream of hot water, I drown myself in all the other features I've somehow memorized about Wyatt Stone's body, his face, his eyes, his hair.

His voice.

I shut my eyes and look up to let the water pound my face. I shouldn't indulge. And I'm sure I'm remembering him better than he really is. He's definitely an asshole. But if Wyatt Stone is going to be the star of every single one of my dad's nightmares this season, what's wrong with letting him make an appearance or two in my dreams?

Chapter Four

Wyatt

I'm not sure how long I've been standing outside the firehouse staring at my dad's name, but it's been long enough for the tip of my nose to feel the burn of the bright afternoon sun.

"Wyatt! Hey, good to see you," the burly man with the full-gray handlebar mustache says to my right. I shake out of my daze and hold out an arm to give Jeff a sideways hug.

"Hey, old man," I tease as I give him a squeeze. Jeff was my dad's captain. They'd been riding the same truck for seventeen years and were on track to retire together.

He shifts his gaze to the wall where my dad's name, Todd Stone, is carved into a thick piece of copper. This firehouse was named after him three months ago. The gesture means a lot, but my heart aches every time I read the epitaph. It's a somber poem about brotherhood and trust.

"He would have preferred a knock-knock joke," Jeff says, and my shoulders shake with quiet laughter.

"Maybe I'll run for mayor one day so I can get it changed," I say.

"Kid, you get to be mayor, I hope to hell you focus on our pensions rather than dad jokes," he coughs out.

I smirk and nod, agreeing to a deal I likely will never be in a position to fulfill. I've learned a lot about public safety pensions over the last six months, mostly about how hard it is to prove a correlation between job duties and a lung cancer diagnosis. Those details matter when it comes to spousal benefits. We've managed all right, though, thanks to the guys in this house. The fundraisers covered the medical deductibles, and the extra funds made it easier to eat the loss on my dad's truck, which we sold, and the move to Coolidge from the Valley. Cost of living was on par with playing time when it came to reasons for us to make this move. It was down to three rural towns, and Coolidge was the first one where Mom landed a job offer. She started last week with the municipal water department. I wonder if everyone will be as welcoming when they find out that their town water bill is processed by Theresa Stone?

"Hey! Baby Stone! What are we buying, and how much do you need?" Alan, the guy who was promoted to Engineer in my dad's place, pushes the foot rest in on his lounge chair, propelling him to stand. I can tell he feels guilty for taking my dad's position. He's always the first to donate to my football fundraisers, and he made the biggest contribution to our online fund before the move. He doesn't have the means to be so generous. He has three young boys at home. But I know it puts his mind at ease to do it.

"Let's see," I say, pulling out my phone and checking the latest spreadsheet of numbers Coach texted the team. "We basically earned enough to cover snacks for one road trip with that car wash, so I need to sell . . ." I pull the stack of restaurant gift cards from my back pocket and snap the rubber band against them. "All of them."

I'm actually not exaggerating. I have sixty of them, and at forty bucks apiece that would just about cover our road trip needs for the season.

"I don't think I can swing that, but put me down for ten. I'll give them out as gifts for the holidays," Alan says, fishing out two hundreds and a lot of twenties from his wallet. He prepared for this, and I feel guilty taking so much from him.

"You sure? I was expecting to sell maybe five today," I say, wincing as I clutch the stack of cards in my palm. I'm hesitant to go through with this.

"Screw that! Give me my cards, and you assholes better act surprised when you get these in your stockings for Christmas!" Alan jokes. The rest of the guys join in with his laughter, and my shoulders ease back down to their natural position.

"Shit, man. Guess I'm gonna need to buy one to give to Alan, then," Shane pipes in from the kitchen. He has a towel slung over one shoulder and a splash of marinara on the center of his shirt. He's lucky he's at this station. Some of the other captains take dress code rules extremely seriously. Jeff has always given the guy who volunteers to cook for the day some slack. That guy used to be my dad.

"Thanks, Shane," I say, slipping a card from the stack to hand to him.

He pockets it and nods toward the sleep quarters.

"My wallet's on the bunk in three. Grab the cash."

I nod as I finish my business with Alan, counting out his cards and marking the numbers on the small paper Coach gave us to keep track. I didn't expect the guys to give this much. I'm a little overwhelmed by it.

I head down the corridor at the back of the station to the sleep quarters for the crew. It's the first time I've walked this hallway since I came with my uncle and gathered my dad's things from his locker. Dad didn't keep much here— the basic necessities like shampoo and toothpaste, along with a few pictures of me and Mom. But his locker was covered top to bottom in news clippings about me. Our trip to state. My record-setting sophomore season. The national rank list that projected me at sixteen overall this season.

"He was so proud of you, you know that?" Jeff's soft voice breaks the careful balance I've been maintaining, and the tear I've been fighting to keep inside finally slips down my cheek. I dash it away with the back of my hand and breathe out a quick laugh.

"Yeah. Wish he could have seen this year," I choke out, coughing in a sad male attempt to mask how I really feel. I know I don't have to, and these guys are like family. But it's one of those things my dad was better at that than me—vulnerability. I missed the opportunity to learn from him.

Jeff steps around me and dips into Shane's room to grab the cash I was sent for. He folds the two twenties but holds up a finger before handing them to me.

"How many left?" he asks.

My head falls to one side, and I suck in my top lip.

"Don't pull that shit with me. We both know I'm gonna get my way, so cough it up. How many left?"

My chest tightens, my dad's voice echoing in my head. *Be gracious, and let good people be good.*

I pinch the bridge of my nose and squeeze my eyes shut as I work through the math in my head. It feels like pity. And on some level, it is. *Jeff is like family.*

"I have nineteen on me. Another stack of thirty at home." I hold my breath, not sure if I want him to balk at the amount or call it good.

Jeff pulls a fat roll of cash from his pocket, a stash he clearly had ready and planned to send me home with no matter what. He doesn't have any kids, and he and his wife have their house paid off.

"Jeff, I don't think I can—"

He plops the wad in my palm, then closes my fingers around it.

"You can and you will. Keep that second stack at home and use them to take your mom out for dinner from time to time, okay?" He winks at me and keeps my hand enclosed in both of his.

"Yes, sir," I relent.

The mix of relief and shame is making me drunk. And I'm sure my expression looks sick enough to discourage Jeff from giving me a hug. He opts for a heavy hand on my shoulder.

I stick around the firehouse for about an hour, long enough to stuff my face with one of Shane's stuffed bell peppers. I'm supposed to meet Whiskey at this BBQ place called The Pit, about halfway between the city and home, but I'd rather not indulge in whatever it is he expects us to get away with. He has a fake ID, and I guess they're pretty loose about rules out there. I'm not looking to give the state a reason to revoke my transfer variance, or force me to sit out the first five games, either.

When I reach the service station near the freeway entrance, I shoot Whiskey a quick text and let him know I'm not going to make it. We don't know each other super well yet, just from summer practices and some seven-on-seven games. I hope he's not the kind of guy who's going to badger me into coming. When he simply sends back a thumbs up, I let out the full breath I've been holding, and the tension in my chest eases.

I step out of my truck and swipe my card at the pump while a group of girls break into laughter on the other side, just out of my view. I smirk to myself and try to listen in on their conversation.

"So, you two are really done now? You aren't going to do that thing where you pretend to ignore each other for the first week of school, then the next thing we know, you're making out at the bonfire?" The girl's question lingers for a second without an answer.

"You roll your eyes now, but that's been the story of you two for the past three years," the girl adds.

I lean against my truck bed and push the nozzle into the tank, my curiosity growing.

"Why are you so interested, Lexi? Is it because *you* want to take your shot with him?" another female voice says.

"Uh, no! I think I had enough of the Bryce Hampton soap opera living vicariously through our friend," the original girl says. My ears prick.

No fucking way.

"More like nightmare," the second girl says, and they all laugh.

My gut says that third person, the one yet to speak but whose white skirt I can see blowing in the wind through the small space between the gas pump and the advertisement for $8.99 12-packs of shitty beer, is Peyton.

My eyes scan for a better view, but without fully moving to the back of my truck, I don't have a clear shot. I spot a squeegee and water bucket a few steps away, so I snag them and make my way to the front of my truck. The view from here isn't much better, but as I run the wiper across my windshield, the other side of the pump clicks, and the girl in the skirt slides off the back of the car and skips toward the vehicle's gas tank. I abandon my window, leaving it streaked with soapy water, and toss the bucket to the side as I rush to my side of the pump. Our eyes meet instantly, about a half second before the water bucket I threw rolls around a concrete pillar and splashes dirty water onto Peyton's white shoes.

"Seriously?" she bites out as her gaze drops to her feet.

I put the nozzle away and peek around the pump, my chest tight with guilt and maybe a touch of panic. I'm outnumbered here—I clearly didn't think through the one of me and three Team-Peytons.

"Yeah. Sorry about that," I say, letting my brow sink as my hands drop into my pockets.

"I literally just bought these," she says, lifting her right foot and pulling the now muddied shoe from her foot. Her ankle is wrapped in a thin pink string, one of those friendship bracelet things, I'm sure. She rips her no-show sock off too, and tosses it in the direction of the trash can. I stop myself before making a joke about littering, instead stepping over the gas hose still linking their car with the pump, and picking up her discarded sock. It's sopping wet.

Shit.

I throw it in the trash and turn around in time to catch her cursing under her breath as she pulls her left shoe from her foot. I catch the second sock—which she threw at me —against my chest.

"That's fair," I say with a chuckle.

"Uh, you think?" Peyton's gaze snaps to mine with her words, a bit of fire in her eyes.

My low, nervous laugh lingers as my gaze drifts to her friends, who are both obviously holding back laughter as one covers her mouth with a closed fist and the other hides behind the thirty-two-ounce soft drink clutched in both hands.

"Peyton, who's your friend?" the one behind the giant cup says. The girl's eyes dim, her lashes heavy and unusually long, and I feel a little bit like prey under her scrutiny.

"He's nobody. Literally," Peyton throws back.

"Wow." My eyes widen with shock. I wasn't expecting her to be that blunt, and mean. I guess I started this. And it's not exactly *her* fault that her school's football team is bathed in gold.

Determined not to let her get at me, I move to the open driver's door, where the first girl I heard is leaning with her elbows resting on the opening. I hold out my hand, and she slides her palm against mine as she blows a bubble. It snaps, and I'm hit with a watermelon scent.

"I'm Wyatt. Nice to meet you," I say.

"Tasha," she says with a quick nod toward her friend.

I glance across the roof of the car where the long-lashed huntress still has me in her sights.

"Lexi. Single," she says, and even reading her signals, I'm still surprised by her boldness.

"You can do better than this guy, Lex. What he's not telling you is his last name," Peyton pipes in. I drop Tasha's hand and sink my hands back into my pockets as I face my new nemesis.

"This is Wyatt Stone. He's the quarterback at Vista," Peyton reveals.

"Damn! Wyatt Stone, you are fine!" Tasha says, dropping her chin to her throat as she peers through her lashes, which are not quite as long as Lexi's but are dusted with gold.

"Yeah, but I heard he's a cheater. Didn't you pull some strings to avoid transfer rules or something?" Lexi seems to know a surprising amount about transfer protocol. A quick glance inside their car reveals why. A blue and gold cheer bow hangs from the rearview mirror. *Of course they're cheerleaders.*

"We submitted my transfer request the same way anyone else would." I shrug but don't offer more. I know I got special consideration due to my circumstances, but I'm not in the mood to talk about our tight finances now that my mom's a widow. Not with them, anyhow.

"You all headed to a party or something?" I glance down and to the left, noting the gold heels Tasha is wearing with her white shorts and black tank top. They're all hot. I've counted at least half a dozen guys ogling them as they wandered from their vehicles into the gas station while we've been out here chatting. But there's something about Peyton that has an extra pull on me. She's curvier, and she seems kind of free-spirited. Her makeup is done up the same as the other girls, but her hair is down in wild waves, and she seems perfectly fine standing barefoot in a parking lot while her canvas shoes dangle from her fingers. Her nails are painted blue with yellow tips, probably for her school's first day and spirit week. The cheerleaders did that at my old school, too. Kiera, the girl I dated my junior year, always painted my number on her thumbnails. It was sweet, even though

Kiera wasn't. She moved on quick when the season ended.

"We're heading back to the resort to spend some quality time in the hot tub. Too bad you can't come with," Lexi says, winking. She slips into the passenger seat, and I turn my attention to my other side, where Peyton is tightening the gas cap, her shoes now tied at the laces and slung over her shoulder. She doesn't seem bothered at all that dirt is getting on the white sleeves of her dress.

"Resort, huh? Sounds fancy." My tone is purposely acidic, but when her brown eyes zip to mine, I'm hit with a twinge of guilt.

Her lips part, and I think she's about to speak, but then they snap shut. She dismisses me with an eye roll and opens the back door.

Fifteen minutes ago, all I wanted to do was get home and flop into my bed while I played my dad's favorite songs on my phone. But now, fuck it. I'm up for a dip.

"I could go for some hot tubbing. I've got shorts in the truck," I say, my head ticking toward my ride just a hint.

Peyton's eyes flash wide, but only for a blip. She bites the tip of her tongue, a faint smirk teasing one side of her mouth.

"You coming?" Lexi says from inside the car. She's leaned into the back seat, over the console.

"Depends," I say, still holding Peyton's stare. "Am I invited?"

Lexi says yes right away, but that's not the invitation I'm interested in. And Peyton isn't so keen on letting me off the hook. She shifts her head, her gaze glued to me, even as it turns into side-eyes.

"Sure. You can come . . . if you want," she finally relents, her lashes batting once in slow motion before she slips into the back seat and closes the door with enough muscle for it to *almost* count as a slam. I feel drunk from her final glance, the mental picture of her tongue grazing her bottom lip right before she spoke. That was so intentional. And so effective. I'm not sure the shorts in my cab are going to be thick enough to hold down my reaction to Peyton, especially in a swim top.

"We're at Canyon West. Say room one-eleven, and the last name Malone," Tasha says through the open driver's window.

I nod as I punch the hotel name into my phone for directions. I was pretty sure I recognized it by the name, but the directions that guide me halfway up one of the nearby mountains clinches it.

When the guys at the gate get a look at my truck, they're going to think I'm there to clean the pool. But that's not what's taking up the real estate in my head right now.

You can come . . . if you want to.

Fucking hell. I just might.

Chapter Five

Peyton

"I don't know when bad-girl Peyton showed up, but I like her." Tasha pats my ass cheek, which this bikini does not cover enough of, as she passes me in our hotel room. I wish I brought a one-piece like Lexi's. Well, not *exactly* like Lexi's. The open cut down to her navel would definitely be a problem for *my girls*.

"I am not a bad girl. And please don't make this into, I don't know, *a thing*." I pull the thin strip of white cloth out of my ass as if somehow that's going to make these bottoms seem modest. I snag my cotton shorts from the bed and slip them on.

"If this isn't a thing, then why are you covering up, *hmm*?" Lexi teases as she clips her hair up on top of her head.

"I just don't want Wyatt getting any ideas." My lie doesn't even fool me, but my friends do a decent job of holding in their snickers.

"Well then, here, take this with you," Tasha says, snatching the heavy terrycloth robe from the hook by the bathroom and tossing it at me. It's heavy and embroidered with the hotel logo. I hold it out with stretched arms and twist my lips.

"I don't want him making fun of me, either, so thanks, but no thanks." I toss the thick robe on my bed.

"Mr. No Big Thing has been sitting down there in the hot tub for the last thirty minutes. If we drag this out any longer, maybe he'll just go home," Tasha says as she grabs the door handle and tugs our room door open. She shoots me a daring gaze, one eye squinting a little more than the other. It's how she calls me on my bullshit. When we were kids, she got me to leap off the roof into the pool with that look. I bruised my heel on the pool floor. Tasha's peer pressure track record isn't great.

"Fine, I guess I'm ready to go," I huff, grabbing my phone and my room keycard so I have a way out if I need one.

Usually, the resort pools are pulsing with music on summer weekends, but college classes started a week ago, which means most of the summer staff and clientele are gone. Left in the wake are high schoolers like us and older couples on getaways. As we approach the hot tub nestled on the far side of the pool deck, Wyatt comes into view, along with an older couple who seem to be really settled in.

"Ugh, I hate sharing," Lexi protests.

Tasha nudges her with her hip as we approach the empty lounge chairs near the hot tub. Lexi has a habit of saying rude things out loud and within earshot. Thankfully, the couple in the hot tub seems to be too rapt by their conversation with Wyatt to have heard my friend. Wyatt, however, isn't. His attention shifts mid-sentence, and the smile on his face that likely matched whatever topic he was discussing with his new friends morphs into a flirtatious smirk that tugs up the right side of his upper lip.

"Ladies," he says, lifting his arms out of the water and stretching them out along the deck. His biceps and shoulders dent in all the right places, his body bronzed, probably from playing shirtless at football camp all summer.

"Who are your new friends?" Tasha says, dropping her phone and towel on a chair, then moving toward the hot tub steps. As revealing as my suit is, Tasha's is ten times so. It's basically a bunch of purple bikini strings with three tiny triangles in—*barely*—strategic places. The older man sitting on the other side of Wyatt definitely notices. He doesn't even mask the gawking as he licks his lips while watching my friend sink into the warm water. But Wyatt's eyes remain on mine. He doesn't even flinch.

"This is Sue and Terry. Am I right? Terry?" Wyatt's question pulls the man's eyes off my friend, yet Wyatt is still looking at me.

"Yeah, you got it, bub," Terry says.

I smirk at Wyatt's new nickname and he rolls his eyes.

"Nice to meet you, Sue and Terry. I'm Tasha, and these are my friends Lexi and—"

"Peyton," Wyatt interjects, taking over saying my name. My skin heats at the way his deep tone seems to stretch out the first syllable. I sit on the edge of one of the lounge chairs and slip off my flip-flops, my towel resting on my lap to hide the goose bumps rushing up my thighs.

"You girls having a little getaway?" Sue asks, moving over to make room for Lexi to sit next to her. Everyone's eyes shift to me, as I'm now the only one not in the hot tub, and now I feel *very* aware of how revealing my swimsuit is.

"Yes," I answer. "We all start school Monday, so this is sort of our last hurrah." I raise my fist to shoulder height for emphasis.

"Gosh, it's good to be young," Sue muses, her gray hair pulled up into a bun on top of her head, her sunglasses nestled against the hair. The pink on her cheeks and pale skin around her eyes leads me to believe she and Terry have been out here all day.

"Oh, I don't know. Being a young man sure comes with its challenges," Terry pipes in. He shifts in the water, moving to the railing along the steps, which he grasps as he climbs out of the water. His shorts drape below his knees, and his hairy belly hangs over the waistband. His chest is as pink as Sue's cheeks, minus a few spots where it appears he smeared some sunscreen.

"Yeah, I hear young white men have it really rough," I let slip out. My eyes widen, and my gaze shifts back to Wyatt in time to see his lips stretch tight to hold in laughter. As much as Lexi puts her foot in her mouth, I'm just as bad. Though, I usually do it intentionally.

"Sure, sure," Terry says, waving his hand at me before

grabbing a towel from the nearby table. He pats his face with the towel, then unfurls it to wrap around his waist. "I get that, believe me. But that's not what I meant."

"What *did* you mean," Tasha says, pulling her legs up to rest her arms atop her knees in the water. This is how my friend group works. Lexi causes accidents. I light matches. And Tasha? She comes along with gasoline.

Terry chuckles as he snags a second towel from the table and moves toward Sue.

"I'm sure Bub here could tell you. What was it you were saying about understanding women?" His amused expression lands on Wyatt as he helps Sue step out of the water, and my attention zips to Wyatt.

"Ha, yeah," Wyatt says through a nervous chuckle. He runs his palm over his face then through his hair, his gaze dancing around all of us before meeting Terry's. "I think I said I *didn't*."

"Yeah, and you never will, bub. You never will," Terry laughs out. Sue nudges him, but he quickly swoops an arm around her and kisses the top of their head. "You kids have fun. And try not to do anything we wouldn't do."

"Have a good night, T," Wyatt says, lifting a palm from the deck. We all look on while the couple flirts their way toward the exit.

I take advantage of the distraction, slipping out of my shorts and moving toward the hot tub's edge. I'm not fast enough to avoid Wyatt's gaze as I drop into the water a step at a time. I feel naked under his stare, his attention tracing the curve of my hip, my stomach, my breasts, and finally, my face.

"So, can I call you Bub?" I ask, snapping him out of his overt dog-in-heat mode. His lip ticks up.

"Depends," he says, a slight quirk in his right brow. For some reason, my upper lip tingles in response.

"They were cute. I hope I have a relationship like that when I'm their age," Lexi says before I can ask Wyatt what *depends* means.

"Same," Tasha echoes.

"How about you?" Wyatt asks, dropping his arms back in the water and shifting so his body is square with mine on opposite sides of the tub.

I blink slowly and chew at the inside of my cheek. My parents *are* literally that couple—or they will be.

I shrug.

"I don't know. Maybe I'm meant to be alone." The notion actually appeals to me on many levels. While my parents have had the fairytale, they've also had the heartbreak. And I'm not sure I want to lose myself in someone the way my mom did when she and my dad first got together. Sure, they found balance as they grew. And my dad would tell you that my mom is really the backbone of their marriage. But as much as she has accomplished, the world still sees her as Reed Johnson's wife.

"That's sad as fuck," Tasha says, splashing water at me.

I sneer and hold up my middle finger.

"No, it's not. It's resilient," Wyatt says.

His quick response, seemingly in my defense, takes me off guard, and my gaze snaps to him.

"Boo to that. It's lonely," Tasha responds.

I shake my head slowly, my eyes on Wyatt's. My lungs open up, and I draw in a deep breath. It feels like he's trying to say so much more through our locked gazes. Or maybe I'm reading into it, looking for signs—signs I don't even want.

"No, it's not lonely. At least, it isn't always." He blinks slowly and moves his focus to my friend as he speaks. A pang tugs at my chest in his attention's absence.

Tasha runs her hand along the bubbling foam in front of her as her lips mash. She's avoiding Wyatt's stare. Tasha doesn't do deep conversations, and I get the sense that there's experience behind what Wyatt is trying to say. Tasha's mom is single. But she dates—*a lot*. And Tasha's dad is not in the picture. Nor has he ever been.

"Drinks?" Her head bops up with the instant change in subject.

"I'd take a water," I answer, knowing that's not the kind of drink she means.

"*Pffft!* Loser," she teases, but winks as she slips out of the water and turns her attention to Wyatt and Lexi.

"Whatever you get," Lexi answers. I'm sure somehow Tasha will come back with beer. She looks a lot like her mom. So much so that she pocketed her mom's driver's license last year and has been using it for a whole host of things my mom would flip her lid over. Drinks at the pool bar fall on the tame side.

"Wyatt?" she asks, now standing behind me.

"I have to drive. So, water. Unless . . ." He turns his head slightly, giving me side eyes.

My gaze narrows as I mentally work through his insinuation.

"No! You are not sleeping here. He'll have a water, too." My tone amuses everyone, but thankfully, after Tasha laughs at my expense, she doesn't push the idea.

It takes about five seconds for the awkward quiet to set in once my bold friend is gone. I'm not sure whether Lexi can feel the extra tension between Wyatt and me or not, but after nearly a minute of silence, she decides to duck out of the hot tub to go find our friend and help.

It's only the two of us in a dozen-person hot tub, yet the quarters feel strangely tight all of a sudden.

"You think they planned that?" Wyatt breaks the quiet.

I shift as I laugh, turning to the side so I can stretch my legs along the bench seat. I shake my head and roll my neck until my eyes rest on his tepid smirk.

"I think planning things would be giving my friends a whole lot of credit," I joke. Truthfully? Tasha may have it in her to scheme and plan, but Lexi is too easily distracted to play matchmaker.

The water stills as the pump cuts off the jets. Wyatt steps into the center of the pool, ripples cascading from his body toward me. He sits where my feet end, and if I were to point my toes, they'd touch his thigh.

"So, is Bryce, like, your boyfriend or whatever?" The

way he makes eye contact with me briefly sends a rush of serotonin down my spine.

"He was. And then he wasn't. And then he was." I roll my neck along with my eyes, and Wyatt breathes out a soft laugh. I think he gets my point.

"And you? Do you have girls stashed all over this Valley that you shack up with at resorts?" I'm fishing, and I'm pretty sure he sees right through it. I don't care. I want to know if this . . . whatever this is we seem to be playing at . . . is a two-person game or a team sport. Wyatt is hot. There's no way he hasn't been with other girls.

His eyes haze a little as he stares into mine, his mouth hinting at a knowing smile. Finally, his head shakes slowly.

"I'm pretty tied up with starting a new school and leading a new team to state. Priorities and shit," he says.

"Mmmm, yeah. Priorities." Fucking football—it's always the priority.

"That's good about Bryce, though," he adds.

My face puzzles.

"That you aren't really dating anymore. He was a real player during camp," Wyatt says, his gaze once again darting to me in short stints, like he's testing my reaction. I'm not surprised by the revelation.

"Sounds about right." I shrug.

"You seem shocked."

My shoulders shake with a tiny laugh.

"Gobsmacked."

"Ha!" Wyatt busts out, his hand forming a quick fist over his mouth as he holds the rest of his laughter at bay.

"He's a good quarterback," I say for some reason, once again shrugging. It's like I'm compelled to make excuses for having been in a relationship with Bryce.

"I'm better," Wyatt says quickly.

My lips instinctively purse as I rest my arm on the deck and tilt my head.

"What? I am. You'll see. And your dad . . . I bet he's seen the tape." His gaze shifts to the surface of the water over my body, and I cross my legs. Thanks to the soft glow of the spa light and the lack of foam, I'm not terribly hidden.

"Volumes of film. I think he has an entire hard drive about you," I tease, though sadly, it may not be much of an exaggeration. Wyatt chuckles, and it doesn't come off as arrogant. There's a modesty to his expression.

"You know . . ." He stops his words and bites the tip of his tongue, his gaze drifting to me as his cheeks dimple with a guilty smirk. He looks away again, and I fear he's going to leave me with more unfinished thoughts. I still don't know what that whole *depends* thing meant about calling him Bub.

"Spill it," I say, stretching my right foot and pressing my toe against his thigh. His focus drops below the water as his hand wraps around my foot. He presses his thumb into my arch, then shifts to face me and takes my foot in both of his hands so he can fully massage it. It's glorious, and I wish I could enjoy it, but I'm too busy staving off the fantasy of his hands roaming up my leg.

"That thing you said about being alone," he begins.

I train my attention on his words even though the devil on my shoulder is whispering naughty thoughts in my ear, thanks to the way his palm presses against my skin. I lift my chin to meet his stare.

"Yeah," I manage to squeak out.

"My dad died at the start of the year, right after the holidays." His confession is so matter-of-fact it's obvious he's made it plenty of times—probably too many times. But despite his emotions remaining in check, his words send a sharp prick to the corners of my eyes. Tears form fast, and I feel instant guilt that he has to see them.

"Sorry," I say, swiping them away.

His mouth forms a soft, lopsided grin, and his hands are still tender on my foot under the water.

"Thanks, but I'm all right. And my mom is a strong woman."

"Resilient," I say, my new understanding sinking in.

"Beyond."

We share a long look, and for once, the quiet between us doesn't feel like torture. The pull is there, though. Wyatt Stone has me so curious. *More* curious. And very confused.

"Two waters for the lame-asses!" Tasha drops the plastic bottles into the hot tub between us, and I jerk my foot out of Wyatt's hands. I don't think she noticed, and the hot tub makes for a nice excuse for my entire body being beet-red.

"I think I'll take mine to go. I should head out," Wyatt says, snagging both bottles and setting mine on the deck. He skips the steps, instead lifting himself to the edge. His workout shorts cling to his thighs, and he tries to wring the water out as best he can. His muscular build—and other things—are still very much on display.

It's a good thing I didn't let him talk me into him spending the night. I'm pretty sure we'd be making out tonight. And I meant what I said about being all right with being alone. At least right now. And certainly not with another fucking quarterback.

"Nice suit," I say, unable to help myself as he runs a towel over his shoulders.

He smirks as he grabs his T-shirt from the nearby table, then slips it over his head.

"Not half as nice as yours," he responds with a wink. He bites his bottom lip, too, and goddamn if my chest isn't completely overwhelmed with thunder.

"Ladies," he continues, holding up his water in thanks to Tasha before strolling away.

Thankfully, Lexi keeps her mouth shut as he leaves. But the moment the sliding glass doors to the hotel lobby shut, both of my besties' glare at me with open mouths.

"We said we wouldn't make this a thing," I warn them, but even I know that this—*tonight*—was very much a thing.

"Fine, sure. Whatever," Tasha says, sinking into the water with her bottle of Canyon Mountain Brew. She rolls her head to her left as she takes a long sip, and her scrutinizing gaze lands on me. "But don't be mad when I transfer to Vista and make him my boyfriend."

I glower at my friend as I splash water at her, which she quickly reciprocates. Our stereotypical squeals of teenage girl laughter echo in the empty space. I plaster my smile wide and will away the nagging jealousy raging in my gut at the thought of Wyatt Stone being with anyone but me.

Chapter Six

Wyatt

I'm not a social media guy.

Sure, I have the apps. And I've got profiles. But every single one of them shows nothing but my highlights and awards. There's nothing social about any of it for me. It's recruiting business.

Yet here I am, staring at a follow request from Peyton Johnson. And yeah, I'm thinking about accepting it. Not so she can poke through my shit, because everything I post is public. But hers isn't. I get why. She's probably endured her fair share of online bullying just for being a famous athlete's daughter. Hell, *I'm* curious about what things look like behind that curtain. I've seen the Johnson Ranch. Getting glimpses of their family room or vacation pics has nothing to do with why I'm considering clicking accept. Fuck if I don't want to look at more pics of her. Maybe a few in that goddamn bikini, too. Forty-eight hours has done very little to erase that visual from my mind. If anything, it's only grown more vivid.

"You're up next, Wyatt!" A heavy hand slaps my upper back, and I shut off my screen before turning to face Jody.

"I'm ready. How was the interview?" I ask.

Jody shrugs, wordless, then starts dressing out for his first class.

It's media day, which means the entire team showed up for the first day of school at five in the morning to get through photos and give interviews to the local press before class starts. A few of the bigger outlets are here, too, because apparently, our new high school is embroiled in an instant rivalry thanks to our cross-town opponent and its famous coach. Plus, a lot of our players wore the other team's colors last season. Whiskey's one of them, and I bet he's getting grilled by reporters. Jody's an outsider, like me. His family lives deep in the desert. His old high school barely had enough to field a team last season, and Jody was worried the program would get cut this year. He's too good to lose out on his senior year.

I grab my helmet and head into the gym, where the photographer is set up. Whiskey is standing off to the side, his arms folded over his massive chest while he rocks back and forth in his size-twelve sneakers. His eyes are intense as he nods to whatever the reporter is asking.

"Wyatt?"

"Huh, yeah. Sorry." I draw my attention away from my teammate and to the photographer.

"Nice to meet you. I'm Cora."

We shake hands.

"You'll be featured in a few places in the program, so if you're up for it, I'd like to try a few different poses so we have a lot to choose from. We'll need something strong for the cover—"

"Oh, no. I'm not the cover," I say, my attention still split between her and whatever Whiskey is saying to the reporter. I can't tell for sure, but I think I heard some talk about Coach Johnson. This season is going to be hard for him.

"But it says here . . ." She flips through a stapled packet until she finds a page with a mockup of the program along with a bulleted list of shots. I lean toward her as she holds it out as proof.

My stomach knots seeing my name so prominent, on top, typed often. It's not that I mind being used to sell ad space or to promote our program. It's that I don't want my teammates to be shafted on credit. And when we're all so new to playing together, at least with *me* at QB, I would really like to start the season with us all on the same pedestal.

"Can we just try some with a few of the guys?" I glance up and meet her anxious expression.

"I mean, I shoot the shots. That's really all they hired me for." Cora shrugs, and I think she's hoping I'll drop this idea. I'm making more work for her, but if it means our boosters have to throw an extra hundred bucks or two her way, I'm willing to wash cars by myself all weekend to make those photos happen.

"Just a few shots. I'll get the players together. I'll handle the pitch to the boosters." She blinks twice, slowly, but caves.

"Whatever. It's all the same to me. But I will need to get the ones of just you to make sure I did my job."

"Deal," I say, grabbing my helmet and getting into place in front of her backdrop.

We run through a few poses, some with me in my helmet, some with it tucked to my side. I do a few tosses of the ball as well, and we finish with a shot of me holding it out in my palm toward her lens. I'm sure the shots make me look tough. My mom will love them. The guys at the station will too. But I can't be the cover. That's the wrong first step. I feel it in my gut.

"Hey, Whisk!" I wave him over before he has a chance to head into the locker room after his interview.

"What's up?" he asks.

"We want to do a group shot or two. I need to get Jody back. And some of the other guys." I pull my phone from my pocket and send a message in our group chat.

"I thought the team photo was before practice?" He glances to the photographer, and her shoulder hikes up.

"Yeah, this isn't that," I explain.

Within minutes, I've managed to gather seven of us for a few group shots, and Cora seems to be getting into it. She spends nearly thirty minutes having us set up tight formations, various poses, and even more individuals for a few of the guys who really get into the whole "growl at the camera" concept.

We finish up just as the first bell rings, so we don't have time to look through more than a few over Cora's shoulder. I'm confident there are multiple winners in the bunch, however.

While most of the guys take off for algebra or English, I hang in the locker room with Whiskey since we both have advanced weight training for our first hour. It's a perk of being a senior, and I was glad to see that the tradition is the same here as it was at my old school. It's sort of a cheat to the system—a way for coaches to get extra time with their team leaders and not have it count as practice.

Whiskey and I dress out for lifting and head through the doors at the back of the gym that lead to the weight room. Coach has been in there most of the morning. I'm sure I could have run my idea by him before I coerced the photographer into shooting my idea, but a lesson from my dad rang in my head the second I thought of it.

Do what's right, and you won't even have to ask for forgiveness.

"You gonna tell me what that was all about?" Whiskey tugs open the weight room door and steps to the side as I pass through.

"Come with me. I'll tell you both at the same time." I lean my head toward the back of the room where Coach is straddling one of the benches and reviewing charts.

Whiskey lets out a low chuckle.

"Why do I feel like I'm being used as a human shield?"

I stop hard and pivot to look him in the eyes.

"Dude, that's literally your job. Lineman. Human

shield." I pat the center of his chest, shoot him a smile, and turn to head to Coach.

"Wyatt, I think I'd take a hundred high school athletes coming at me at once over whatever the hell you're walking me into," he mumbles behind me.

I glance over my shoulder.

"And yet you're still with me."

"Bro, you're my only friend in this place. I ain't got a choice."

I laugh hard. That's not even remotely true. At least half of our line came over from the old school with Whiskey, and I don't think there's a damn human in town who isn't his friend. But I like that he sees me as more than his quarterback. I like that we've moved to *friends*. If anyone in this scenario only has one of those, it's me.

"Gentlemen. You trying to score bonus points for being early?" Coach Watts glances up over the golden rims of his glasses. He might not have the pro pedigree Reed Johnson has, but he's paid his dues in high school football. He's been coaching a small school up north for the last sixteen years, and he's managed to win six state titles with a group of guys who habitually play in a division above their size. My dad would have loved him.

"I wanted to make a proposal about the program, sir."

He blinks at me a few times, his mouth a hard, indiscernible line. After a few seconds, he pulls his glasses off and folds them before setting them on top of the clipboard resting on the bench. He folds his arms over his chest, and a deep grumble emanates from him. Whiskey takes a step back, and I shoot him a glance.

"What?" he whispers.

"Chicken," I utter back.

"Wyatt, do you know how many hours of my life have been spent on this program? With a committee of twelve booster parents? All with *very* different opinions?"

I'm no stranger to the politics and big personalities on a booster club. I know what a pain in the ass every single project is. It's half the reason my mom didn't want to step into the board elections when we came for orientation.

"I do. But this is important," I say.

He blinks at me again, then sighs before rolling his palm out toward me, urging me to continue. I swallow hard.

"We need to have a group shot on the cover. The leaders on the team. Guys from each platoon." I was thoughtful when I sent out the plea for guys to come back for the extra shoot and made sure to ask for a leader from special teams, defense, and offense.

"I agree." His quick response surprises me, and the relief that drops my shoulders is instant. But it's short-lived. "But Don Atkins wants you on the cover. He bought a sponsorship because of it."

Coach's frustrated tone gives me pause, but it's not really *me* he's frustrated with. It's the fact ads and photos are taking up his time.

"I'll talk to Don. Joey's dad, yeah?" I should know this

by now, but there are a lot of new names for me to get down.

Coach nods.

"If you can sell him on the idea, and if I don't have to be involved, like, *at all*—"

"Yes, sir," I say, nodding with a tight smile. I turn to face Whiskey and give him the full toothy grin along with a thumbs up kept close to my chest.

"Hey, one thing," Coach says as we begin to walk away. Whiskey stops with me, and we both turn to face Coach. I lift my brows.

"Why is this important to you?"

I'm not sure if Coach is truly curious or if this is a test. My answer is the same, regardless.

"Because I can't be the only one on the cover. Not when it's the *team* brochure."

His nod is slight, but the approval is obvious. He goes back to his charts, slipping his glasses back on and not glancing up again. Whiskey pulls me into the side of his body with a massive one-armed hug, his other hand busy rubbing my hair from my head.

"You big softy, you," he teases.

I'm pretty sure he's the one looking soft here. Or at least we both are. But it feels good to have won him over completely. A friend.

I'm used to practices kicking my ass. I thrive when facing physical adversity. But Coach Watts takes practices in the high heat of the Arizona desert to an entirely new level. We went hard for two hours straight. Tomorrow we go for three. Then four after that. I'm starting to see why the southern schools are so much tougher when playoffs roll around. The lungs can't help but step up to the task.

Of course, the gallons of water I ingested are probably just as key.

"It's definitely hotter down here," I say as my head falls back against the cold metal of my locker, the bare skin of my back sticking on contact.

"Yeah, somehow the city feels cooler. Always has. You're going to be shocked when you never get winded again, though." Jody slaps his arm across my chest after sinking down on the floor to sit next to me.

My chest is still huffing pretty good, and it's been twenty minutes. I roll my head along the metal, my pads and helmet piled next to me.

"You mean this feeling of death will eventually end?"

"Ha! Yeah, you'll see," Jody laughs out. He draws his legs in to make room for Whiskey to pass. For a big guy, he doesn't seem nearly as wiped out as I am. He doesn't bother sitting before ripping his way out of his pads and practice uniform.

"The fuck? How have you recovered already? We had the same practice out there," I say.

Whiskey's head rears back with his coughed-out laugh.

He slings a towel over his bare shoulder and toes off his cleats.

"Today," he says, bringing one foot up to rip away a soaking sock and then the other.

I widen my eyes and shake my head.

"Uh, yeah. Today." I glance to Jody, hoping he can decipher what Whiskey means. He simply chuckles, then gets to his feet to finish stripping down to shower.

"You know what? I'll show you. Get your ass showered, then come with me." Whiskey grabs a protein bar from his locker and rips it open on his way to the showers.

I linger behind my teammates for a few seconds, mostly because my calf muscles are twitching from sprints. Knowing I can't just sleep here, though, and wait to shower in the morning, I drag myself to the shower after peeling off my pants and leaving a reeking pile of clothes for the equipment manager. That's one perk we get, at least.

After ten minutes of standing under a stream of steaming hot water, I almost feel human again. My muscles feel spent, in a good way. But I'm going to hit the pillow hard tonight.

I talk Jody into going on this excursion with Whiskey and me. On our friend's direction, we follow him from the school lot to the nearby grocery store so we can pile into Jody's car for the rest of the trip. I'm not sure why Whiskey insists we take Jody's compact hatchback that can barely contain our massive bodies, but he's adamant about it, so we go along. However, his reasoning becomes clear when the glow of the Coolidge High lights comes into view like a set of suns against the darkening pink swatches of sky. For such a new facility, there's a comforting vintage quality about those lights.

"I'm not spying, Whisk. We should go," I say as Jody pulls up to the stop sign right before the parking lot entrance.

"Nah, we're not spying. But you should know what you're up against. Just . . . trust me. Turn here, before the lot." He reaches between Jody and me from the back seat and points to a back entrance that appears to lead to the maintenance area.

Jody makes the turn, guiding us around a few temporary buildings and into a space tucked between two dumpsters. We get out and follow Whiskey into a nook between what looks like the gym and maybe the library. He tugs a metal ladder extension down and latches it, then immediately begins scaling his way up.

"Sorry, but how is this not spying?" I whisper shout as he climbs away from me.

All Jody and I get for a response is Whiskey's annoying-ass laughter. After a few seconds, I give in and start my climb, with Jody a few rungs behind me. We get to the flat roof and follow Whiskey to the far corner, crouching about a dozen feet from the edge and basically army crawling the rest of the way.

"Whisk, I'm not so sure about your vocabulary skills, man. Because *this*? It's fucking spying," I growl at him.

He bobs his head side-to-side, still wordless, then nods toward the edge, urging me to look.

I glance to Jody, who is making what I imagine is the same *WTF* face I am. My glare shifts back to Whiskey, lips pursed, and eyes narrowed as I shake my head. I give in anyway and move to the edge, lifting myself enough to peer down at the football field from across the tennis courts. It's basically a sea of bodies, everyone moving non-stop in matching compression pants, shirts, workout shorts, and shoes. It's like the world's biggest Cross Fit studio, from the timed sprints up the bleacher steps to the clapping pushups on the track to the sand pit with massive tractor tires being flipped by one lineman at a time.

"What is this?" Jody asks as he finally slides up next to me.

"Second practice," Whiskey explains.

I sit back on my heels, feeling the soreness in my lower calves. My eyes shift to him, and he shrugs.

"Second. Practice? As in, they had a first practice?"

"Now who's the one with the vocabulary problem?" Whiskey responds.

"They do this for season prep?" I move back to my space and look over the massive team. We took half of them, and there are still so many.

"They do this every day. And on Saturdays. Coach Baker started it around the time Coach Johnson was a senior, and well . . ."

"Coach Johnson kept it up," I mutter.

No wonder Whiskey's in such good shape for a big guy. Until three months ago, he was following this regimen. Shit, he's probably backslid under our current plan. And here I thought it was tough having the occasional two-a-day at my old school.

"We should be doing this," I say, expecting resistance from my teammates. But instead I get two *yeahs*.

"You think we can get some tires like that?" I ask and Jody nods toward the sand pit with a quiet laugh.

"Don't see why not. They came from my uncle."

I scan the grounds, looking for my rival, and find him doing footwork through an obstacle course in the far end zone. As amazing as this facility is, with its huge stands and all-weather track painted in the school's blue and gold, it's the simple stuff happening on the field that will make the difference. It's the respect the guys have for the program—the way they're all bought in. I catch sight of the large figure pacing around the middle of the field, checking in with every platoon and assistant coach, pulling individual players aside.

"Reed looks like he could step right in behind the Arizona O-line and take snaps tomorrow," I admit.

"Ha, yeah. Probably," Whiskey says.

The longer we sit up on that roof, the more resolved I am that starting tomorrow, we're going to be doing double practices, too. And when Coach Watts takes us to four hours, we'll be putting in the extra one all on our own. I think I can get Jody and Whiskey on board, and if the three of us set the tone, it will make it part of the culture.

The blast of music from the speaker anchored closest to us hits me like paddles to the chest, and I fall back on my ass along with Jody. Whiskey, however, finally gets closer to the edge.

"Now, this is what we should be spying on," he says.

I roll my eyes but find myself moving back into position just as the cheer team finishes a tumbling pass across the track. They're dressed in blue leggings and yellow sports bras, matching shoes for practice, and their matching bags all hung on the fence. But there is one that stands out.

Peyton's stronger than the others. Her jumps are twice as high, her extensions perfectly straight. I don't know much about dancing and stunting or whatever this is, but I can tell that for Peyton, this work is serious. She leads, nodding to teammates when they form bases and throw other girls in the air. Peyton isn't the one who flies, but she sure lifts. And dances. Her body moves like a serpent at times, hips undulating as her palms trace her own curves. They're getting to do everything I've been dreaming of since the night we met.

"This music sucks," Jody says, though he sure doesn't seem ready to stop watching.

"It's the worst," I add on. After a few seconds, he and Whiskey laugh. We're all so painfully basic and predictable.

I have a feeling I'm the only one zeroed in on the dirty blonde in the center. I better be. Especially as she drops down on her hands and knees to toss her hair around like some hypnotic weapon. I could literally stand here all day and never get bored. I'd need my own ear pods because this music is truly terrible, but I could handle it. Security detail for Peyton Johnson has a nice ring to it.

I snap out of my own fantasy when I realize the music has stopped, and Peyton's gaze is fixed right on mine. I drop down behind the wall and bury my head under my hands.

"Oh, fuck!"

Whiskey and Jody follow me.

"What? Coach Johnson see us?" Whiskey sounds panicked. I knew this was a bad idea.

"No, but Peyton did," I admit.

"Oh, ha. She won't care. I mean, she might about you, though, since she hates you after the car wash thing." I scowl at him, but he laughs right through my hard stare. He's the reason I'm here in the first place. And he's sort of the reason I snapped at her at the car wash.

"Let's go," Jody says, crawling his way back to the ladder.

Whiskey follows.

But before I join them, I take one more peek over the concrete. Her hands are linked and resting on her head as she walks slowly in my direction. She's not making it obvious, not rushing over here, or calling us out. But she sees me. And she wants me to know it. If I had any doubt of that, she erases that with a simple smirk and a nod. And a goddamn wink.

Chapter Seven

Peyton

Thursday night before the first home game is always a big deal in this house. Even when my dad was playing professionally and not home for it, he always called in for the early September Thursday night "meeting of the genius minds" to talk to Grandpa and a few of the other old-timers who eat, live, and breathe Coolidge football. Now that my dad is actually the coach, though? Those whiteboards and game charts that my grandpa kept around to throw in his two cents—that never went beyond this house—have been elevated to actual foundations for the season.

My mom brings a fresh batch of bacon rolls into the family room and swaps out the new pan for the now-empty one on the coffee table.

"Nolan, you're an angel," Coach Jacobs says, kissing my mom on the cheek. My dad eyes him with that jealous look, and he holds up his hands as he backs away.

"Just appreciating a good woman," he defends. My dad grumbles.

"*Mmm*, yes. I am. And Saturday morning, I expect I'll see you all back here to help me clean up the mess," my mom jokes. Well . . . half-jokes. I think she'd revel in the help. She refuses to hire party planners and help for anything other than the charity. She may love the horse rescue and rehab ranch, along with the neurodivergent therapy program she's built more than my father. It's at least a close second.

"You don't want help tomorrow?" The new special teams coach, Cory Lumis, grabs one of the cocktail napkins from the top of the stack, then glances around a room of suddenly stunned faces.

Everyone exchanges glances while poor Cory stands in the middle of our house with his piping hot bacon roll perched on his napkin-covered fingertips. He spins slowly, his brow arched, probably desperate for someone to clue him in. My grandpa is the first to break the quiet with his signature laughter. He even pulled his oxygen from his nose to really belt it out in all its gravelly glory.

"It's okay, honey. You're new and still sweet. Don't let these guys ruin that about you, but you are going to be pretty busy tomorrow. You know. Friday and all?" My mom pats Cory on the shoulder, then gives it a quick squeeze as she moves to leave the room.

"Dumb-ass!" My dad tosses a pen at Cory from across the room.

"Hey, don't get mad at him for showing you up and being a gentleman," Grandpa piles on.

"*Pfffft*, whatever. I'm a gentleman," my dad defends, catching my mom by the waist before she scurries out of the room. He pulls her onto his lap and tips her back before basically lip-tattooing her in front of us.

"Gross," I protest, slapping my laptop shut and packing up my homework from the dining table.

"Oh, don't pretend you don't love how romantic your parents are," my dad teases. My mom giggles as she pushes up from his lap, taking care to wipe the hint of red lipstick she left behind on his mouth.

I glare at my dad but stop short of rolling my eyes because he's kind of right. I do love how much my parents love each other. But I also remember how hard the last few years of his career were. There were nights when my mom cried because she was tired of being alone. Others when she dreaded the next week's game, praying that my dad made it through without getting knocked out of the game. So, while the romantic gestures are kind of sweet, the heartache along the way makes me wonder if that kind of life is worth it.

"I need to get supplies for the bonfire. I'm taking the Jeep," I announce. My mom has my baby sister on her hip, and Ellie tries to hand me a half-eaten chicken nugget. It's wet, probably from her mouth.

"Oh thanks, El, but I'm full," I say, rubbing my tummy. She persists though, and the threat of crying breaks my resolve. I take the nugget and pretend to eat it—*and love it*—then promptly duck into the kitchen where I can throw it away.

"Drive carefully," my mom warns over her shoulder. Our eyes meet, and I cross my heart to let her know I heard. My mom doesn't love me driving through the desert while the sun is setting. It gets the darkest of darks on the roads to our house, and my parents survived a pretty nasty accident with a distracted driver when they were my age. While I think my mom's worries are overboard, I also respect the reality they're based on.

I grip the keys and snag my CHS hoodie from the counter on my way out the door. It's still a hundred degrees out, but I'm manifesting fall weather. And something about wearing an oversized hoodie makes me feel safe.

The sun is positioned between the jagged tops of the western mountains as I open up the Jeep on the back roads into town. Our city is growing. It's not quite a suburb of Phoenix yet, but the edges are definitely meeting. Still, our main downtown feels special. And our hardware store is still run by one of my grandpa's oldest friends, Cliff Norman, and his wife, Bitsy. I pull into the space right in front of the entrance, the giant windows already painted for the season's home openers. There may be a new school in town, but it's clear where Cliff's allegiance lies amid all this blue and gold.

The bell dings as I push through the door, and Bitsy pops her head up from behind the register.

"Ah, she's here, Cliff!" she shouts toward the back of the store.

"He's expecting me?" I draw in a full breath. Cliff's a talker, so I may be here a while.

"Your grandpa called in a special order. It's a big season, you know." She winks, and my head falls back with a sharp laugh.

"Oh, I know, Bits. Believe me, there's no escaping it for me!" I head toward the back of the store and find Cliff pulling together a few massive boxes of lord knows what.

"I only brought the Jeep, Cliff. Should I have asked for Dad's truck?"

"Oh, no. This stuff isn't yours. Jeep should be fine for the bonfire kit and what your grandpa added on." He climbs a ladder while he's speaking and I move to hold it, not really liking the idea of him scaling this rickety thing back here unobserved.

"Is the kit up there?" I ask.

"No, no. Just getting the last of the clearance down. Bunch of leftover stuff from the years." He snags a long, skinny box and balances it on his shoulder as he moves down. The box begins to teeter before he reaches the ground, so I abandon my ladder post and grab it before it crashes to the floor.

"What is all this?" I say, peeling the already disintegrating box top open. I recognize the yellow posts just as the acrid scent of old plastic tinges my nose. I back up a step and wave it away.

"Yeah, got to let this breathe before that kid comes to pick this stuff up."

That kid?

Oh. Oh no, this is not happening to me again.

I swallow hard.

"You donating this stuff to Vista or something?" His back is to me, so he can't see the way my eyes flutter with hopeless hope.

He lets out a heavy sigh, hands on his hips as he stares down at the pathetic pep rally leftovers he's culled together.

"Yeah, I mean. I can't really give them the shaft and refuse to do business. That's not the kids' fault they live in the wrong end zone." He snickers at his joke and I put a smile on my face.

"Right, *right.*" I step forward again and slide the stacked boxes apart so I can look inside the other two. I recognize two small cans of paint that were our returns at the end of last season. The wrong color. Of course, they aren't really the Vista colors either.

"And they want this stuff?" I set the orange paint can back in the first box and peek inside the third. It's mostly plastic sheets, a few rolls of butcher paper, and two wheels. I lift one and Cliff shrugs, taking it from my hand.

"Kid I talked to said he knows a guy who can make them a gear cart or something. He came by the other day to scope out my stuff, and I pulled together what I could. I guess they don't have a budget for much yet, and you know the district doesn't give any of you all shit."

I nod in agreement about the district, but my cheeks feel heavy with guilt because I know there is a massive order somewhere around here that didn't cost our booster club a penny. My family paid the bill.

"You got room for the wood tonight? Or you sending one of the guys over tomorrow morning?" Cliff asks over his shoulder as he heads through the stock room door.

"You talking to her or me?" Wyatt's voice startles me, even though I knew in my gut this order is for him. He's "the kid." Some kid. He looks like he's ready for the NFL draft today.

"Oh, hey! You're here too. Perfect. I got those donations boxed up for ya. If you hold on, I can help you carry it out. And if you've got room for your wood order, we can load that up, too." Cliff scratches his head, glancing from us to the back room.

"I got it. I've done my share of stock inventory," Wyatt says through a crooked smile. His gaze slips to me for a second, and I suck in my lips, my cheeks suddenly warm.

"How 'bout you, Peyt? Take the wood too?" Cliff asks.

"Oh, uh. *Hmm*." I mentally run through the square footage in the Jeep, and even with the back seat pushed down, I don't think I can haul our lumber for the fire. My dad usually picks it up in the truck anyhow.

"I can take it for you if you want. I've got my pickup," Wyatt says as he hoists the three boxes of random hardware and junk into his arms.

"Sure would like to sleep in tomorrow instead of meeting your dad at my back door, Peyt. You sure don't mind?" Cliff's gaze passes over me and goes right to Wyatt. Not that I have the guts to say no, but it would be nice to have the chance. Perhaps he simply saved me the embarrassment of more stammering.

"Nah, I got it. I'll pull around and make life easy for both of us. I can load your order, too, if you have something." Wyatt's back is to me as he strides through the center aisle of the store with his boxes.

I look back to Cliff, who simply shrugs, then disappears through the back door to gather my s'mores roasting sticks, metal mini-bonfire tubs, fuel, torches, and the large vinyl banner sheets I added to the order on a whim.

Wyatt doesn't even have the right color paint.

Overcome with awkward nervous energy, I scurry down the same aisle as Wyatt and jog to the Jeep, which is parked right next to his pickup. He's feeling for his tailgate latch with his left hand as I step up, so I unlatch it for him.

"Thanks," he huffs out, dropping the boxes into the bed of his truck. He pushes them back then jumps into the back himself, his movement smooth and easy, as if the weight of his body on his bicep is nothing. I maintain focus on the spot where his muscle fills the sleeve of his black T-shirt. He squats to shove the boxes against the back of the cab, and my gaze shifts to his ass. *Could I be any more predictable?*

"Hey, I didn't mean to butt in or whatever. If it's weird, me helping you out, I get it. I was really just trying to make it easy on the manager guy." He shoots me a glance over his shoulder, and I'm pretty sure he catches me staring. I suck in my bottom lip, and Wyatt lets out a deep chuckle. He doesn't say anything about my gawking, thank God, and I back up a few steps to make room for him to jump down.

"My dad usually picks the lumber up in the truck, or he has one of the guys—"

"Like Hampton?"

My head snaps up, and Wyatt bites the tip of his tongue. His mouth forms a faint, bashful smile.

"Sorry, I shouldn't say things like that. Your relationship with him is your business," he says, taking a step toward me.

The ground crunches under the weight of his sneakers. I shove my hands into the front pocket of my hoodie but stand my ground, my legs peppering with goose bumps from the slight breeze, or perhaps it's the company. I'm in my shortest workout shorts, and with the length of my hoodie, it probably looks as if I'm not wearing shorts at all.

"Bryce and I don't have a relationship. I told you. We have a past."

I hold his gaze as he moves another step in my direction. He stops when we're maybe a foot apart and reaches forward with his right hand, tugging my hoodie string.

"You did say that." His voice is soft, low. Pretty fucking sexy. He grabs the other string and twists both around his fingers, gently pulling me toward him. I give in—mostly because I want to—and have to look straight up at him as he towers over me.

"So, what do you say, Miss Johnson. Can I carry your wood for you?" His smirk is so intentional. I'm hit with a minty scent from his gum, and he snaps it against his molars behind his smile.

"Sure, Wyatt. You can carry my wood." I back away

and fish my keys from my pocket as I amble toward the Jeep. "But you're going to have to meet my dad, just so you know. Because he's at the house—with the *entire* coaching staff."

His Adam's apple shifts in his throat.

"That's not a problem," he says, his voice cracking just a little—a tiny betrayal that pleases me.

"Meet you 'round back." I turn my back to him and round the Jeep to the driver's side. We both rev our engines. Wyatt follows me around the storefront to the back loading dock, where Cliff has already switched on the flickering bulb he has dangling above the garage-style door. It's finally getting dark.

"I've got a pretty good dolly if you think that will help, but I'm afraid you're gonna have to handle most of the lifting. I'm not the young lad I used to be," Cliff says through a laugh.

"I think Peyton and I can handle it," Wyatt says, glancing my way.

My eyes widen at first, but then I size up the lumber bundles and do some quick mental math. I'm actually flattered he considers me an equal in strength.

"Yeah, we got it," I say, pushing my sleeves up over my elbows and moving to the opposite side of the first pallet.

"Well, wait a second. Let me at least get you gloves," Cliff says. I don't fight him on the offer because the pallet is pretty rough, and the bundles of lumber are rather jagged.

Cliff comes back with gloves in a flash, and I slip them on before squatting to lift my half in sync with Wyatt. It's a little heavier than I expected it would be, but I maintain my composure. It helps that Wyatt doesn't ask me anything while we carry the wood from the storage space to the back of his truck. I move in next to him, our biceps touching as we both shove the wood deeper into the truck bed.

"Pretty impressive," he acknowledges while I clap the sawdust from my gloves.

"Well, you did scout me at practice the other day, so you must have some idea what I am capable of," I tease. His gaze snaps to mine, and his cheeks dimple with his tight smile. I think he's embarrassed.

"I knew you saw me." He shrugs, trying to play it off, but the fact he trips over his own feet as we make our way to the second pallet gives me a nice little ego boost.

"Yeah, I saw you guys. You know, my dad would lose his mind if he knew you were up there spying," I say, lining up to lift with him. We both squat and get our grip.

"We weren't spying. Whiskey just wanted to show me why he was in such good shape. I gotta admit, your dad's conditioning routine is pretty impressive." He grunts as we lift, and I focus on the way his jaw works as he strains. He's on the heavy end, and this time he is definitely doing the bulk of the lifting.

Once I get my edge on the tailgate, I let him take over. Taking a few steps, I marvel at the way he easily climbs into the truck bed again, then pushes the massive pallets together and off the tailgate enough to close it.

"You know, losing Whiskey was really hard on the

team," I say. What I mean is my dad. Something about that guy had him burrowed into my dad's heart.

"I bet," Wyatt says. I wait for him to lay on another comeback, something like, "He's with a better team now." But that part never comes.

"Don't forget these," Cliff says, jogging out to where Wyatt and I linger between his truck and my Jeep.

He hands me a plastic bag that's wrapped around a flat stack of boxes. I give him a sideways look.

"Am I smuggling cigars to my grandfather again?" I begin to unravel the plastic but maintain a slight scolding expression as I stare at Cliff. He drops his hands into the pockets of his saggy jeans.

"Oh shoot, Peyt. You know I won't buy him any more of those. I'm just as interested in him sticking around as y'all are." My Grandpa Buck snuck a lot of extra smokes after his first heart attack. And he got away with a few more after the first stroke. One batch was delivered by me, but in my defense, I was six and thought it was a box of chocolate. Not that he should be eating that, either.

The bag finally drops with the weight, and I reach in to pull out one of several boxes of sparklers. A sea of memories tickles my upper lip, and I'm smiling before I'm aware of it.

"What is it?" Wyatt scooches in close. Mint again. Warmth.

I hand over one of the boxes.

"Sparklers? You know, the fourth was . . . " He glances

up under his lashes, and his head bobs with his silent counting. "Three months ago?"

"Buck asked me to keep some from the holiday stock." Cliff winks at me, and I can't help but feel this sudden urge to tear up for all sorts of happy reasons. I stave off the full unloading of emotions by giving our old family friend a hug.

"Thanks. It will make my day," I say softly.

"Good," Cliff responds. "Oh, and don't forget your order."

"I got it," Wyatt says, rushing into the storage space before I have a chance to make the move myself. He stacks my boxes and carries them in pairs, loading the back of the Jeep while I tuck the sparkler box back into the bag.

I help Cliff lower the sliding door and turn to find Wyatt waiting by my driver's side door. He opens it and leans against the edge as I near, his eyes glancing down to my bare legs at least twice before I reach him.

"So, are you gonna tell me what the big deal is with those, or not?" He taps on the plastic handle of the bag where it wraps around my finger. I hold my story in for a breath and consider keeping it to myself, but something about Wyatt Stone makes me want to share personal things.

"It's my birthday on Sunday, and ever since I was maybe two or three, my grandpa and I light sparklers and try to spell things in the air while my mom takes slow-exposure photos." I look up from the bag in my hands, half expecting him to look uninterested or to maybe find my tradition lame. But his smile . . . it's soft.

"What's the longest word you captured on film?"

His question sounds genuine, and the way he's now wrapped his arm through the open window of the Jeep, his weight fully resting on the steel, makes me believe he's not just putting on an act to get in my pants.

I blink slowly and hold my tongue behind my teeth as I riffle through the years of fire-writing, as my grandpa calls it. Then it hits me, and I laugh out hard.

"Was it a bad word?" Wyatt teases.

I shake my head.

"No, not like that, at least. My dad was playing for Detroit, and I was a pre-teen and always angry at him for something, and well . . ."

"You didn't," Wyatt says, seeming to have an idea about where my story is going.

I nod.

"I wrote GO COWBOYS." I slap my hands over my face and cringe.

"Ohhhhh, that's . . . Peyton, no!" He lets go of my door and crouches down, his hand covering his eyes. He peeks at me through the spaces in his fingers on one hand while he bites the thumbnail of the other.

"It took two photos to piece it together. I actually spent time on my mom's laptop merging them into one. And I emailed it to him." I cover my face again, laughing at the memory and also feeling a slight burn of shame.

"That's diabolical!"

I nod, curling my fingers until their fists over my mouth.

"I know," I say, my words muffled in my hands.

Wyatt pulls himself up with the edge of my door and hooks his arm back through the window. I move to slide into the driver's seat, and he gently pushes the door shut when my legs are inside. He hovers at the window, his forearm resting on the edge, for a few seconds while I crank the engine and manage to overcome my flushed face. I twist to rest my elbow on the steering wheel and meet his gaze. God, his eyes are perfect. They're basically straight out of a cartoon prince fantasy, down to the almond shape and the light creases at the corners.

"That's a really sweet tradition," he says. His gaze trails the contours of my face.

"Thanks." My voice is just above a whisper.

"Maybe," he starts, stopping with his tongue caught between his teeth. His eyes drop down for a second and he shakes with a short laugh before his gaze comes back up to mine. "Nah, never mind."

He backs away, but his hands grip the window edge. On instinct, I cover his left hand with my palm. His fingers flex under my touch, but I don't pull away.

"Tell me. What were you going to say?" I'm still hanging on to the other night in the hot tub when he said "depends" when I asked if I could use his new-found nickname—Bub.

His attention remains on our stacked hands. I shift my focus to his mouth. The way he wrestles with his smile is like he's trying not to let it get out of hand, to betray his thoughts. Maybe I'm projecting, but there's an electricity between us right now. It practically crackles.

He lets his head fall to one side before his gaze shifts to mine.

"Maybe Sunday you can try writing my name."

His lips fall into a comfortable smile, and I think he intends to draw out this staring contest until I cave under the pressure of looking him straight in the eyes without speaking a word. I'll lose, and I know I will. So I'm the first to blink and look away, taking my hand away too.

"Depends," I say, smirking as I look out toward the purple skyline that's rapidly transforming into a midnight blue.

Wyatt chuckles as he takes a step back.

"Good enough," he says. "I'll follow you."

My entire body thrums with energy, every word we shared bouncing around my mind like a chemical reaction. Like an explosive bomb. It's those last three that carry me home, though.

I'll follow you.

Makes me wonder . . . how far?

Chapter Eight

Wyatt

I drove by this house with my dad once. It was around the time of Reed Johnson's last season. I was obsessed with his story, the fact he came from my state, played for the college I want to go to, and held all these records that I had listed as my own personal goals to beat. It has never been a negative feeling. Opposite, in fact. I looked up to the guy. In my youth, I idolized him.

Right now? The mere idea of him scares the shit out of me.

I pull to a stop just behind Peyton, off to the side of a massive driveway where a basketball hoop is lowered to about six feet, probably so someone can dunk.

"You play?" I gesture to the hoop as I get out of my truck.

Peyton glances toward the backboard and puffs out a short laugh.

"I can't even win HORSE. My dad likes to shoot,

though. A lot of the coaches come over to play." She moves to the back of my truck, but I linger for a moment, picturing the scene of Reed and his staff blowing off steam out here. I miss the way my old coach used to have family events. It wasn't just the coaches at his house; it was all of us. My dad always rolled up with the BBQ. Some firefighter stereotypes are true, and Todd Stone made a mean brisket.

"Can I get a hand with this?" Peyton says, peeking at me from behind the tailgate.

"I figure you can handle it," I tease, forming a bicep curl to my side. Her head falls toward her shoulder as her lips purse.

"Kidding," I say, jogging over to hop into the back to move the load close to the edge.

I have to basically plank behind the wood to get it to budge, my feet planted on the back of my truck bed as I push the base of the pallet with my palms.

"All right, who gets a get-out-of-sprints-free card for helping you haul this home?"

I freeze at the sound of Reed's voice, my face still hidden behind the pile of wood and boxes. I drop my head while my arms flex, part of me hoping that Peyton speaks up and sends her dad away. After a few long, very wordless seconds pass, I know I'm screwed.

"Not one of yours, Coach. And to be honest, I like my sprints," I grunt out as I pop my head up and meet his eyes.

If humans could shoot fire from their pupils, I think it would have happened just now. Reed's stare bores into my face, and I think I hear his jaw crack. I'm almost grateful that I'm in this strained position, pushing this massive weight along my truck bed. At least I have something to do.

I give it a good shove as I grit my teeth and growl, my eyes closing with the exertion. My truck dips and I glance up, expecting to see Peyton joining me. Maybe I was simply hoping.

"Scoot," Reed barks, sweeping his hand toward me. I shift to my right to make room for him, and within seconds, we have everything that needs to be unloaded pushed to the edge.

"I could have done it," I say between breaths. *Why did I utter that? Fuck if I know.* I'd give anything to eat those words before they hit Reed's ears, but since I don't have superpowers—at least, not *that* one—I'm stuck facing the most belittling expression I've ever seen an adult make at me.

"Sure, kid," he says, clapping the dust from his hands as he leaps from my truck. Funny, he kind of hits the ground with the authority of a superhero.

My eyes meet Peyton's, and I convey my best silent plea. *Help.* She chuckles, though, and puts her arm around her dad.

"I had to help him load the truck," she says.

Motherfuck.

"I bet you did, sweetheart," he says, kissing the top of her head as she rises on her toes.

Another man who looks familiar comes jogging

through the front door. A woman who looks a lot like Peyton, only with dark brown hair, hovers in the doorway with a toddler on her hip. She leans against the door jamb like she's getting comfortable. They're all loving this. Their amused smirks are a dead giveaway.

"Ohhhh, wait a second," the new guy says, coming to a hard stop a few feet away from my pickup, his hands raised as though he just walked in on a murder scene.

"Should we be letting this guy on the property?" he says, his eyes darting from me to Reed.

This guy?

All of a sudden, I'm not in a hurry to leap down from my truck bed. At least I'm taller up here.

"Maybe we should ask Peyton that question." Reed's tone isn't exactly welcoming, and the way Peyton's head falls to one side and her eyes slit makes me wonder if they've had a conversation about me.

"You know what?" I suck in my top lip and stare at the void between the three people staring up at me. I shake my head, hands on my hips, and breathe out a short laugh before making direct eye contact with Reed—my one-time idol. Hell, maybe he still is, but things have gotten really weird.

My shoulders rise and fall in a kind of defeat.

"My dad worked in public service, and he had a pretty strict code of ethics he stood behind. Tip your waiter well. Call your mom often. And if you come across a woman who needs a hand, offer." I jump down and pat my hand along the side of the bundle of lumber. "While it was tempting to see if Peyton could make this stuff fit in the back of that artifact on wheels, I'm pretty sure my dad would have kicked my ass for not offering to help. And if my gesture happened to save an old man from having to wake up early on a Friday when it's obvious he's planning on staying out late to watch his favorite football team's opening game, then it seems like it's twice as right to do."

I hold Reed's stare, his eyes hazed, and mouth closed in a tight line. I think a part of him wants to hate me, either because I clearly followed his daughter home or because I'm slinging the ball for his brand new rival.

He nods. Once.

"Hey, Coach Jacobs. Why don't you help him load that in my pickup?" His eyes meet the other man's, and I now understand why I recognize him. He's the Coolidge assistant coach, and he spent a lot of years at former Coach Baker's side. My freshman year, the only time my old school played Coolidge, I saw him having a chat with the refs on the sideline before the game. For the next forty-eight minutes of play, we were nailed with a record-setting twenty-seven holding calls. We lost by a six. Because the touchdown I threw at the last minute for the win was called back. *For holding.*

With four of us working, we have the wood loaded in Reed's truck in less than two minutes. Reed pushes my tailgate up with some zing in his wrist, and his curt smile is obviously him being polite. His gaze moves to his daughter as he leaves us alone *to say our good-byes. His exact words.* I'm pretty sure there was a low growl mixed in there, too.

"Is he still mad that I refused to wash his Jeep or some-thing?" I ask as soon as he's out of earshot. A part of me anticipates him rushing back out of the door, though, because he has super-human hearing.

"Oh, he doesn't know about that. It wasn't your best moment, and I didn't want to do you dirty," she says.

My attention snaps back to her from the still-closed front doorway.

"Do me dirty, huh?" I arch a brow.

"Ugh, not like that," she says, and I instantly regret making an innuendo. Fuck, it's so hard with this girl. I can't read her. She is literally the *last* girl in this town I should be putting my energy into getting to know. But damn, if she ain't got me stuck.

I clear my throat and drop my gaze to the ground with my hands in my pockets.

"I know what you meant," I say, my voice low. "And I'm sorry. I was a dick. But to be fair, you didn't tell me who you were when we met. And I have a new team full of hot-headed teenage boy-men. I needed to earn their respect."

"And they respect you now, do they?" she fires back.

"Ouch."

I glance up at her with wide eyes, acting as if her words cut a little deeper than they did. They grazed for sure. She doesn't say anything to let me off the hook. And the longer the silence extends with her eyes on mine, the more I feel the power tilting completely in her favor. Hell, I may have never had any at all in this dynamic.

"I can't tell if you like me or not, Peyton Johnson."

She blinks a few times, rapidly, as her arms tighten across her chest, her hands half tucked into the sleeves of her hoodie. She shifts her weight, but she doesn't back away. And she doesn't back down.

"I can't either," she finally says.

My lips pucker into an awkward smile, and I bite the inside of my cheek. This time, I definitely feel the sting. I rock back on my feet, hands still tucked in my pockets, and I chuckle at the ground. My shirt sticks to my back, my body still hot from hauling wood around. The moon is cresting over the pitch of her family's rooftop. It's the most Halloween-looking thing, and to be honest, it fits the mood. The landscape lights flick on along her driveway, lighting my path out of this place like a sign from God. Or maybe a signal from her father, who likely sped up the timer or triggered them from whatever window he's spying from.

"Don't forget your sparklers," I say, giving in to my urge to give up for the night.

I hop behind the wheel of my pickup and shut the door, leaning my elbow on the open window and adjusting my side mirror. My truck is old, and every trip I take in it rattles things out of whack. I catch a glimpse of Peyton in the mirror as she walks to the Jeep. It's still halfway caked with mud, and I feel a little guilty about leaving it that way. Not that she or her dad can't run a hose over the thing

"Stupid," I mutter to myself, running my palm over my face and through my hair. I give my scalp a good scratch, then crank my engine. With a little luck, maybe I'll manage to fall asleep at a decent hour. Between the pre-game jitters and, well, whatever the hell I'm doing here, I have a feeling racing thoughts are in store for me until at least one a.m.

Shifting into reverse, I pull back and to the side so I can flip around and head down the world's longest driveway and toward the town's darkest road. I zip past Peyton and the Jeep, but after a few yards, I'm hit with rapid flashes from her high beams in my rearview mirror. I slow to a stop, and I'm not sure if it's my truck's crappy alternator or my nerves vibrating my body. Peyton leaves the headlights on so I shade my eyes and search for her in my side mirror, finally seeing her jogging toward me. She stops just short of my window, panting a little.

"Here," she says, handing me a single sparkler. I take it from her, and it seems we're both careful not to let our fingers touch on the exchange.

"Uh, thanks," I say, holding the thin firework upright in front of me. I admire its length for a few seconds while I rack my brain for what the hell to say next. I shift my gaze to Peyton in time to catch her taking a half-step back as she pushes her hands into her front hoodie pocket. She looks nervous, and it's not a look I've seen on her yet. Not to this extent anyhow. My mouth twitches to curl on the right the longer I look at her.

"I don't *not* like you, Wyatt Stone."

Yeah, it's a full grin now.

I nod slowly, then shift to rest the sparkler in the cupholder on my console. By the time I look back, Peyton's walking away. I let myself watch her form blend into the beams of light for a few seconds, then pull away. Stopping at the end of her driveway, I pull my phone from my pocket and open the follow request she hasn't yet rescinded on my social media. I click accept, then immediately message her.

ME: *Happy early birthday, Peyton.*

I hit send and wait for a few hopeful seconds. I set my phone in the other cupholder and check the pitch-black roadway in both directions for any sign of eighteen-wheelers taking shortcuts to Phoenix. My phone vibrates before I turn right, so I lift it just enough to read her response.

PEYTON: *Good luck tomorrow.*

I stare at those three words for a few long seconds, and eventually, my smirk reappears in full force. She likes me just a little.

Chapter Nine

The season always starts with a blowout. It's purposeful, the game schedule choreographed to up the challenge for the Coolidge Bears a little week by week. Game one? The blowout for confidence.

Poor Mountain Sky High. They shouldn't even be in our division.

The clock is under a minute, and Bryce just ran in a touchdown to up our score to an even seventy.

Seventy.

At what point does this become obnoxious? My gut says anything after forty.

"I'm really getting tired of the leg kicks," Tasha complains as she puts her arm over my shoulder so we can kick along with the fight song, this time seven more times than the last.

"We definitely get to skip leg day," I laugh at her side.

Our kicks last through two and a half rounds of the band playing the fight song, and the clock hits zero somewhere around kick fifty. The stands have cleared, and the players have all pooled in the end zone for the game wrap-up with the coaching staff.

"The dance was good," Lexi says, joining Tasha and me as we pack the poms into the gear bag for Coach.

I shrug. I hate the dances. They aren't challenging, and nobody really watches them besides the booster parents. And there's always a whistle from some creepy guy. There were only two of those tonight—whistles, not creepy guys. At least, I think the whistles came from the same man.

"I can't wait for real practice tomorrow," I groan.

"Ugh, that makes one of us. Practice is throwing a major wet blanket over the party tonight. How am I supposed to get tanked and show up at seven the next morning to do roundoffs?" Tasha zips the gear bag and slings it over her shoulder.

"Maybe, and hear me out, but perhaps you take it easy tonight?" I plan on being the designated driver. I had my fill of getting shit-faced last year. It's how I ended up getting back together with Bryce after the first game. Beer makes me flirtatious, and Bryce is a bad habit.

"Fuck that. I'm getting lit," Tasha says as she marches across the track and through the gate.

"She always shows up." Lexi shrugs next to me, and I nod because she's right. Tasha will be shit for the rest of the day, but somehow she'll muddle through practice. She won't be sharp, though. And I really want us to be sharp this year. It's my captainship. And we have a chance to go to nationals and place, maybe even win. Our stunt team is good. Lexi is good. How she flies and pulls off mid-air splits beats me, but I guess some people say the same thing about my ability to catch and throw her.

It feels good to get out of my uniform. It's the one part of high school cheer I don't love. The uniforms are all about show and very little about practicality. The choker-style neck covered in sequins sometimes makes me feel like gagging. I can't wait for winter when at least we get to switch out for leggings and oversized sweatshirts. Of course, those make tumbling hard. But I have to remember that game nights aren't about practicing and perfecting. They're about the game. About Dad. And Grandpa.

"I'll meet you guys at the Jeep," I say, pushing through the women's locker room door and skipping out to the faculty parking lot right outside the back entrance to my dad's office.

"There she is," my grandpa says, his arms outstretched, his oxygen tank fixed to his electric chair. My mom and I decked it out for the game tonight, complete with a CHS football-themed license plate that reads BUCK#1.

That was his number years ago when he threw the ball on this field. Different grass, different time. But the legend was born then. And when my dad took the spotlight, my grandpa relived his glory years. Sometimes, I'd like my dad to be as excited about my cheer competitions as Grandpa was back then watching him play.

"What did you think of our dance, Grandpa?" I squat down so I can snuggle into his side. He coughs out a laugh.

"I'm with you. More flipping and pyramid-building, less of that clappy dance stuff."

I giggle at his choice of words, but my chest warms with his sentiment. He's heard me gripe about it enough, and while I'm not totally convinced he fully gets competitive cheer, he at least gets me. That's enough.

"Ah, and there he is, the man of the hour," my grandpa says over my shoulder.

I release him and stand, expecting to see my father eating up the praise when I turn around. Instead, I'm hit with Bryce's bare chest as he reaches toward my grandpa to shake hands. His gaze passes mine, and I blink away, but too late not to get caught for a moment.

"Looks like you're inching closer to that passing record. You keep it up with games like tonight, you'll be putting your name on top of my son's on that plaque in there." Grandpa gestures toward the weight room where football achievements are etched in black and gold.

"Ha, maybe. Better me than that asshole over at Vista," Bryce says. He doesn't look at me, but I'm certain he brought up Wyatt for my benefit. To get a reaction. I refuse.

"*Pffft*, he doesn't have talent to throw to. You'll be fine," my grandpa says, and Bryce's head falls back with a heavy laugh.

I'm not sure what's so funny. I know who transferred over there, and while it wasn't our best receivers, Vista still got some top-tier talent. And with Whiskey on the line, they're going to be formidable. In fact, I'm curious just how well Vista did tonight. They had a tough match-up against Phoenix Prep.

Pulling my phone out, I open the scores app as I back away a few steps from prying eyes. It takes me a minute to find Vista on the list, probably because it's their first year and they don't yet have the huge following that we do, but when I open up their box score it looks like Wyatt had a pretty productive night, too. While they didn't beat Phoenix Prep by sixty points, they did win. By ten. And given the reputation of Phoenix Prep, my guess is people are going to start paying attention to the Vista Mustangs.

I don't notice the headline right away. Maybe because I'm not exactly looking for it. But Wyatt's name catches my eye, and when my eyes compute the rest of the words, I swallow hard.

QB WYATT STONE ON TRACK TO BREAK NFL STAR'S HS NUMBERS

My eyes grow wide and I lift my gaze, coming eye-to-eye with Bryce, who seems to be done reliving his best moments from an hour ago. His gaze narrows and his lip ticks up about a second before he walks toward me. I click my phone off and shove it in the hip pocket of my leggings just as he leans into my other side.

"What was that look for?" I'm sure he assumes it was about him. Everything is *always* about him.

"No look. Just checking the time," I lie. My eyes flit to

his T-shirt, which he still grips in his left hand. I nod at it. "You gonna finish getting dressed?"

My mouth forms a crooked line as I glance back at him lazily.

"You know I hate it when the cotton sticks to me after a shower," he says, shaking the dark blue T-shirt out and pushing his arms inside.

"*Hmm*, is that it?" We both know he likes to show off his physique. He's proud of his defined abs and his fairly impressive biceps. And the tattoo across his right pec that reads, for whatever reason, *ride or die.*

"Oh, Peyton. What's with this cold shoulder act?"

"It's not an act, Bryce. My shoulder is, in fact, cold," I explain.

He slings his arm around me, cupping my shoulder with his palm and rubbing vigorously. It feels terrible, and I shirk him off by taking a step to the side.

"I didn't mean literally. I'm in a sweatshirt." I'm well aware of my tone, but he's not bringing out my best qualities. And he deserves the tone he gets.

"This is about Wyatt, isn't it? I heard he stopped by the house."

My gaze darts to his. He swallows hard, and I can't tell if it's from jealousy or rage. Are those emotions really that different?

"Who told you that?" I doubt my dad brought it up. He seems happy to erase it from mental existence. He didn't even bring it up at breakfast this morning.

"I have my sources." Bryce shrugs, dropping his hands in his pockets. Good, now he can keep them off me.

"Coach Jacobs," I guess.

Bryce's lips purse and his shoulders twitch slightly. I guessed right.

"I borrowed his truck to pick up the lumber." I simplify the situation a little—okay, a lot—but I really don't want to get into this with Bryce.

Thankfully, my dad comes out, so Bryce can redirect all of his affection where it belongs. I never really thought Bryce was into me simply to get close to my dad, but I do think he has a lot more respect for my father than he ever did me.

I let Bryce get his fix for a few minutes, then butt my way in so I can congratulate my dad and indulge the speech —the same one I get every time I go out to the desert on Friday nights.

"Seventy was a bit much, don't you think?" I tease as he hugs me to his side.

"It's never enough. I told you—"

"I know, you once came back from a forty-point deficit in a single quarter, so what's to stop someone else from doing it," I mimic, doing my best impression of my dad's glory days voice.

He rolls his head, then pokes my nose with the tip of his finger. I squeeze him tighter and look up with a crooked grin.

"Good win, though. Even if it was a bully move."

"Ha! Like you wouldn't keep your foot on the neck of

that Tucson cheer team if you had them beat." He cocks his head a tick, and I roll my eyes.

"Cheer doesn't quite work that way, but I get your point. You leave it all out on the mat. Well, field in your case."

"You're going tonight, right Peyt?" Bryce cuts in.

"I am," I say, doing my best not to look him in the eyes. I'm sure he wants to peg me for his designated driver, and if the situation demands I do it, I will. But I'm a last resort. Bryce is a lot sober. Drunk? He's a foolish prick.

"You know the rules," my dad begins.

I sigh and stare at his chest, zeroing in on the embroidered COACH stitched on the right of his polo shirt.

"Home by two. Text if I'm taking people home and running late. Keep the phone tracker on at all times. And do not accept drinks from anyone that I did not pack myself, especially if it's from Tasha." I flit my eyelashes and give him my best daddy's-girl expression, all doe-eyed and innocent.

"Especially Tasha," my dad teases, kissing me on top of my head and sending me on my way.

My parents know I drink. I tried the sneaky route my sophomore year, but an entire weekend spent vomiting lord knows what made it tough to disguise. I was grounded for a month after that, but when last year's season started, my parents set some ground rules. They do not necessarily condone me partying, but they mostly push responsibility. And I never drive under influence or let others when I can help it. I fought hard to move the curfew to two this year, too. The phone tracker was our compromise.

"Hey, Peyt! Wait up," Bryce hollers from behind me.

I grit my teeth and push my hands in my front hoodie pocket, then turn to walk backward as he catches up.

Just be pleasant, Peyton.

"Home by two, huh? That's new," he says. My dad let me stay out until one when I was out with Bryce, and I never told him but I think my father would have given in for a full overnight if Bryce asked.

"Well, I am almost eighteen."

Bryce stops in his tracks, and I wince as I keep walking. I shouldn't have brought up my birthday. He never remembered when we were dating, and now he'll probably try to do something annoyingly romantic in an attempt to win me over.

"Is it really here? Wow. I can't believe how lucky I've been," he says, walking again, which unfortunately means he's by my side. Still. *Again.*

I try so hard not to react.

"You know what I mean? Lucky?" He is not going to let this go.

I stop this time and let out a heavy sigh.

"No, Bryce. How are you lucky on my birthday?" To be honest, making my birthday about him tracks.

The way he saunters up to me makes my pulse pick up, but not in the good butterflies way it used to. And when his fingertips reach for my chin, a move that used to work so well on me, I stiffen my jaw. He must feel my rejection because he drops his hand almost immediately.

"Because I got to see you grow up," he says, his tone actually apologetic. And now I feel like an asshole.

"Oh, that's . . . that's sweet."

"Happy birthday, Peyton." His gaze lingers on my face, and that familiar tug beats in my chest for a moment.

Our vehicles are parked on opposite ends of the lot, so he walks backward a few steps before turning his back to me. I let out a ragged breath, one riddled with nerves, and clamp my molars together to remind myself that this is all part of the routine. I really want off this ride.

I gave Lexi my keys, so she and Tasha are sitting on top of the seat backs in the Jeep, their arms waving in the open air as my stereo thumps Tasha's latest favorite rap song. I vaguely know the lyrics, but it seems Lexi and Tasha know them all because I'm serenaded as I close in on them. In unison, they stand and belt the chorus.

"Girl's a playa, never date her, all the boys, they gotta taste her!"

I slump into the driver's seat and crane my neck to stare at them.

"Is that supposed to be about me?" I grimace.

"We're just sayin' . . . you seem to have the two hottest guys in Coolidge fighting over you. So the song kind of fits, no?" Tasha's right shoulder scrunches up to her ear.

"Nobody is fighting over me," I huff, spinning around and turning the music down but not off.

"Not yet," Lexi says through one of her signature self-righteous giggles.

I breathe in and hold the oxygen in my chest until it burns, letting it out slowly through my nose. It's going to be a really long night as the designated driver if it's anything like this.

Thankfully, we switch topics to the college guy Lexi's been chatting with. By the time I weave through the edge of town and into the thick desert brush that leads to the dry riverbed where post-game parties have been going down since my grandpa was QB, I feel grounded again. I back into my usual spot, tucked between two boulders, and we all hop out. Lexi and Tasha blow me kisses on their way to the keg, and I flip them off with both hands.

"Not our fault you have a super functional family who wants to celebrate your birthday!" Tasha teases.

I let out a mocking laugh, but smile to myself as I turn back toward the Jeep. Last year, I probably would have thrown a fit about not being able to drink after the first home game. But this year, it hits different. If I end up going far away for school next year, I'm going to miss my super-functional family activities. And those moments with my grandpa are becoming fewer and fewer.

Since nobody seems to have music going, I take on the task and slip between the boulder and my driver's side door to reach through the open window to press the power button. I pull my phone out of my pocket and sync it with my system, then crank up the volume. The first song is a bit country, which always seems to bring out the amped-up testosterone leftover from the game. But when I hear a familiar voice call out *yeehaw* from somewhere near the bonfire, I flip on my high beams to see if my gut is right.

Whiskey Olsen is here. This song? It's his favorite. And these parties? They're what he lives for. Except now he's wearing rival colors. And damn if he didn't show up here tonight with a few of his new friends, including one who is leaning against the hood of his blue pickup truck with a beer dangling from his right hand. And his eyes are set right on me.

Chapter Ten

Wyatt

This is a bad idea.

I should have listened to my gut.

"We'll be fine. They're still my boys, at least until the last game of the season, when we crush them." Whiskey hands me a beer that he snagged from one of *their* coolers.

I don't think I need to be drinking tonight, but Whisk has been hyping the post-game desert party all week. He and the other guys who came over from the old school see things differently. Maybe that's what it's like growing up in a small town with only one football team. There's no concept of territory, of bragging rights. At my old school, it was a big deal if we got midnight pancakes at the wrong Denny's.

"We'll see. I'm gonna hang back a while," I say, taking a sip of my beer and getting comfortable against the hood of my truck. I should also stay close to our exit route out of here.

It doesn't take long for the dry river basin to fill with trucks and cars, and the bonfire in the makeshift campsite pit is roaring pretty good. It's hot as shit out here, so why there's a fire beats me. Another part of the Coolidge tradition, I suppose. Might be time to start some Vista traditions.

Whiskey blends easily, slapping hands and hugging his old teammates. A few of our guys do the same, but not all of them. Tony and Dillon, who both caught passes from me in the end zone tonight, are hanging back too. I nod at them across the swath of desert between us, and Tony raises his beer. Dillon's hands are empty, and I can't help but suspect he's staying ready for anything . . . just like I am.

The air breaks with electric guitar, and the song Whiskey was playing in the locker room after our win blares in the desert. Ten seconds in and he's yelping like he's some cowboy. I chuckle and indulge in another sip, turning my attention to the source of my favorite lineman's favorite song. My gaze lands on Peyton about a half second before she lights me up with the Jeep's high beams.

"Shit," I mumble to myself, half because the bright lights have seared my pupils and half because that ominous feeling in my gut just doubled down.

My tongue passes over my dry bottom lip, and I lift my beer in her direction to acknowledge her. She should keep her distance tonight. I should. But she's just flipped the Jeep lights off, and I'm pretty sure that's her body I see walking toward me. I'd know for sure if I could fucking see.

Welp. I take an even bigger drink, then rest my beer on my hood and meet her halfway.

"What are you guys doing here, Wyatt?" She punches her hands into the front pocket of her hoodie. Her hair is pulled into a ponytail damn near on the top of her head, a yellow bow wrapped around the base yet a tad off-center. I nudge it toward the middle with my right hand, and she blinks up through thick eyelashes.

"What? Ugh. Just, I forgot about that," she grumbles, ripping the bow from her head. Her gaze comes back to mine, and I laugh a little at her sudden mini temper tantrum.

"You're pretty cute sometimes."

Her mouth snaps shut and her eyes dim. I've either stunned her or offended her, both entirely possible.

"You're avoiding my question." She stuffs the bow into her hoodie pocket, then crosses her arms over her chest.

I debate whether or not to mention the glitter splashed across her cheeks, but thankfully, Whiskey saves me from myself, slinging his massive arm around Peyton and pulling her into his side.

"Ahh, there's my favorite cheerleader," he says, his burly body knocking her ponytail loose. She pulls the hair band out and shoves it into her hoodie along with the bow, her curled locks falling around her face.

"Jack Olsen, what the fuck are you doing out here? You trying to start a fight?" Her hands land on her hips, and her brow lifts with her wide eyes.

Jack Michael Olsen? She's gone full mom mode.

I chuckle.

"Hush," she says, waving at me. It only makes me laugh more.

"Oh, come on, Peyt. Most of us grew up together. This is the party spot. Just let it be." He finishes off what I somehow think is already his second beer and tosses the bottle into a gully behind my truck. I grimace at him and go pick it up.

"Sorry, Wy. I get too comfortable sometimes."

"More like *all* the time. The amount of recycling I've cleared out of this place on fall weekends could fund my future tuition," Peyton says.

I set Whiskey's empty bottle in the back of my truck and meet Peyton's stare.

"Starting my own fund, in case the full ride to Arizona doesn't pan out," I say with a shrug. I have a pending half-scholarship with them now, but I'd like to see them cover the whole thing. Which means I need to make sure this season goes one way—perfect.

Unfortunately, fucking Bryce Hampton is striding toward me right now, looking like he has zero interest in how well my season goes. He's ready to start some shit.

"Now, you see, Whiskey . . . *this* is why I thought this was a bad idea." I nod toward the incoming piece of shit, and they both turn just in time to witness him lunge at me. Bryce's hands grab either shoulder, and I stumble back a few steps until my back hits the side of my pickup.

"Fuck, that hurt," I grunt out, shoving back to get the hothead off of me.

"Bryce, what the hell?" Peyton shoves him, and he moves a little from her force. I smirk and wonder if he hates that she's strong enough to move him.

"You okay?" Peyton asks as she steps between us.

"He's at the wrong fucking party, that's what he is!" Bryce says, pointing at me over her shoulder.

I twist my lips and stand up straight. I have him by two inches, and while he might have me by weight, something about being just a little bit taller feels pretty good.

"Man, Bryce. Don't be like that," Whiskey says, laying his hand on Bryce's shoulder.

I wince, mostly because I think I might be able to see the future. Bryce isn't drunk on alcohol. He's drunk on ego. And that? It's far more dangerous and self-destructive.

He swivels his head and drops his gaze to where Whiskey's hand rests on him. I don't know about their lives before Vista was built, but knowing the kind of player Whiskey is, I'd venture to guess he and Bryce were friends. Friendly, at the very least.

"Fucking Mustang traitor. Get your hand off me!" Bryce jerks his arm away and takes a step back, giving himself just enough room to lean forward and spit on the ground between him and his old lineman.

"Are you being serious right now?" Whiskey sounds genuinely shocked. I, on the other hand, saw this play out almost verbatim in my head.

Dillon and Tony have made their way over, and we all exchange uneasy glances. Whiskey is too big for any of us to stop. And he's pretty hyped from the game and the chugging he's gotten in already. If Bryce decides to provoke him much more, it's not going to be pretty.

"Yeah, I'm serious. We aren't on the same team anymore, bro. And this place? It's ours. It's been that way for years. Go find your own fucking traditions. And find your own fucking girls, too, while you're at it."

Oh, now, that shit? That was for me.

I'm about to step up and do something stupid when Bryce shoves past Whiskey, ramming into his side with a stiff elbow, and everything turns to slow-motion. The chest of my new, ginormous, soft-hearted friend fills up and his face reddens with white-hot rage, and Whiskey grabs the entire sleeve of Bryce's T-shirt. The seam tears at the neck as Whiskey's jerk spins Bryce around, and about half a second before anyone's fists are thrown, I get the brilliant idea to thrust myself into the middle—just in time to take Bryce's knuckles to my upper lip. I instantly taste blood.

"Bryce!" Peyton screams, pulling what's left of her ex-boyfriend's T-shirt away from me.

My head flung to the side, my hat who the fuck knows where, I touch two fingers to the numb section of my mouth, then stare at the blood on my hand. I've been hit before. I've busted my lip plenty of times. Usually, I'm braced for the blow. Still, it could hurt worse. It could hurt *a lot* worse. And that thought makes me laugh.

"Wyatt, let me see," Peyton says, cupping my face in her cool hands. She cradles my chin and nudges my head back so she can get a good look. And while she's inspecting me, my gaze drifts to Hampton, who looks jealous as fuck, his eyes slitted and his lip curled in a snarl.

I grin at him, my teeth likely stained with blood.

"What's so funny, dickhead?"

I laugh again, and Peyton's hands slip away.

"Maybe your girl wouldn't be looking at guys like me if you knew how to throw the ball." I let my gory, toothy grin linger on him as his jaw tightens under the heat of my stare. Before he can lunge at me again, Whiskey wraps his arm around him and drags him about a dozen feet back. My laughter picks up. Bryce Hampton and I have been competing for records and rankings for years, but since we were at the same quarterback camp this summer, he's risen to the number one spot on my list of least favorite people. Not only because of the way he collected girls all summer long like they were trading cards, but because of his complete inability to consider anyone but himself. Bad plays weren't his fault. Great plays were thanks to him. And the lies that fell off his lips—especially the ones he told about his ex-girlfriend back home—let me know all I needed to about the kind of man he's on track to be.

My eyes flutter, my focus a bit out of whack, but eventually my gaze returns to Peyton. Judging by the way her mouth is weighed down at the corners and her eyes have hazed, she's not as amused by my comeback as I was. I swallow my remaining laughter.

"Sorry," I utter.

She nods, only once.

"Yeah, well. You probably need stitches. You should go

get some of those." Peyton's glare sticks to me for a full second, but nothing more. She's gone, and I'm being helped into the passenger side of my pickup by Tony, who I gladly hand my keys to.

Whiskey opts to stay at the party, and I tell Dillon to stay behind and keep an eye on him. I don't want him taking up a vengeance against his old quarterback on behalf of his new one. I don't need him taking things too far and turning this into something that gets back to the district.

"Hey, just so we're clear. I dropped a wrench on my face," I say, my head resting on the seat as I try to hold my eyes open and keep my gaze on Tony.

He nods.

"You should maybe make sure Whiskey and Dillon know that," he says, flickering my lights to get people to clear out of the way. Seems my little altercation with Bryce drew quite the crowd. There are a lot of blue and gold shirts out here tonight. I knew this wasn't a party for us.

"I'm not worried about it getting back to Coach. My mom, however? She's going to flip her lid."

"It's pretty bad," Tony says. He glances at my busted face, then back to the dirt road that winds through overgrown brush.

"Feels like it," I admit.

I sit up tall and flip down the passenger visor to check things out for myself in the mirror. The dome light in my cab is dim, but I can clearly see the split. I might get away with a single stitch if I'm lucky.

It takes us about an hour to weave our way back to the

highway and through the west side of town to the urgent care. I call my mom when we're five minutes out, and she meets us there. As I predicted, she immediately jumps to the worst possible conclusion, and even though Tony does a good job selling my story, I don't think she's buying it. Probably because as little as I drank, my shirt still smells like beer. And this isn't the first time I've been punched in the face at a party.

Luckily, I get fixed up with one stitch and some really good glue. Not that I'll grow much of a mustache now; it'll probably have a small bald spot for the next several years. I tell Tony to keep the truck for the night and pick me up tomorrow for film review. The ride home with my mom is deathly silent. I know it's because she's worried. It's me and her now, and I went and got knocked around.

"You should see the other guy," I finally utter, unable to take the tension any longer.

She sighs and leans her elbow on the window.

"Fighting? Wyatt, that's not like you." Her brow is drawn in so tight I can see the wrinkle on her forehead in the dark.

"I've been in fights before."

"You were twelve. And you had a bully! Not the same as—" She whirls her finger in my direction.

"I didn't really fight, if that makes you feel better. I sort of got in the way of one, for the good of the team."

She glances at me and her hard eyes soften a touch.

"It's what Dad would have done. I actually thought about it when I made the decision."

Her lip quivers.

I reach over and hold my hand out for her to take. She does, squeezing my palm while I squeeze hers back. She turns the final corner to head to our house but slows when we spot the Jeep idling at the edge of our driveway.

"Someone coming back for more?"

I shake my head.

"No, not exactly." Peyton may have words for me, but she's not going to knock me out. At least, I don't think so.

When she hops out of the driver's side and Whiskey climbs out of the passenger side, my mom sinks back in her seat with relief. She idles at the end of our driveway, and I get out to talk with my visitors.

"I'll be right in," I say. I feel guilty I pulled her out of bed in a panic. She has work in the morning and was already out pretty late for my game.

My mom pulls up the driveway and into the garage, leaving it open for me after she heads inside.

"How bad is it, dude?" Whiskey steps up as I tilt my head to allow the streetlight to glow on my wound.

"Oooof." He winces.

"Eh, looks worse than it feels," I lie. It definitely feels worse than a single stitch.

"You tell her how to get here?" I nod toward the Jeep where Peyton is still hovering outside the door.

"Yeah. I hope that's okay. She was pretty insistent. And to be honest, she's always scared the shit out of me," he says, whispering that last part.

I chuckle.

"I get that," I agree.

I glance back to Peyton and nod. She lifts a hand, but not really in a wave. More like a silent agreement that we're both here, that she came to my house, and there's a weird fucking vibe going on because of tonight.

"You wanna stay the night? We have a guest room. Tony's picking me up for film in the morning, so you can just come with."

Whiskey nods and runs his hand through his sweaty hair. It's too hot to party in the desert. *What is up with this place? Why don't they simply pick someone's house?*

"I'm gonna shower if that's cool with you?" he asks as he begins to trek up my driveway.

"Yeah. There are clean towels by the linen closet. We haven't gotten around to unpacking the boxes yet, so look for the one with a T on it."

While Whiskey heads into my garage, I shuffle toward Peyton, my chest tight because I'm not sure what to expect. She rests her back against the side of the Jeep and tucks her hands in her hoodie as I step in front of her.

"How's the lip?" Her brow arches.

"You tell me," I say, turning my head slightly as if I'm showing off a new piercing or a close shave. She stands up and leans in close, her hand reaching up and brushing my chin. Her eyelashes flit as she studies my wound, and a second later she's staring into my eyes.

"It's pretty gross."

I laugh at her unkind bluntness, but I don't back away.

Neither does she. And her hand, its touch only becomes more certain. Steadier.

"I brought you a dime," she says, her other hand slowly bunching up the center of my T-shirt. The toes of our shoes are touching now.

"A dime? Do they still make those?" I say.

"*Hmm*, it's an artifact, for sure. But I wanted to buy that bottle off you. You know, for my collection. Contribute toward your tuition fund."

I move my hands to her elbows, then slowly glide my palms up her arms, then neck, until my hands cradle her face.

"I think I can get more than a dime for it," I tease, our mouths now inches apart.

Peyton lifts up on her toes and blinks slowly. She runs her fingertip over the cut on my upper lip and I twitch. Her gaze flits to mine.

"You get more for recycling in Michigan. You're welcome to try that if you want. Or you can take my deal."

The healthy side of my mouth raises with a tiny smirk. She's so funny and smart. Smart-mouthed for sure, but also . . . just smart. And so fucking beautiful. My chest tightens again, and the thumping inside gets louder.

"I'm sorry about starting shit with Bryce tonight," I say with a hard swallow.

She shakes her head slowly.

"That wasn't because of you. And Whiskey told me it was his idea to come. I shouldn't have made you all feel unwelcome."

I squint one eye and dimple my cheek with the good side of my mouth.

"You were a little harsh," I tease.

She shakes her first against my ribs, her hand still clutching my shirt. She can have it. My shirt. My heart. My rib. Whatever she wants. She can take it if she'll just give me one shot. One kiss.

"I'm not Bryce's girl," she says, a point she's made clear many times. Still, I can't help but hate that guy for having had something with her. And having cheated on her. And spreading stories about how clingy she is, and making her sound like a crazy ex to every other girl he bragged to. He used her as clout, used the fact he dated a famous man's daughter as a way to up his own cachet.

"I know," I say in a hushed tone. My eyes zero in on her mouth. I feel her breath against my chin.

"I'm nobody's girl. I belong to me." Her eyes are open, and I lean back a tick to meet her gaze and prove to her that I hear her.

"Okay," I say.

Her attention once again dips to my mouth, and her tongue peeks out between her lips. While her left hand twists my shirt into a tighter hold, her right one nudges my chin toward hers, and I bend down just enough for her sweet, perfect mouth to touch my bottom lip. It takes every ounce of self-restraint in my body not to say *fuck it* and kiss her the way I want to. But I'd only bust open my stitch and probably bleed all over both of us. So I'll have to settle for slow.

I indulge in her being in charge of this. She takes my bottom lip between hers and sucks in lightly, her tongue passing along my skin as she holds my mouth to hers. I forgo breathing. In fact, I don't fill my lungs once after her feet flatten back on the pavement. I definitely don't draw in air when she unfurls my shirt from her grip. It's not until her hand falls from my chin and I let go of her face and look into her almond-shaped brown eyes that I remember air exists at all.

"I've decided," she says, climbing into the driver's side. I ease the door closed.

"Oh, yeah? What's that?" My eyes don't know where to focus. What mental pictures to snap most. Her mouth. Her face. The stray blonde hairs blowing across the bridge of her nose. Back to her mouth.

"I like you, Wyatt Stone. Quite a lot, I think."

The full grin sneaks up on me, and I wince when it stretches my stitch. I touch the spot with my fingertips and Peyton giggles, then promptly rolls up her window and drives away.

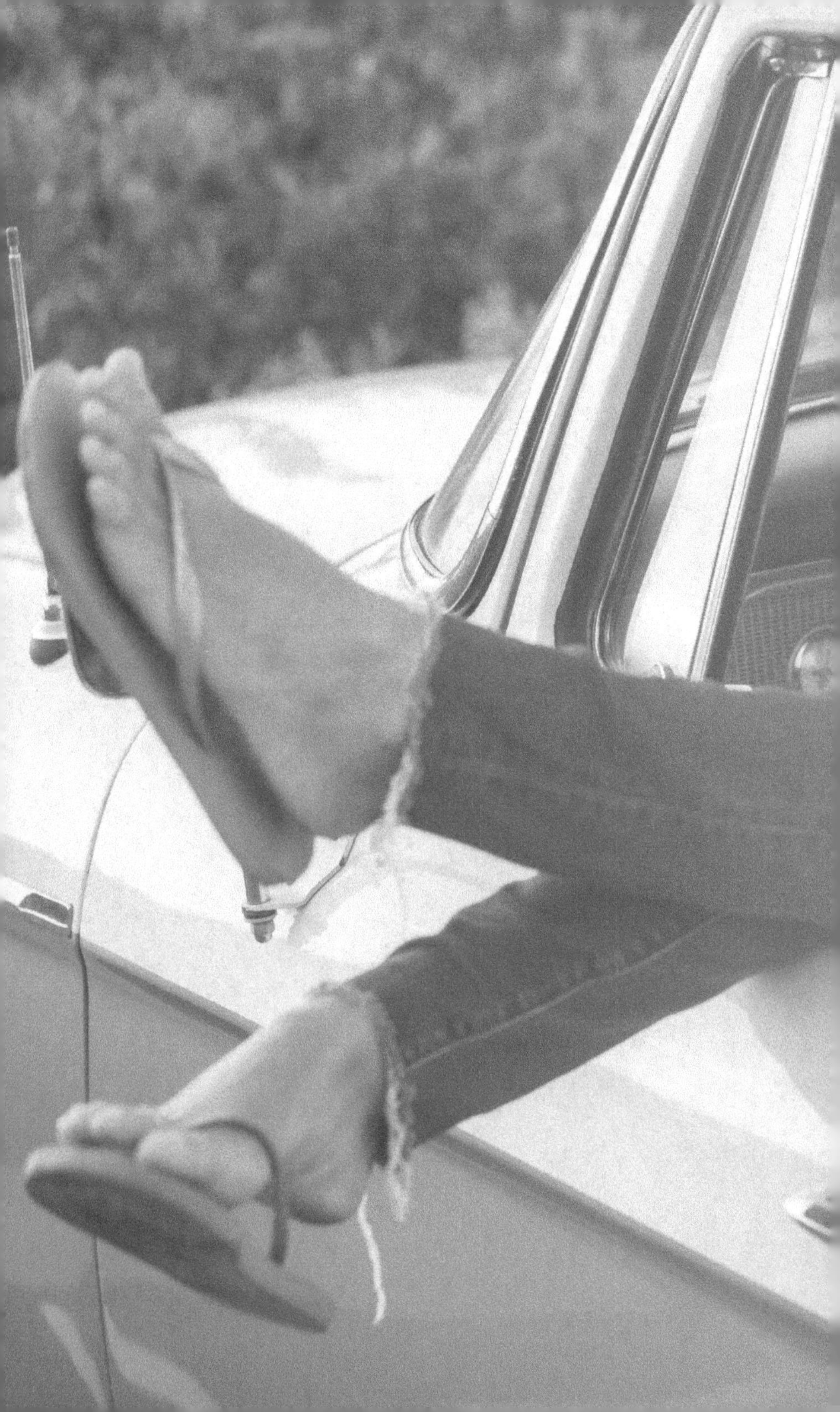

Chapter Eleven

Peyton

Eighteen.

I can vote and gamble on scratchers.

It's a pretty epic day.

"Now, don't forget about our big date tonight," my grandpa says.

I cross my heart with my index finger, as if there were a chance I would ever miss fire-writing with him.

The Cardinals game is on, and my Grandma Rose is heating leftovers from the massive family dinner she made last night to celebrate my birthday. She tosses the red beef in with some fresh eggs so it qualifies as breakfast. It's one of the few times she will let my grandpa indulge in eating off of his medically curated menu. Usually, she's a stickler. Even now, I know she whipped that dish up with egg whites.

"Who's ready for pancakes?" My dad claps as he jogs

down the stairs, then rubs his palms together when he meets me at the bottom.

"Honestly, I'm still full after last night," I admit.

My dad snags his keys and wallet from the sofa table and turns to walk backward toward the door.

"Me, too," he says, pointing at me and winking. "But it's pancakes."

I drag my feet along the wood floors toward him, only half acting reluctant. I really am full, but these birthday traditions mean the world to me. I've been having pancakes with my dad ever since he retired. And before sunset, I'll go for a long horse ride with Mom. The first year we did this one-on-one thing, which was totally my mom's idea, I spent half of my time with my parents whining about it and insisting I had nothing to say. Funny the difference a year makes, though, because last year, these dates marked some of the most meaningful conversations I've ever had with my parents.

"Okay, the world of pancake syrup is at your fingertips. Where are we heading?" My dad turns over the engine on the Jeep and shifts into drive but waits for my final decision.

"I know it's weird to want to eat where I work, but—"

"Oh, thank God! I love Jack's," he says, racing down our driveway and hitting the roadway with a bit of a fish-tale move that thrills me. Mom would be so pissed.

The restaurant lot is fairly full, but I don't see anyone waiting in the entry when we park. I feel a little guilty because I normally help open on Sundays. It's the only day I work during the school year, and mostly because I love the owner, Maggie. Her son Neil went back to college this week, so she's probably running around like crazy this morning with the two floaters she calls in when things get busy.

I snag two menus from behind the counter when my dad and I walk in, and I wave to Maggie from across the restaurant where she's taking a couple's order.

"Wow, this place is hopping," my dad says as I guide him to two open stools at the end of the counter.

"I feel bad," I admit, glancing around the joint. Everyone seems happy at least. That's part of the charm of Jack's.

"Nah, it's your birthday. Plus, this place prints money, doesn't it Douggie?" My dad sits up tall as he peers through the kitchen window. Doug, Maggie's husband, pops his head up from the griddle.

"Hey, what's my favorite quarterback of all time doing here?" Doug slips around the wall and through the swinging door as he wipes his hands on the front of his apron. He and my dad went to high school together, though Doug was two years older. Looking at him now, full grizzly beard tucked into a net, long hair knotted into a bun, two full sleeves of tats, and the upper body of a bouncer, you'd never guess he was once Coolidge High's kicker.

I let the two of them have their trip down memory lane

for a few minutes while I scan the menu, which I have memorized. It wouldn't be right to come here and *not* get pancakes, but I'd kinda like something lighter. I decide to get a short stack with berries and cream, and I'm about to make my request to Doug when a sudden chill takes over my dad's face.

I follow his gaze to my right and spot Wyatt three seats down, doing his best to hide his face behind a very obvious propped-up menu. He's pinching his brow with his other hand, probably wishing he could visualize one of those cartoon rabbit holes to dive into. I know I am.

"Speaking of great quarterbacks," my dad says, his volume purposely lifted. Doug follows my dad's gaze, and now half the restaurant is staring at Wyatt. He flattens the menu and forms a panicked smile on the good side of his mouth as he raises his hand.

"Coach. Good to see you," he says, his eyes reaching mine briefly and flickering. I don't think he really meant that.

The couple between us tosses down some cash and nods to Doug, complimenting the best breakfast they've had in ages. They must be out-of-towners because they don't seem the least bit interested in the wild west show-down happening at the breakfast bar. I feel their absence immediately, however, and I'm sure Wyatt does too. Now there's nothing between his lonely seat and my father and me.

"What brings you into this fine establishment on a Sunday morning? I would think you all would be watching our film. I know you had a guy there." My dad shifts, getting comfortable in his seat. Doug's gaze meets mine, one brow higher than the other. He's probably trying to figure this scenario out.

"Dad, stop," I say, not bothering to keep it under my breath.

"Doug, this is Wyatt Stone. He's—"

"Oh yeah, you're the kid about to break ole Reed's record," Doug interjects. My dad clears his throat as Doug moves around the counter to shake Wyatt's hand.

"I don't really pay attention to that stuff, but I guess so," Wyatt says, his eyeline sliding to Reed, then back to Doug.

"Sure you don't." Doug covers the back of Wyatt's palm with his other hand, giving it a healthy couple of slaps as he verbally ribs my father. Doug's grip is massive, and I catch Wyatt stretching out his fingers when he lets go.

"All right, birthday girl. What will it be?" Doug finally turns his attention to me. I place my order, and my dad orders his black coffee and a mega-stack, which is basically a week's worth of carbs on a plate.

Maggie slides a plate of pancakes in front of Wyatt, and he drops his attention to the syrup and butter. I can literally feel the heat of my dad's stare crossing me as he watches the poor guy try to eat, so I let out a heavy sigh and twist in my stool to face Wyatt.

"Why don't you join us?"

"Oh, whoa—" my dad pipes in. Wyatt's mouth is hanging open, and I'm positive he wants no part of my suggestion. But it's not like we can sit here now with two seats between us and carry on as if we're two separate parties. And if I ever hope to somehow find a way to see Wyatt again without feeling like I'm sneaking around, the massive block of ice between them is going to have to start melting.

"It's my birthday," I say to my dad. "And clearly, you have questions for him. I'd rather not spend the next half hour pretending he doesn't exist and you aren't obsessed with him."

"I'm not obsessed. *Pffft.*" My dad turns his attention to Maggie as she sets down a mug and fills it with coffee.

Maggie's gaze slides to me and I roll my eyes. She laughs silently, then tightens her lips into a straight line before pulling the invisible zipper.

"Well?" I say to Wyatt. He sets his forkful of gooey pancake on his plate and slides off his stool, pushing his plate and glass of orange juice over two spaces to the open seat next to me.

"What's with the banged-up face?" My dad taps his finger to his upper lip.

"Game injury. It's not that bad," Wyatt lies. My stomach tightens because I don't want him to have to lie about what happened, but I also don't think it's the right time to get into a debate about what a dick Bryce is.

"Looks like you got yourself a stitch or two. That's more than a scratch," my dad needles. He takes a loud sip of his coffee, slurping, and eyes me.

"Watched your film yesterday, by the way," Wyatt says, and I zip my gaze to him.

"We're engaging in this?" I say.

Wyatt shrugs.

"He started it," he defends.

I take a deep breath and snag a straw from the container in front of me. I peel the wrapper off and poke the straw into my water glass merely as a distraction.

"You learn anything from it?" My dad chuckles, turning his body to the side completely. At this point, I should trade him seats and let the two of them spar without having to endure being in the middle.

"Nothing new," Wyatt quips. I give him side eyes and he smirks through his bite.

My dad grumbles, but thankfully, Maggie shows up with our plates, and for the next few minutes we're all able to lose ourselves in good food.

I may not be getting my one-on-one time with my dad, but it's hard to argue that this breakfast hasn't been a standout.

"I was going to stop by today to give you your present," Wyatt says. His plate is now cleared but I'm only halfway through my meal. My barely existent appetite vanishes with his words.

"So, he got you a present?" My dad doesn't bother to look our direction this time, instead opting to talk while chewing, eyes set on the small TV set above the kitchen window. It's Sunday morning news, and I know my dad—

he's waiting to see them replay highlights from Friday night.

"I heard about the sparklers the other night when I brought over your bonfire wood," Wyatt notes.

"Yeah, nobody asked you to do that," my dad says, not even masking his dislike.

Wyatt slides from his stool and whispers, "Sorry," at my side. He pulls cash out to cover his bill and tip, then steps around me to hold out his hand for my dad.

"Sorry to interrupt your breakfast, sir," he says. My dad lets his palm linger for a few seconds, but before I have to intervene, he wipes off his palm with a napkin and shakes Wyatt's hand.

"Good luck with that record," my dad says, one side of his mouth flashing a very short-lived grin.

"Which one?" Wyatt says as their hands part.

I let my eyes flutter shut. Here my dad always thought Bryce was his mini-me. Their gazes wrestle for a few awkward seconds.

"You got her present with you now?" my dad asks.

My stomach grows so tight I think my pancakes might come back up. I push my plate away.

"Oh, it's nothing that can't wait." Wyatt drops his hands in the pockets of his Vista football shorts. He probably spent the morning lifting or getting in some cardio.

"Well, if it's nothing, why not give it to her now? Save yourself a trip to my house." My dad pulls a piece of bacon from his plate and snaps off a bite.

"It can wait, Dad," I urge, no longer amused by this pissing match—if I ever was.

"Well, you've got a pretty busy day. And you know Grandpa doesn't like to share his time, and if the kid says he's got it with him now . . ." My dad is in rare protective father form. And he's digging deep to pull out his old self —his 18-year-old self—whose ego can't stand that someone he didn't have a hand in helping might just beat his record. Correction—*records*.

"It's not really much. It can wait until whenever, really," Wyatt says, clearly squirming where he stands.

"Well, then, it won't take long." My dad pops the rest of his bacon in his mouth, the crunch of his chew somehow loud even when his mouth is closed.

Wyatt's gaze drifts to me, and as much as I want to save him from this, I also meant what I said the other night. I like him. And I need my dad to respect him. On his own terms.

"I'll wait," I say.

His eyes widen for a beat, then he drops his gaze to the floor, his shoulders shaking with a quiet chuckle.

"Okay," he relents.

He shakes his head as he leaves the restaurant, and I follow him with my eyes as he moves to the passenger side of his truck parked on the opposite side of us. No wonder I didn't spot his truck when we pulled in.

"I thought he was just a guy who stopped in for pancakes?" My dad is referencing our first chat about

Wyatt, when Bryce tried to sour his reputation with my dad.

"Seems he really likes pancakes," I say, turning my attention to my water, which is draining fast as I keep taking nervous sips.

"*Hmm,*" my dad grumbles.

Wyatt comes back in with a plastic grocery bag in his hand. He grabs the back of his neck with his opposite hand as he approaches.

"I didn't have anything to wrap it in, sorry," he says, giving me a sheepish expression before handing over the bag.

"Wrapping paper is wasteful," I say, throwing him a bone. My dad never wraps presents. He leaves it for Mom, so he better not offer any commentary.

"Thank you," I offer, meeting Wyatt's eyes.

He smiles through tight lips, but the only emotion I sense in his expression is worry. I write it off to the gauntlet my dad is putting him through, but when I pull the jersey out of the bag and the iconic silver and blue registers, I realize what had him so nervous.

It's a fucking Cowboys jersey. Which I love. Because I know why he got it for me. He was paying attention to me, and he remembered the story I told him about taking a dig at my dad when I was mad at him. But his timing could not be worse. It is, however, hilarious.

"Thank you," I say, unfurling it and pushing my arms through the bottom. "I love it."

I pull it over my head, on top of my CHS cheer shirt,

then twist to my side as I stretch it out to show off for my dad. He deserves this.

"Huh," my dad reacts, his brow lifting as he chews at the inside of his mouth.

"It's sort of an inside joke," Wyatt utters, his voice vibrating.

"Is it?" My dad knows exactly what makes this funny. And he knows that means Wyatt and I have talked more than a little. We've shared stories.

"I don't really like the Cowboys, though. I mean, I would play for them. Of course. But they aren't really my team. I like the home team. And I grew up watching Seattle with my dad. And—"

"It's a nice jersey." My dad's words are abrupt, and he's reaching into his wallet to pay the bill, clearly done with this ego-match.

"I meant it to be fun. Just as a nice gesture. *Shit.*" Wyatt mumbles that last part.

"Yeah. Fun." My dad holds the bill and his credit card out for Maggie to run. Thankfully, she does it quickly.

"Anyhow, I have a thing I have to get to. I hope you have a happy birthday, Peyton. And good luck Friday, Coach." Wyatt steps toward me but stops short of stretching out his arms to hug me. He glances in my dad's direction for permission, which he won't get—ever. So I take things into my own hands and step up on my toes to wrap my arms around his neck and kiss him on the cheek.

"Thank you, Wyatt. It was really thoughtful," I say. I am pretty sure he's trembling.

"Uh, yeah. I mean, glad you like it. Anyhow, I have to—"

"Where you headed?" My dad was done with this a second ago. I'm not sure why he's now pulling Wyatt back into his web.

"It's sort of a team thing I started. I mean, I hope a team thing. I might be the only one to show up. Well, Whiskey will because I'm picking him up." Wyatt's gaze shifts between me and my dad.

"Like a tradition, huh?" my dad pries. He signs the bill and tucks his card back into his wallet.

"Something like that," Wyatt says, stepping back to make room for my dad to exit first.

Surprisingly, my father holds the door open for Wyatt, though maybe it's simply because I'm trailing behind. I'm just glad our vehicles are parked far away from each other so we don't have to continue making small talk in the parking lot. I can't wait to fill my mom in on everything when we go out for our ride.

"Well, good luck with your tradition thing. Whiskey's a good teammate. Take good care of him," my dad offers. It's the nicest he's been, and of course it's about one of his old players.

"I will, Coach. Thank you," Wyatt says, his gaze passing over me before he spins around and heads toward his truck.

I twist my lips and shoot my dad a glare. He laughs out hard, not even hiding his feelings about all of this.

"I'm sorry, Peyton, but that? You are ditching Bryce for

that guy?" He chuckles as he adjusts his keys in his palm and presses the unlock button.

I shake my head and bite my tongue, but when I get into the Jeep, all of the words I've been eating for months bubble to the top.

"You know why Bryce and I broke up every summer?"

My dad shrugs, almost indifferently.

"You're young. It's what young people do," he says. He's not so naïve that he assumes every relationship is like his and my mom's, but he's not exactly savvy on teenagers, either.

"Because Bryce wanted to sleep around while he was at camp. We broke up because he knew he wouldn't be faithful. I knew he wouldn't. It was this understood contract, and we'd break up so he could go have guiltless fun in California, or up north, or wherever y'all sent him for camp that year. And then every fall, I'd take him back."

My dad hasn't moved his hands from the wheel since I started talking, and his eyes study the leather wrap between his palms. A pathetic laugh slips from my lips.

"I guess I liked the hype as much as everyone else did. I liked being Bryce's girlfriend. At least, I thought I did. The last time we got back together, it just made me sad. And then I realized that I was sad a lot. He might be a great quarterback for you, Dad. But to me? He's just a shitty boyfriend."

I breathe out a soft cry, mostly out of relief for finally getting things off my chest.

My dad's lashes bat, his gaze working overtime as he

burns a hole through his steering wheel. He breathes in long and slow through his nose before shifting his attention to the gear shift on the center console.

"That thing on his lip. He didn't get that during a game." It doesn't come out as a question because my dad doesn't need to ask. He simply wants to confirm.

"You know how he got it," I say, giving him just enough.

My dad nods once, then shifts into reverse to take us home. He doesn't mention the jersey I'm wearing or our special guest for breakfast for the entire trip.

Riddell
Riddell

Chapter Twelve

Wyatt

The first Sunday swim went well, I think. The guys might hate me for it a little when winter months roll around, but that's when the toughness comes out.

Truth is, I was motivated when Whiskey took me by the old campus and I saw how much work the guys put in above and beyond regular practice and drills. But there's something about having an organic thing happen that starts with the players. I wanted Sundays to be a thing *we* start and that Coach finds out about. It's a gift to him in that way, I guess. It's gotta feel good seeing your players put in overtime on their own. But beyond the pats on the backs, if we can get to a point where most of us—at least the nucleus of the team—show up for laps on Sundays, our bond is going to be unbreakable.

As it is, I swear my cardio is better today because of the hour straight swim about twenty of us did on Sunday. Now, to put in the work for my passing. I'm not in sync with Jody yet. I can lead Tony and Dillon deep downfield, but Jody needs to be my top target at running back. He has the speed, and from what I could tell when we watched the Coolidge game, they struggle defending the short pass. It's their weakness. And in a few weeks, I need to exploit it.

Coach Watts is still in his office when I finish dressing out, so I lean into his open door and knock to get his attention.

"Got a minute?"

He nods, so I take a seat in the metal chair on the opposite side of his desk.

"I got something for you," he says, opening his side drawer. He tosses a key on the desk, and I stare at it for a moment.

"That way you guys don't have to hop the fence to get in laps at the pool." His mouth is a straight line, and I'm not sure if he's impressed or irritated with us.

"Thanks," I say.

"*Hmm*," he grunts, and nods.

I slide the key into my pocket while he goes back to reviewing something on his iPad. He's always studying film.

"That the Marcos game from Friday?" I crane my neck to get a better view and he turns the tablet a tick.

"Yeah, they're gonna be tough. We front-loaded our schedule. It will pay off, though, I think."

I nod at his assessment and watch the game play with him.

"They're sloppy with the handoffs," I say, pointing to the screen.

He drags the video back a few seconds and watches them run the play again.

"Good spot. We'll need to work on that with the defense tomorrow." He makes a note, then turns his attention back to the screen.

"So, what's up?" he asks, his gaze not on me. He's such a hard man to read. Harder when he's not looking at me. I swallow.

"I want to get in some extra pass work. You think I can get the end zone lights on?"

He stops the video and leans back in his chair, studying me.

"Tonight?" His brow pulls in.

"I was . . . well . . . yeah. Tonight. Tomorrow. Next day—"

"Yeah, yeah. I get it. Uh, man, I don't know if I can get facilities to stick around. And the AD is up my ass about costs and raising more money. It's something like two hundred for every extra hour the lights are on or some bullshit." He chews on his pen cap as he stares hard into my eyes.

"Forget the lights, then. Just give me a key to the back gate, and I'll use my headlights."

Coach chuckles and tosses his pen on his desk.

"Hell, if you're willing to go that far to get better, I may as well get out there with you." He stands and closes his laptop as I push back in the metal chair, the legs scraping along the concrete floor.

"I didn't mean to make extra work for you," I say,

feeling bad when his phone buzzes and I see an image of his wife pop up on the screen. He holds up a finger.

"Hey, babe. Wyatt and I are going to work out a few things. I'm gonna be an hour. If you want to bring the boys, though . . ."

"Really, it's o—" I try to let him off the hook. He holds up a finger, though, and listens as his wife talks. A second or two later, he holds the phone away from his ear.

"You like rice or chow mein?"

My face puzzles.

"Rice, I guess? Is she—?"

He repeats my answer and is off the phone and heading out of his office seconds later. *What just happened?*

"My boys are starting pee wee next week, and they've been dying to meet you. So, hope you don't mind having some helpers out there. And apparently, my wife is hungry, so we're getting dinner delivered."

"Oh, wow. Umm, okay." I try my best to keep up with him, shutting off the locker room lights and snagging my duffel as he holds the locker room door open for me. My mom is working late, picking up all the extra hours she can so it hurts less financially when she takes off Fridays.

I follow Coach down to the field, the sun still up just enough that we might be able to get away with some work before I have to pull my truck around. He stops at the equipment room to grab a bag of balls and wheels out a basket I think he wants to use as a target, but as he slides the door back down to lock it again, an acrid scent hits my nose.

"You smell that?" I ask.

His head snaps to mine and a half-second later, he drops the balls and we both rush around the building to get a clear look at the field. The flames aren't terribly high, but they trail across the width of our end zone.

"Call nine-one-one!" Coach shouts, sprinting down to the field. He hurdles the fence and scrambles to open the box for the automatic sprinkler lines, flipping them all on at once. He races through the middle of the field, water blasting him from all directions, and stops at one of the large corner jets. He cranks it to point the spray directly at the flames, and the air fills with white smoke just as I finish telling the operator there's a fire at the school field.

I pull my collar up over my nose and cup my hand on top. Our field backs up to desert, so it's not like someone drove by and flicked out a cigarette. *Do people even smoke cigarettes anymore? I don't think throwing a vape pen out a window has quite the same effect.*

"Fuck!" Coach's voice reverberates off the bleachers.

I jog up behind him, and when I get a clear view of the burn marks, I see what led to his reaction.

The letters CHS are charred clearly in our end zone. My mind instantly flashes back to last Friday. To Whiskey telling me it wouldn't be a big deal. The uneasy feeling I had going in for the party. The stitch in my lip. My bruised upper gums that makes it feel a lot like my teeth are falling out.

"I don't suppose that fat lip of yours has anything to do

with this?" He starts pacing with his hands threaded over his head. Sirens blare in the distance.

"I wish I could say no, but I have no fucking idea, Coach."

His gaze snaps to mine, and as hard as he normally is to read, I can tell right now he's lit as hell.

"I'm not instigating anything. I swear." I hold up my hand in pledge and shake my head, my body thrumming with a jolt of adrenaline.

"Go get the emergency gate," he barks, tossing his keys to me.

I clutch them in the air and jog to the access road to undo the padlock and open the gate wide. Coach's wife shows up with their two boys, who look to be about six and eight, just as the firefighters finish off the last bit of flames. I toss a ball with them on the track to keep them away from danger as the crew works.

"You must be Wyatt," his wife says as she approaches. I direct her oldest boy to run deep and toss the ball to him.

"I am. Nice to meet you, Mrs. Watts," I say, taking her hand.

"You can call me Jamie."

I nod, but I don't think I'll ever be able to do that. My dad taught me to always respect coaches and their families. Jamie feels much too casual.

Coach walks over with one of the police officers who showed up at the scene. My stomach drops in anticipation of his questioning, but it seems he's got things pretty sorted without me having to give a statement.

"Hey, Wyatt. Officer Caldwell," he says, shaking my hand and pressing his card into my palm. I scan it, then slip it into my pocket. "We anticipated some of this might happen. Coolidge High has been all alone out here for years. And I'm sure you've learned that people in this town take their football pretty seriously. It's some pretty extensive damage, I'm afraid. But the district has a policy for this stuff. No one will want to throw the other guys under the bus, given that half of the administration graduated with Coach Johnson over there. So I'd expect things to get swept under the rug pretty quick."

I'm baffled how nonchalant he's being. I'm also kind of pissed at the clout Coach Johnson apparently has. Mostly, I'm mad that he made me feel like an idiot yesterday in front of his daughter and now he's screwing up my practice.

"I should take off. My mom probably heard about a fire and I don't want her to worry," I say, using my mom as an excuse.

"Yeah, sorry, Wyatt. We'll figure this out in a few days and start working something out. Me and you, okay?" Coach holds out a fist and I tap it, relieved that he doesn't seem to be blaming me. Of course, if he knew I was driving straight to the Johnson house to lay into our rival coach, he probably wouldn't be so calm.

I give knuckles to his two boys and thank his wife for being nice enough to bring us dinner. She insists I take my order with me, so I plop the container on top of my truck's cupholder before speeding off to the Johnson Ranch.

The driveway is filled with cars when I pull up, so I

leave mine near the roadway. I'm still fuming enough to power my march up to the house, but when I realize Reed's truck isn't among the vehicles puzzled together on their property, my nerve wanes.

"Wyatt?" Peyton's voice behind me pretty much zaps whatever courage is left.

Caught at her front door with her walking up the path behind me, essentially blocking me in, I spin around and force what I hope is a casual smile on my face. I must be failing in my effort, though, because she's setting down the gallon-sized containers of fruit punch she was hauling in either hand and is moving closer to me with a serious look of concern weighing down her cheeks.

"You smell like a BBQ," she says, moving in to me. Her arms swing around me without warning, and suddenly we're hugging.

None of this is happening the way it should with her.

"We had a fire," I blurt out.

"Oh, my God!" She takes a step back to look me in the eyes. "Is your mom okay? Did it burn your house down? Where?"

"Oh, shit. I meant at the school. Well, the field. The end zone, to be precise."

Her arms slowly cross over her chest. She's wearing a white T-shirt with bear paw prints and her short black cheer shorts. As my head clears and I begin to recognize the squeals coming from inside, I realize why the driveway is so full.

"Cheer meeting?" I point my thumb over my shoulder.

Peyton nods, but her eyes are still dim, and her mouth is a taut line.

"The guys burnt letters on the field, didn't they?"

I laugh out once, and hard, but quickly control my expression. I'm shocked at how exact her guess is.

"I thought they were kidding with that shit," she says, moving past me and opening her front door. She waits for me to enter behind her, so I timidly step onto the rustic wood floors and into a home that smells like pumpkin spice and popcorn.

"Oh!" a woman says as she steps from what I think is the kitchen to peer into the foyer.

"Mom, this is Wyatt," Peyton explains.

Mom. Yeah, I figured that from the other night. They look so much alike other than the color of their hair. And I kind of think if Peyton lost the highlights, she'd practically be her mom's twin. Well, younger twin. I suppose it's more fitting to say daughter. I shake my head to clear my scattered thoughts as her mom wipes her hand with a towel and moves to shake my hand.

"Wyatt, it's so nice to meet you finally. I've heard—"

Peyton coughs and her mom snaps her mouth shut and glances in her daughter's direction.

"It's nice to meet you, too, ma'am," I say.

"Oh, yeah . . . *no*. Don't do that. I'm Nolan. Please, I'm begging you. Never say the word ma'am again. Like, ever."

I chuckle and nod, noting that I now have two women who insist I use their first names. I think maybe my dad missed out on being progressive. Still, it's going to be hard not to call them something formal.

"We're just finishing up with the board meeting for the trip to nationals. You're welcome to come in and grab a bite," she says, nudging me toward the kitchen.

"Oh, thanks. But I have dinner in the car, and well—"

"You have dinner in the car?" Nolan's brow furrows and she glances at her daughter.

"His mom works a lot. And he just got done with practice." It's nice to have her make the excuses for me, but also, hearing it said out loud like that, the obvious void of my dad in the conversation cuts inside.

"Is Dad on his way? Do you know?" Peyton asks.

"I think it's a late night. You know how they are when they get to talking." Nolan rolls her eyes, then mouths, "Coaches," to me.

"You don't have to make this a thing, Peyton," I plead. All of that bravado and hot-headedness I had about five minutes ago has turned into wanting to run out of here and join the golf team. I can't possibly be the source of more strife for her dad. Not when all I want to do now is kiss her. I'm not going to have many chances to kiss her if I keep pissing off her dad like this.

"I'm not making it a thing. And *you* didn't make this a thing. Childish fools made this a thing, and it's about damn time some of them felt consequences." She's fired up, and her mom's interest is piqued in that way only an involved parent's can be.

"Nobody needs to do a thing. I'm sorry I came here. I

was just in my feelings and needed to rant about it to someone."

While I'm doing my best to dismiss everything, Peyton is busy filling her mom in on the actual details. When she gasps and meets my gaze, I drop my chin to my chest.

By the time I look up, the shock seems to have faded. But now Peyton and her mom, who is married to my rival coach—the coach of the guy who lit my field on fire, no doubt—are making plans without me to take things up a level.

I grab the officer's card from my pocket and flash it to them, and thankfully, it seems to get them to stop.

"It's being handled. As best as things in this town are handled when it comes to football, I mean." We all get silent for a moment, and I think they both understand the politics involved.

"Just maybe mention this to your dad," I say when my eyes meet Peyton. "So he's not surprised. And maybe if there's a way that it didn't come from me?" I shrug, already feeling a foot shorter around Reed, thanks to the hole I keep digging myself into.

Peyton nods, then leans into her mom's shoulder, whispering something.

"Wait here. I'll walk you out," she says.

I agree, but my twitchy muscles are aching to sprint out of here before one more cheerleader peeks around the corner and giggles about something. *About me. They are giggling about me.*

I shake her mom's hand one more time and pretend I

don't notice the knowing smirk on her face. The fact her daughter has talked about me didn't get past me. I'd love to know what she said.

Peyton comes back after a few seconds, a salad bowl filled with popcorn and two cupcakes balanced on top. Rather than argue with her, I let her carry them to my truck as she walks me out. I presume she's about to hand the treats to me as she sends me on my way for the night, but instead, she hops into the passenger side of my truck and buckles up. I pull the door open and gawk at her, kind of impressed with her audacity.

"What? If you're not coming in for dinner, I'm coming out to eat mine with you. But if you don't want my dad joining us again, I suggest you get in and drive." She pinches a kernel of popcorn and tosses it at me. I catch it in my palm, then pop it in my mouth. It's kettle corn. Sweet and salty. And amazing. *Of course it is.*

"Well, all right, then." I slide into my seat, buckle up, and crank the engine as she eyes the takeout my coach's wife brought me.

"Where to?" I ask her.

"Anywhere," she says, a playful smirk on her lips. "Anywhere but here."

Chapter Thirteen

Peyton

"I give you the freedom to drive me anywhere, alone, at night, and you take me to an abandoned driving range by the state fairgrounds. Wow, Wyatt Stone. You really know how to woo a lady."

He laughs hard, letting his head fall back against his seat, which leaves his eyes off of the chicken and rice I've been smelling the entire drive out here. I snag the bag and turn my back to him in an attempt to keep it to myself.

"Hey! No way you're getting all of that," he says, his seat belt clicking as he unbuckles and lurches over the console to put his arms around me. I fumble with the wrapper on the fork, tugging it off with my teeth while he fights to take the box container of food from my other hand.

"Hey, buddy. Get your own!" I twist back and forth in an attempt to shirk him off, but his arms only get tighter around me. And then I stop fighting because his palms are wrapped around my biceps, and he's squeezing me against his chest, and his mouth is at my neck. Our laughter stops. My chin moves to my shoulder, where all I can see are his parted lips, tongue caught in his front teeth. He breathes out as a soft smile forms, the air against my neck sending goose bumps down my spine.

His hands glide down my arms, and I release the container and fork when he takes them from me. He sets them on the dashboard with his left hand, which quickly returns to me, his palm gentle against my face.

My gaze settles on his mouth, on the healing spot on his upper lip, the stitch there but the skin no longer pink or bruised.

"Does it hurt?" I reach up and lightly run my finger across it.

He shakes his head, his eyes flitting to meet mine for a moment before his attention immediately returns to my mouth.

"You took that punch for me, didn't you?"

His head tilts an inch or two away from me as he glances up.

"I really took it for Whiskey, but sure, you too."

I shake with a soft laugh and twist in my seat and his arms so I'm facing him more head-on.

"We need to work on your game, Wyatt. First, the abandoned driving range, then you give away heroics meant for me to a two-hundred-pound lineman."

"Two fifty-seven," he says with a shrug.

His smile comes in sharp and fast, and I look up at the

ceiling of the cab with exasperation. His hand moves along my jaw, though, coaxing my attention back to his face.

"You know it was for you."

A new kind of quiet settles in, his eyes roaming my face as his thumbs caress my jawline. I move my hand up his chest, his muscles hard underneath the soft cotton of his T-shirt. I snake my palm around his neck and shift my weight, coaxing him to sit back in his seat as I climb over the center console to straddle his lap. His chest rises and falls faster, my body moving with every breath he takes as my palms flatten against his chest and I let my weight sink down on him.

I can feel how hard he is under his shorts, and a low grumble escapes his mouth as I position myself so the neediest parts of us meet. I lean into him and kiss his upper lip gently, careful not to hurt him. His hands slide to my hips and he pulls me up into him, then urges me to rock back again, his want unmistakable. I nip at his bottom lip, and his teeth graze against mine as his hips shift to push his hardon against me.

I give in and kiss him deeper, still careful to keep my attention on his plump bottom lip, my tongue meeting his. I've never had a kiss feel so instantly perfect. It's as though our mouths are meant to be together, to connect like this. He coaxes my head to the side so he can kiss his way along my jawline and to my neck, and I grind my hips on him to relieve the impossible need growing between my legs.

"You're so fucking beautiful, Peyton," he murmurs in my ear.

I give him more of my neck to taste, and his tongue draws a seductive line up to my earlobe, which he nips with his teeth. My hands drop to the bottom of his shirt, and I gather it up his abdomen, my knuckles grazing against every ripple of his abs and over the hard contours of his chest as he lets me pull his shirt up over his head.

"How are you built like this?" I half tease, dropping my mouth to his shoulder to take a soft bite of his salty skin.

His hands shift from my hips to my back, roaming up either side of my spine and over the elastic band of my sports bra. They deftly slip underneath, rolling the stretchy fabric up my back a few inches before his thumbs hook into the taut fabric under each breast. I sit up and meet his heated stare, nodding before slipping my shirt over my head. His gaze drops from mine to my chest, his thumbs sliding across my nipples underneath my sports bra before his hands work to push the fabric up to expose me to him completely.

He sits up quickly, his mouth covering one of my nipples while I wrap my arms around his head, holding him to me. I never want him to stop. His tongue flicks my tender skin as his hands drop to my waist and encourage me to rock against him more. I roll my hips, feeling my own wetness in my panties and I'm sure my cheer shorts. His hands move to the backs of my thighs, his fingers clawing under my shorts until his hands are basically cupping my ass cheeks as I roll my body against him harder.

I can feel the edge coming closer, my core tightening as

every rock of my hips brings a new promise of pleasure, and I let his name slip from my lips.

"Wyatt," I plead again.

He tugs on my nipple with his teeth, then sucks it into his mouth, soothing the tip with his tongue as he works me against him in his lap. I begin to pant, and I press one palm on the ceiling as my other hand holds on to his shoulder for leverage. The wave comes soon after, and Wyatt isn't far behind as his mouth opens and his eyes roll back.

I collapse against him, my glistening skin sticking to his. He rakes his fingertips lightly up the small of my back to the curve of my shoulder blades. The gentle tickle sends shivers across my skin, and Wyatt reaches to the passenger seat, grabbing his T-shirt and slipping it over my head. While I wasn't done feeling his bare chest against mine, I also wasn't going to refuse him taking care of me. Of getting inside his clothes and smelling him, keeping this shirt and taking it home. Wearing it to bed at night. Dreaming of him and this, and when we can do this again. When we can do more.

W yatt slips into a pair of sweatpants he pulled from his gym bag. I sneak a peek at him as he changes outside the truck, though all I can really see is the curve of his ass as his back is to me and the moon is barely a sliver.

I haven't said it out loud, but my inner voice keeps asking me what I'm doing. Did I really trade one quarterback for another? And this one should be, by all terms and conditions, off limits. Yet no kiss has ever felt so right. No person has ever made me feel so seen. In all the months I spent with Bryce as his "lucky girl," as he called me, never once did he make me feel the way Wyatt did just now.

Beautiful.

The chicken is cold, so Wyatt and I share what's left of the kettle corn and the pumpkin cupcakes I brought. He flips down his tailgate then lifts me by the waist so I have a place to sit, and we look out at the dry, rolling hills that are going to be turned into some housing project in the next year.

"What's the story with the driving range?" I take a nibble of my cupcake as I glance his way. Our eyes meet for a second and he pivots as he laughs, eventually making his way to the space next to me. He pulls himself up to sit and takes the second cupcake.

"It's going to make me sound like an angry rage-head or something," he says, his fingers struggling to peel away the paper cup from the cake.

"Here," I offer, resting mine on my thigh. I pull his paper back easily with my fingernails.

"Universal tools," I say with a shrug.

He smirks and touches the tip of my index fingernail.

"And weapons."

I wince and he leans into me, dropping a soft kiss on the tip of my nose.

"Don't tell anyone, but I kinda liked the scratching," he

whispers. He takes his cupcake back, and I cover my heated cheeks with my hands.

"Come on, don't get shy on me now," he laughs out.

I bite my bottom lip and uncover my face, but quickly dive into eating my cupcake to take the attention away from the fact I got worked up enough to scratch him like a werewolf.

"Okay, now you have to tell me how you're a rage-head because I feel like a horned-up vixen."

He coughs out an instant laugh, sending crumbs from his mouth.

"Wow, I wasn't going to call you that, but since you said it—"

I lean into his side and he quickly puts an arm around me, so I decide to stay.

"It's not much of a story, but I found this place on accident the day we signed for the new house." He takes another bite, then sets his cupcake to his side, glancing to me then out into the very still, extremely warm night.

He runs the back of his hand over his eyes, squinting with thought.

"You remember what I told you about my dad?"

He drops his gaze to me, and I nod.

"We were close. Like the way you and your dad are. At least, I *think* you're close."

I nod and utter, "We are." I'm hit with a sudden appreciation of the fact.

"He was a firefighter, and he got cancer. Everyone knows the risks of the job, and it's hard not to believe that his cancer—the type he had—was related to all the shit he inhaled over the years."

I thread my hand with his and squeeze, and he brings my wrist to his mouth, pressing a soft kiss against my veins. He holds his mouth there for a few long seconds as his eyes close, then moves to hold the back of my hand against his cheek as he looks at me.

"I'm so sorry." I know he's heard those three words a lot, but it's all I can think to say. His soft smile lets me know it's enough.

"Thanks," he says, loosening his grip on my hand but keeping our fingers linked, moving his touch from one finger to the next.

"Losing him was—" His shoulder lifts slightly.

"Impossible," I finish for him, remembering the first time I was old enough to realize my dad was really hurt on the field.

"Yeah, definitely that. And then we were moving because it was expensive to stay where we were, and I don't think my mom wanted to wake up in the same house every day and remember."

"I get it," I say.

"Me, too," he adds with a long exhale. "That was home, though. My dad taught me to throw in the park across the street from our house. He coached my teams there. We held team BBQs in our backyard because he was the *man with the grill*. And, I don't know, we drove down here, and my mom handed over a cashier's check for a deposit on our new place and I . . . just . . . lost it. I drove out here while my mom walked through design choices and picked a lot, and I found this empty, sad plot of land that looked the way I felt inside. And I just screamed."

My gaze drifts to the nothingness, and I try to remember how this place looks in the daylight. We haven't been to the fairgrounds near the driving range in years. It's not an easy place for my family to come without people recognizing my mom. My dad wouldn't be able to make it through the gates without being swarmed. But I remember this driving range. I remember how the grass went from green to brown in the summer. I can visualize the torn-up netting that no longer keeps a ball from flying through without turning to dust on impact. The shreds of turf where golfers once made divots now grown over with weeds.

"It's a good place to scream," I say.

I slip down from the tailgate and take a few steps toward the broken concrete where the parking lot dissolves into dirt. Cupping my hands around my mouth, I yell so loudly that my throat burns. I think about summers wasted waiting on some boy to come back home and decide to pick up where we left off. I think about how much my dad thinks they're alike when they're nothing alike at all. I picture the smug look on Bryce's face when I overheard him today bragging about knocking Wyatt out. I hate that I didn't march into the middle of his clique and set the record straight. Tell them all he didn't knock anyone out, and that the guy he hit is twice the quarterback he is.

My voice curdles as the air runs out from my lungs, and I'm dizzy by the time I spin around to face Wyatt.

"Wow, that was some good—"

"Rage?" I finish.

He leans back on his palms and lets his legs swing off the tailgate as his head falls to the side.

"Yeah. That was some well-earned rage. How do you feel?"

I draw in a deep breath, my lungs filling a little more than normal. I smirk.

"I feel amazing."

Chapter Fourteen

Wyatt

If I've learned one thing about towns like this, it's that secrets have a way of spreading like wildfire.

Fire.

Ironic that's the thought I have given that just about everyone at Vista High knows about the CHS burnt into our end zone. I didn't say a word to anyone, and it was only me and Coach out there to discover it. He made it pretty clear to me, as did the police officer, that this was getting deemed an accident. Rivalries like ours tend to get amped up when talk about retribution gets involved. I know Peyton didn't say anything on her end either. Keeping her mouth shut was actually her mom's idea, so I'm sure things are buttoned up in their house as well.

Her mom agreed that giving this more attention will only add fuel. Petrol in the form of a two-hundred-twenty-pound former NFL quarterback who doesn't put up with bullshit in his hometown. Or with his team. And as much as I want Bryce to get his due, I want to be the one to give it to him—on the field.

Someone talked, though. Just enough. And the conversation is still going on in hushed tones across the bus aisle as we head home from our big win tonight against Marcos.

"What do you think? Coach said he just saw a fire, but someone posted this photo," Whiskey says, leaning over the back of his seat and showing me his phone screen.

I take his phone in my hand and zoom in to get a better look. Someone was watching Coach and me that night. Luckily, I'm out of view. I must have been dialing nine-one-one at the time because otherwise, I would have been right behind him. Regardless, it's pretty clear in this shot that the burn was in the form of Coolidge High's initials. I'm not sure how Coach scalped it clean after the fire department put it out. I'm sure he got help from a few of the firefighters. Hell, maybe even the cop.

I hand Whiskey back his phone.

"I don't know, man. People can do a lot with Photoshop, and you know how AI is now." I swallow down the lie.

"Yeah, I guess. But there's a lot of talk. And it wouldn't shock me after the way Bryce acted at the desert party. Speaking of, you up for a little repeat tonight?" Whiskey arches a brow.

My chest puffs with a short laugh.

"Uh, no. I was pretty sure it was a bad idea *before* I got

punched in the face, and now that my stitch is out, I'm certain of it. You shouldn't provoke them." I lower my gaze and hold his stare to make my point clear.

"Ehh, I think that was a one-time thing. He was jealous and shit, you know, because of you and—"

"And nobody," I fill in for him. My eyes flit to the seats around us and Whiskey covers his mouth. Somehow his goofy smile still sticks out the sides.

"Dude, I didn't know it was a big secret."

I sigh.

"It's not. But I don't think it's a thing either of us are talking about with a lot of people yet. And I'm pretty sure her dad hates me, so . . ."

"Coach J? No way! If he gets to know you, he'll love you. You're his perfect player. You throw so much like him, man."

"Yeah, I don't know. I think he's pretty committed to Hampton." My stomach turns at the thought of Bryce with Peyton. I don't begrudge her for her past, but I hate that he got to have anything with her. He doesn't deserve the memories.

"That's just 'cause Bryce wins. I promise you, if they drop more than a game this season, that guy's status will dive big time in Coach J's eyes," Whiskey says.

"Hasn't he only lost, like, two games in three years?" I don't know why I qualify that. It has only been two. I know exactly the ones. When a guy constantly bumps you out of the top QB ranking for the state, you pay attention to everything he does. You use it for motivation.

Whiskey shrugs and drops down into his seat.

"Yeah, but he doesn't have the team he had around him before. You have that team, plus some."

His phone begins to play music a second later, so I don't bother arguing with him again. And anyway, he's kind of right. I do have Bryce's old team—half of it. And the pieces we have are committed and full of heart.

I scoop my bag from beneath the seat and dig out my phone. My mom sent me her videos, which I appreciate, but she's still not great at following the action. I'll get the video clips from our assistant coach next week, but I text her *thanks* anyhow. I hope she left in the fourth like I told her to. It's a long drive from the Valley back out to Coolidge.

The next message is from my dad's old captain, Jeff.

JEFF: *I smell a new record, kid! Your dad is looking down proud.*

I heart his message and silently read it over a few times. My dad predicted I'd close in on some state records by now. God, he would have loved to be here for it.

I swipe to my contacts and hover over Peyton's picture. I stole it from her socials, and I'm sure she'll be pissed that I took one of her in her cheer uniform, but I am not ashamed. She's hot. And the cheer uniform? Yeah, it does it for me. Big. Time.

As if somehow the universe whispered to her that I'm thinking of her, my phone buzzes in my hand with a text from her.

PEYTON: *I saw the score. Nice win!*

Ours was a much closer game than theirs. Fourteen to three compared to their thirty-six to zero. Coach Watts told me Coach Johnson likes to stack the schedule that way to build his team's confidence, but I don't think it's the right move. I think that route gives false confidence. And when the real tests come, how can they know if they're really up to the job?

ME: *It wasn't a shutout like yours.*

PEYTON: *Shutouts are boring.*

I laugh out loud, then sink down before anyone notices.

ME: *I wouldn't mind one.*

PEYTON: *Maybe you should practice more.*

I smile at her comeback. We were up, probably too late, last night talking about my schedule and practice regimen. My dad instilled me with my discipline. It definitely does not come from my mom, who is habitually about five minutes late to everything in life.

Not my dad. My grandpa, his dad, was a former Marine, and growing up in their house there was a strict respect for sticking to a schedule. My dad loosened up a little over the years, likely from never being able to convert my mom to being a time-obeyer, but when it came to reaching my goals in my sport, there were definitely charts involved.

ME: *I did skip my morning run. I was sleepy for some reason.*

I was exhausted because I stayed up until two talking to Peyton. I fought through sleepy eyes just to keep her on the phone. My ass paid for it tonight, too, because I was definitely gassed by the fourth quarter. On fresh legs, I probably would have made it into the end zone on that last drive. Twenty-one to three is definitely a bigger statement win. But we won. And I'm not in the hunt for rushing yards. I'm chasing throw touchdown numbers and passing yards.

PEYTON: *Was it worth it?*

I don't even have to think about it.

ME: *Absolutely.*

In fact, I'd rather spend tonight learning more about her over the phone than sitting on the outskirts of some desert party where my presence is clearly not wanted. Unless, of course, she'll be there, and I can learn things about her in person. While touching her. And kissing her.

ME: *Whiskey plans to show up again. FYI*

PEYTON: *Really?*

ME: *He insists it's no big deal.*

The flashing dots indicating she's typing last for several seconds, then stop. Maybe she's already back at the school. Their game wasn't quite as far away as ours, and the cheerleaders travel in a van, separate from the bus. I wish quarterbacks got the van treatment. Not that I don't love bonding with the guys on the way there, but damn, I'd really like to get to the showers faster on the way home.

I'm about to check in on her and ask if she's planning to go to the desert tonight when Whiskey pops up over the seat back again, his brow pulled in like an angry bear.

Maybe it's the eye black smeared down his cheeks that makes him look so mean.

"Dude, you fucking snitched on me? What the hell?"

Nope, he's mad.

I sigh and fall back into my seat, bringing my phone up to read the message I just received.

PEYTON: *I forbid him.*

My gaze shifts to my friend's disappointed expression, then back to my phone screen.

ME: *So he says. Can't we just put him on a leash or something? He looks so sad.*

"Is that her you're texting? Can we call her?" He reaches over the seat to grab my phone, and I twist to keep it away from him.

PEYTON: *Good luck with that. I'm going with the girls. I have to drive. We have a regional competition tomorrow, and I need them to stay sober-ish. Tell him I'll be watching.*

It stings a little that she didn't ask me to come, but I get it. Things between our schools are rough right now, and after seeing that photo Whiskey showed me, putting me and Bryce in the same vicinity anytime soon isn't a good idea for either of us. My resolve is only so strong. I don't need to tempt my worst instincts to the point that I fuck over my future.

I glance up and meet Whiskey's eyes.

"She said you're to behave. And stick by her. Can you do that?"

His stupid big grin says he'll try his best.

"I'm serious, Whisk. Coach Watts doesn't want us starting shit," I plead with him.

"You mean shit they already started?"

I grumble and level him with a serious look.

"Yes, *Dad*," he bemoans, disappearing behind his seat and immediately shouting across the aisle. "It's party time, boys!"

Fuck.

I start to write back to Peyton to warn her that she may need to babysit more than one of our players, and that maybe I should come too, when someone behind me rips my phone from my hand.

"What the fuck?" I shout, spinning around and stepping on my seat. My phone gets passed back through a few hands, the first set from our backup center, who thinks he's being funny. I shove him into the corner of his seat, ignoring the shouts from Coach at the front of the bus warning us to sit the fuck down.

"You updating your dating profile, pretty boy?" This time the barbs come from Noah, my defensive back.

"Ha ha. No, but my phone is my business, so give it back." I dive for it but Noah quickly flicks it behind him to Ransom, my back-up who would probably love to see me get my ass sat for a game. He's shit, though, so I'm pretty sure he's the only one rooting for him to step foot on the field during a game.

"Your business, huh?" he says, holding his foot up and pressing it into my gut as I lurch into his seat. His eyes scan my phone, and my chest tightens. I know what he's reading.

"You got business with Peyton Johnson?" He drops his foot and I snatch my phone from his hand but stay close enough that he has no choice but to smell my breath. I hope it's rancid.

"I said, my phone is my business," I bite out, lunging at him so he flinches.

I go back to my seat and hold up my palm to Coach, who is now standing in the aisle.

"Sorry, Coach. Won't happen again," I growl.

My eyes meet Whiskey's, though I doubt he can read my thoughts. I would give anything for him to stay away from that desert party tonight, and keep the other guys away, too.

"Your girl there know anything about the fire on our field, Wyatt? You let her in to set it?" Ransom is provoking me, and I squeeze my eyes shut, willing myself not to respond.

"Should we ask her ourselves?" he continues, and I snap.

"You don't say shit to her. Ever. Got it?" I point at him, but keep my ass in my seat. I hold his stare, and his smirk turns into garbage laughter. I fantasize about smacking it from his face.

I return my focus to the front of the bus, and my phone vibrates in my palm. I expect Peyton, but instead it's Whiskey.

WHISK: *I get it. We'll start our own tradition tonight.*

My shoulders drop a hair in relief, but my body is still tense. I type back, *Thank you.*

I should probably go with him if it's something just for our team, but now I'm *really* not in the mood. Plus, I'm sure I'd get more questions about Peyton, which would only fuel more rumors and questions about the fire. At this point, I want to throw Bryce Hampton to the wolves—or rather, the Mustangs. Let them have him.

Chapter Fifteen

Peyton

My baby sister is at that age where she absolutely loves me, but she wants nothing to do with sitting still and watching me do what I love.

I've spotted my mom running the bleachers at Eastern College at least a dozen times in the last hour, either chasing my sister up and down the steps or scooting her off to the bathroom. Our squad is up next, and my mom is nowhere to be found. But someone else just showed up, and suddenly I'm sweating bullets.

I assumed when Wyatt said he would come to my cheer competition he was being nice, but when he confirmed the time with me early this morning, I realized he was serious. Still, he had film review today. And if his coach is anything like my dad, I can't imagine they got through everything before ten. Yet here he is—ten-fifteen and fifty miles away from home.

"I take it things between you two are . . . progressing?" Tasha hugs me from behind and rests her pointy chin on my shoulder like a dart. I squirm and she only holds on tighter, her teased out ponytail mingling with mine.

"It's all kind of overwhelming," I admit to my friend.

"*Hmm*, I see that. But still," she pulls away and twists me to face her. "It must be nice. I mean, Bryce never shows up for competitions. Hell, none of our guys show up. Yet, look at that corner of the gym."

She points up to the second-level seats above where Wyatt is standing, and it takes my eyes a minute to adjust to the sight. There are a dozen of them, maybe more, all wearing their Mustang jerseys. Some of them have signs covered in glitter.

"Did they make those themselves, you think?" I ask Tasha.

"My guess is yes. Did you see those bubble letters?"

I squint at the sign that reads GO LADY MUSTANGS and chuckle.

"It's a little scrunched up at the end," I say through my laughter.

"Peyt, it looks like they turned that shit on its side with the glue wet," Tasha jokes.

I give it another inspection and nod.

"Yeah, but at least they showed up. We have to be at their game every single Friday, and yet they can't bother to show up once." My stomach sinks at my own words because that statement? It covers my dad, too.

We both look on as the group of bulky guys squeeze into the bleacher seats amid hundreds of cheer moms. A quick survey of the gym proves they're the only football team to show up for their cheer squad. And my gut tells me the reason they're here is because Wyatt convinced Coach and his teammates that they needed to show their support.

Tasha leaves me at the practice room doorway, and I linger for a few extra seconds until Wyatt spots me and lifts a hand. He nods up the stairs toward his teammates, and I shake my head with a silent laugh and a pang of jealousy that they all showed. He gives me a thumbs up, and I remind myself that at least one of them is here for me.

I return to my squad as he heads up the steps to join the rest of his team. The girls are all sitting in a circle, stretching and visualizing, when I step up behind two of the younger members.

"She's only on the squad because her dad is who he is," one of them says. I stop a few steps behind them and hold my breath.

They think they're being quiet, covering their mouths with the fronts of their hoodies pulled up, like pitchers talking to catchers in the middle of a game. Only those guys? They're plotting the best pitch to throw. These girls are just being mean. About me!

"I wonder if Coach will cut her ass when her dad finds out she's hooking up with the Vista QB. I bet she's doing that for attention, to make Daddy angry." This one is named Stephanie, and she laughs like Cookie Monster as her mean-ass friend, Langley, spots me in her periphery. She turns ghost white in a blink, like, as in even her freckles vanish.

"Hey, ladies. Make some room?" I part my hands as if I'm parting the sea, and they quickly scoot in opposite directions. The pale one looks sick, but Stephanie, the one who thinks Coach will *cut my ass?* She seems up for a challenge.

I've been talked about most of my life. That's part of the curse of having a famous dad. And when you're a teenage girl, it's like you instantly have a target on your back for bullies of all ages. In their eyes, nothing I get is ever because I earned it. It doesn't help that cheer is so intertwined with football, so the leap that my dad is involved isn't a big one. Sometimes I wish like hell I was drawn to anything else—figure skating, sculpting, the piano. *Anything!*

But I love tumbling. I love making my body strong and being part of a team. And if I'm honest with myself, I even love the goddamn Friday nights. What I don't love, though, is overhearing people disparage me. It's not only that their words hurt—which they do—it's that I know they've said those things a lot, all of the times I wasn't listening. Meanwhile, I've been nice to their faces. And when it came to these two, I cast the final vote to put them on varsity.

I hold all of that in and instead turn my attention to Stephanie when it comes time for me to lead us through stretches.

"Why don't you take this one?"

Her eyes widen briefly before blinking a few times.

"You mean, lead?" She leans her head toward the inner circle.

I force my laugh to remain breathy and light—friendly.

"Yeah. You want to be captain one day, right? This will be good for you. Get us hyped. First big comp of the year. Take us out to mat."

Tasha leans forward from a few people down and meets my gaze. I drop my smile for a blip, my mouth a hard line as my eyes bore into her. We've been friends long enough for her to get a sense of what I'm doing. Also, this is not how my friend would handle this. She would call Stephanie out in front of everyone and probably threaten to punch her in the throat. Then there would be detentions involved, and we'd be down two girls for the next two weeks.

My way is better. This is how my mom taught me to handle things. By letting people have the floor and either rise to the occasion or dig their holes deeper.

"Are you sure?" Stephanie whispers.

"Uh huh." My smile is Teflon.

"O-kay," she says, her voice vibrating as she stands and moves to the middle.

"Girls, Stephanie is going to take us out today. Let's give her our best," I say, my palms flat on the floor between my legs as I prepare to stretch.

"I'm so sorry you heard that," her friend mutters from next to me. I wondered how this would go when she was alone.

I tighten my lips and breathe in through my nose, following along as Stephanie leads us through our first stretches.

We all lean forward, stretching our palms to the center, and I maintain my focus on the small space between my two thumbs.

"Don't be sorry," I say. "I'm glad I heard it. It's nice to know what people say when they don't think you're listening."

While the spirit of that statement is true, it also sucks. It's not that I wish I didn't hear their words, though; I wish they never said them at all. That's the difference.

"Can I teach you something, though, Langley?" I roll my head to the side and meet her waiting stare. She looks petrified, and her eyes are glossy. She may have just gotten caught up in things, which is good. It means this lesson will be good for her. Good *to* her. In the long run.

"People who say things behind other people's backs . . . are probably also talking about you that way when you aren't around to hear it." I sit up slowly, sliding my hands along the floor as Langley does the same. She swallows hard.

"I'm sorry," she croaks.

And all I can seem to say is, "Okay."

We finish our stretches and Stephanie pulls us all into a tight cluster to start our hype cheer. I keep my promise and let her run the show, though she's not as good as I am. It's good enough for today. And maybe she'll walk away with a better perspective on things. Or maybe not.

The Chandler High team finishes their routine to massive cheers, which I can tell intimidates some of my teammates. They need more than the hype session Stephanie left them with, but they also deserve my entire heart in it. And right now, I need to go somewhere and cry.

There are ten minutes between routines, time for the judges to tally scores, and for the inspectors to check the mats and set up our props. I mumble something about going to the restroom as I move toward the hallway and deep into the bathroom. I step into the far stall and pull the door shut just as my eyes begin raining tears. But as I close the door behind me, someone tugs it the other way.

I gulp with fear at first, not wanting to get caught, but then I see it's Tasha and let everything I've been holding on to so tightly go.

"Hey, come on. Step in there," she says, ushering me toward the toilet so she can squeeze in with me and shut the door.

I laugh at how absurd this is, but the tears are still welling up. I fan my face with my hands and blow out through my mouth like my mom does with her hot flashes.

"My mascara—"

"Oh, babe, that's toast. Don't save it. Just let it go," Tasha says, pulling me into a hug. She still has her sweatshirt on, thank goodness, so I sink against her and let my tears run down my cheeks, destroying the glitter bear paw print Lexi spent an hour perfecting this morning.

"Those girls are bitches. I told you we shouldn't have taken them on varsity," she says.

I quake with sad, pathetic laughter because she was so mad when I fought to save them. Irony. Sad fucking irony.

"They aren't bitches. They're young," I say, trying to be what I preach.

She steps back and holds me at arm's length, hands on my shoulders, and I meet her hard stare.

"Peyton. I love that you want to believe women are inherently good, because yes, we are so much better than males. But some of us? Just plain bitches."

This time, my laugh is genuine and a little louder.

"I fucked up Lexi's paw, didn't I?" I blabber.

Tasha shakes her head but proceeds to nudge flecks of gold and glue on my face with the sharp tip of her fingernail. I still don't know how she tumbles in those.

We breathe together for nearly a minute, and when my emotions are finally in check, I unlock the stall door and check my friend's handiwork in the mirror. The paw print is missing a toe, but I doubt anyone will notice. Even Lexi.

I follow my strong best friend to the exit, touching her spine before she pushes the door open. She glances to me over her shoulder and I mouth, "I love you."

"I love you more," she says.

Her faith in me is enough to push me to be the leader my team deserves.

With five minutes to mat, I gather everyone behind the set and prepare the new team members with what to expect.

"There will be fog when you run through the balloon arches and it will smell terrible, like burnt popcorn. Smile anyway," I say. "The bases will run out first and set our spots, the rest of you will work around us. It's imperative that we leave our tumblers enough room to really stretch. We don't want a repeat of last year's championship."

A few of my teammates nod while others scan their faces, not entirely sure what I'm talking about. Lexi knows since she's the one who tumbled right off the stage.

"The most important thing of all is that we are one. We do this together. If one of us falls, we pick that person up. If one of us nails it, we celebrate them loud. We smile through everything. We are proud of every stunt. We wait until tomorrow to pick apart skills. Today—right now? We rule. Are we ready?"

"Yes we are!" the upperclassmen shout.

"I said *are we ready?*" My voice almost sounds hoarse, but it's worth it when every single member of our squad joins in. I don't have to look to know we're turning heads. I feel it.

It's exactly twenty seconds from the time our school is announced to the first beat of our music. And for the next two minutes and fifteen seconds, we are precise and loud. My legs buzz with energy, partly in thanks to adrenaline but mostly thanks to the energy drink I pounded before I saw Wyatt was here.

I throw and catch with confidence, and when it's time for me to do my standing back tuck, I've mostly forgotten that the girl flipping next to me hurt me at all. Our hands link for the final stunt, and we catch our flyer together, setting her on the floor and falling into splits just as the music ends.

"We are Coolidge! C - H - S!"

We're a bigger squad, so we're usually louder than most of the teams we compete against in the state. But we sound twice our size today. And the reaction from the crowd fills my chest with warmth, like everyone is somehow hugging me from the inside.

We scurry off the mat, and the usual post-show energy takes over. Everyone loves everyone right now, but there's a nagging burn in the center of my chest when Stephanie pulls me into a hug. I want to give her the benefit of the doubt, to believe she'll be a better person now that she's been taught a lesson. But that ache in my heart tilts me otherwise. Tasha is right. Some girls are just bitches.

"You have a fan," Tasha says, nodding over my shoulder.

I spin around and find Wyatt waiting near the hallway that leads to the restrooms and the small lounge with the vending machines. I jog over to him, but slow before I reach him, nervously balling my hands into fists at my sides. All I want to do is throw my arms around him and let him tell me he's proud, but I can feel the eyes on my back. The *knives* at my back. Maybe they're imagined, and perhaps if I hadn't heard those terrible things, I wouldn't be so afraid right now. But I did. And I am.

Wyatt scans the group behind me and drops his hands into his pockets, seeming to be all right with playing it cool about us too.

"That was bitchin'," he says, and I spit out a hard laugh.

"I'm sorry, but the eighties called, and my grandma wants her word back," I tease.

His neck turtles a bit, but not for long.

"I'm bringing it back. I've been using it all day. Just ask Whiskey. I've got him on board."

"Uh, do you think it's smart to teach Whiskey new words?" I joke.

We both laugh, but it dies out in seconds, leaving an awkward quiet in its place.

"For real, though. You guys were awesome. You're going to take first or whatever at this. Is it gold? How do they rate these things?"

"It's first. Sometimes it's gold, though. And sometimes it's Superior, or points."

His eyes flutter as he shakes his head.

"I think I'll stick with touchdowns and extra points."

"Fair enough," I say. I glance behind me and catch a few people still looking in our direction.

"I'd take you home today, but I sort of turned this into a thing so now my truck is full." He shrugs and gives me a crooked smile.

"You know, Tasha was pretty impressed to see you all show up like this. Our team doesn't turn out for cheer comps." I don't mention my dad and his lack of presence in that statement, but the way Wyatt winces makes me believe it's silently understood.

"They're missing out," he says, his eyes softening a touch. *Your dad's missing out.* I hear what isn't said.

His gaze lingers on mine, and my lips buzz with nervous energy.

"You really turned this into a team activity just so you could watch me?" Maybe I'm jumping to conclusions and the guys decided to tag along on their own. Maybe they finished film early. Maybe—

"I'd walk through hell to watch you shine," he says, cutting me off mid-thought.

And suddenly, the eyes fixed on the back of my head matter so very little. I'm wrapped around him in a blink, and my mouth covers his before either of us can take a breath. My lips cover the small scar forming on his upper lip as he holds my thighs, my legs wrapped around his waist. He turns me slowly, and I can feel his smile stretch along my mouth as some of my teammates whistle. A few of the girls from other squads catcall, and my neck and cheeks burn from the attention. But his smile keeps growing, and I kiss it until it stretches so wide it's impossible for me not to reciprocate.

"That was . . . unexpected," he says, setting my feet back down on the floor.

"You were unexpected," I reply.

It's cheesy, and I suck in my bottom lip, a little embarrassed that I'm being so soft and mushy. But I needed that kiss. I needed this boy. I needed him to show up today, and he did.

"I'd like to see you tomorrow," he says.

"I'm working at Jack's. Building character and all that."

"Good, because I'll be hungry. For two, maybe three

meals. I hear the pancakes are amazing." He backs away with a wink, that same fucking wink that pierced my tough exterior almost a month ago. And when I finally face the girls who made me cry, I decide that Tasha is on to something, but so am I.

People will surprise you in so many ways.

Chapter Sixteen

Wyatt

I wasn't sure everyone would be on board for my whole Sunday team swim thing, but every single guy showed up for this morning's session. The pool was brisk, too. It's still hot as fuck out here by noon, but six a.m. swims don't give the water much time to heat up. The cold, however, is half the point.

"Your dad's polar plunge lives on, I see?" My mom picks up the soaking towel I left on the wood floor on my way from the front door to the bathroom.

I grimace.

"Sorry, I had tunnel vision on the hot water," I admit, taking the towel from her and hanging it on the bar in my bathroom. I pull a clean one out of the cabinet and dry the floor.

"I'm about to make some pancakes if you want some," she offers over her shoulder on her way to the kitchen.

"Oh, I actually . . . have breakfast plans." I hold my

breath behind a tight-lipped smile. My mom spins around and studies my face, a slow smirk growing on her face.

"You have plans, huh?" She's using that teasing voice.

"Yes, I do. And no, you can't come," I say, a little prevention warning.

Her knowing grin lingers as she turns around and continues into the kitchen. I trail behind her, running my hand through my wet hair a few times before snagging the Vista ballcap I left by my phone, my wallet and keys.

"Would this happen to be about that girl who was parked in our driveway the other night?" She pours herself a cup of coffee, and I swear the only reason she did was so she could eye me suspiciously through the steam.

"It may," I answer, backing my way toward the door. She's not done, but she's also likely happy to see me, well, happy. Things like dating haven't really been on my radar since my dad died. I've been going so hard at football, partly to drown out the hurt. My mom has brought up me needing balance a few times, but she never pushes.

Of course now that there is a real girl involved . . .

"And may I meet her?"

I just turned around to face the door and was almost out of here. I was *so* close. Squeezing my eyes shut, I recognize that strange tingle in my belly, the adolescent embarrassment that comes with a meddling, though loving, mom. I've missed it.

"You may. Or you may not. Time will tell," I tease, leaving her with a wink, the same way my dad would when he was being coy. Or, as she would say, *being an ass.*

I shut the door and hear her call out from the other side, "I have eyes everywhere, Wyatt!" I chuckle on my way to my truck but pause when I realize how true that statement is. I always thought I didn't hide things from her by choice, but maybe I simply know it's not really possible.

By the time I get to Jack's, most of the booths are full, so I take a seat near the register, the same stool her dad sat in the day I met him.

"Hi, sugar," Maggie says, sliding a menu in front of me. I wouldn't say I'm a regular here, but I guess I have been in a few times since I met Peyton. Those first few trips were in hopes that I'd see her again. The last visit, though, I hoped I didn't, but only because she was with her dad. And I can't seem to right the ship with that guy.

"I think Maggie likes you," Peyton says, squeezing my shoulder as she passes behind me with a tray filled with short stacks and bacon.

I indulge in being an overt spy while she doles out everyone's order. She's quick to compliment the two little girls at the table on their high ponytails. They both peel out of their booth seat to show off their cheer uniforms, and Peyton squats to give them high-fives.

"She's a good soul," Maggie says, catching me in the act.

I twist in my seat to set my legs straight ahead and own the bashful smile crawling up my cheeks.

"Seems like it," I agree.

"It's been hard on her, growing up with the spotlight always ready to turn up the heat. It's not as bad as being a movie star's kid, but around here, her daddy is a pretty big deal. Lots of people were rooting for her to screw up as a teen. Lots of people rooting *for* her too. But those negative voices are so much louder than the good ones."

"*Hmm.*" I nod and recall the few times I felt the pressure of my dad's reputation, and he was just a local firefighter. He was a hero to a lot of families, though, and there was always this subtle expectation that I be the perfect kid. I nearly failed my freshman year of high school out of some weird rebellion that overtook me. Football was the only thing that saved me—you can't fail and still play.

And then my dad died, and football saved me again. It's the one place where I swear he's still with me; where I feel him. Always.

After Peyton finishes her rounds, she stops at my end of the counter, leaning across it and propping her chin on her hands.

"I'm not sure which I think is cuter, by the way," I say.

She quirks a brow.

"The cheer uniform or the waitress one."

I shrug when she scowls at me, but when she drops her palms on the counter, I take her hands in mine and lead her around the counter until she's standing between my legs. When she rests her hands on shoulders, I straighten her name badge clipped on the right side of her chest.

"Come on, don't tell me you don't like me in the uniform," I tease.

She slides her hands down and grabs the front of my shirt, clutching it as she leans her head to the side.

"Can't say for sure. I haven't seen you in it."

I give her side eyes, and she leans her head back with an exasperated sigh.

"Okay, sure. I've seen photos and maybe a few videos here and there. You're, like, constantly playing on my dad's laptop, just so you know."

I flinch a little at that fact. I figured he was scouting me for our match-up, but I have to admit, I'm a bit honored to be on such high rotation.

"I think I need to see you in person to really make a fair judgement, though," she says, and I feel a sudden jolt of hope tickle its way up my chest. It's a bye week for her school.

I lower my gaze.

"Should I reserve a seat for you?"

She glances up playfully, then drops her gaze to mine as she nods.

"Do not expect me to wear your jersey or anything like that, though. I will remain utterly neutral."

I tip my chin, luring her closer so I can press my lips to hers.

"Now, you in my jersey . . . that is an outfit I haven't explored."

She kisses me again, then steps back, a coy expression on her face.

"Yes, you have, and you know it," she teases.

I shake my head, but she's right. I've fantasized about her wearing a lot of my clothes, and being in my bed, and taking *off* my clothes.

Before I carry our flirting on, I notice her gaze get hijacked somewhere beyond my left shoulder. I glance behind me and spot the blue jerseys right away. The two guys wearing them avert their eyes the second I look their way, suddenly overly interested in their plates of food. When I return my attention to Peyton, she's busied herself by wiping down the counter.

"Are some of them bothering you?" The thought of people giving her a hard time because of me makes my stomach sick, yet at the same time, it fills my fist with blood.

She shrugs.

"It's fine. Sometimes, people take high school football way too seriously." Her lips form a curt smile as she tops off my water and sets up my place setting.

"Tall stack? Extra syrup?" she says, predicting my order but also changing the subject.

"Hey." My head tilts as I implore her with my eyes to let me help.

She swallows and glances at my menu for about a half second before snagging it and uttering, "I'll get your order in."

I wait for her to disappear into the kitchen before I turn my attention back to the table of Coolidge players. I wish Whiskey were here. Other than Bryce, he seems to be able to bridge the gap between our teams. The one who I caught snickering before glances up and meets my gaze. Unlike him and his friend, though, I'm not ashamed of getting caught staring. In fact, I think I'll settle in and make myself comfortable while doing it.

He mouths something to his friend, gesturing my way, and the bigger guy glances over his shoulder. I lift my palm in a wave, but we all know I'm not really waving. I keep my periphery alert in case Peyton pops back out of the kitchen, but until then, I plan to make these guys as uncomfortable as they were making her.

Without the aid of checking my phone for the time, I'd say I get a solid five minutes of gawking nosiness in before one of them walks up to the counter with their check to get Maggie's attention. His friend gets up to wait behind him while they settle their bill, and I turn in my seat to make certain they know I plan to watch their asses all the way to whatever vehicle they came here in.

The taller one who paid slides his credit card back into his wallet, then turns to face me while he puts his wallet away.

"How's that field of yours, Rebound?" His smug expression really pisses me off, but I manage to swallow my desire to blow up at him.

"Cute nickname," I say, instead of the line of insults I want to spit out.

He glances down at the floor as he slowly makes his way closer, his friend behind him wearing a massive grin. They're such a stereotype. Bulldog and his terrier.

"You know she's just trying to make Bryce jealous. That's why—"

"Yeah, it's why you called me Rebound. Clever. I got it," I interject, taking some of the power out of what I'm sure he's been practicing in his head the entire time I stared at him.

He chuckles and glances to the kitchen door, where my periphery picks up a flash of Peyton's blue apron. His chest puffs with a bigger laugh as his attention returns to me.

"You better get those yards in before we play you. That's all I'm saying." He sniffles and gazes out toward the parking lot as if he's one of those gangsters in the movies. It's comical. And sad.

"Noted. Just one thing?"

My smart mouth. This is how I get myself into trouble. This is why I've been hit before.

"Yeah, Rebound?"

"What if . . . I don't care?" My mouth rests in an easy, flat line, and my pulse is right as rain. I actually think I mean those words. I *don't* care that these guys don't like me. I don't care if they call me a rebound, mostly because I know I'm not. The more I get to know Peyton, the more I learn just how honest and genuine she is. And high school cafeteria drama bullshit? That's not in her wheelhouse. But I'm guessing it is in theirs.

The big guy leans in, placing a hand on my shoulder. It's offensive, and my hand balls into a fist along my thigh, but I leave it there.

"You care. And she should too," he says at my ear. When he pulls away, I catch Peyton's eyes on me from across the dining room. She looks pissed, but I'm not sure at whom.

Rather than tag along behind them and keep this conversation going, knowing full well I'd probably end up getting myself into trouble, I stick to my seat and simply grin as they turn and head out the door.

Maggie sets a plate of pancakes in front of me, and Peyton strolls in my direction with a pitcher of syrup dangling from one hand. Her lips pursed, she holds the syrup hostage as she levels me with a cautious look.

"You don't have to fight my battles, you know," she says. I reach for the syrup, but she pulls it into her chest and holds my stare.

I breathe in deep and exhale through my nose.

"I know. And I'm not fighting yours, at least not entirely. I'm fighting mine."

She blinks slowly but seems to buy my response, setting the syrup down and nudging my plate an inch closer to me.

"You better eat up. You'll want to be full of energy so you can impress me when you take the field Friday."

A sheepish grin tugs one side of my mouth up, and I unwrap my knife and fork while I gaze at her.

"We need to find a field first. Ours isn't ready yet." I laugh out, then dive into my pancakes, slicing up a few bites, then dousing them in syrup.

"Well, wherever it is. I'll be there. And I guess I could wear your sweatshirt or something. Just no jersey. I'm not *that* girl."

I smirk as I glance up at her mid-bite.

"You're definitely not. You're something else entirely."

She taps my nose, seeming satisfied for now that I've let

the beef with those two CHS players go. But I'm not letting her leave this place alone. I'll dig out my homework from my truck and set up camp in the corner until she's off. There's just something about that guy's threat that rubs me wrong. They can fuck with me, my field, all they want. But when people start coloring outside their lines, I can't let that go unchecked. At the very least, I can make sure she gets home safely.

By four in the afternoon, I've written notes for a history paper and studied for my economics quiz. I pack up my backpack while Peyton clocks out, and I take her hand when she slips out of her apron and rounds the counter.

"You didn't have to stay all day," she says when I hold open her Jeep door for her to climb inside.

I shrug.

"I wanted to. I don't like you walking out to the parking lot by yourself."

She laughs and reaches for her door, but I hold it in place until her eyes meet mine.

"The gesture is sweet, Wyatt, but I've been walking to my Jeep alone for a while, and I've been fine."

"Doesn't mean you shouldn't have someone watching out for you, though. Just means"— I shrug—"You haven't." It's a dig at Bryce for sure, but also maybe her dad.

She sucks in her lip and nods, and I let her pull her door shut on her own. She turns the engine over and rolls her window down as I walk to my truck.

"You might as well see me home, then," she shouts.

I chuckle and lift up my hand.

"Planned on it."

Peyton's out of the parking lot by the time I get into my truck, but I catch up to her by the first light. I keep her within a few car lengths for the entire route home, catching her gaze on me in her rearview whenever we pause at stop signs and lights. I pull up behind her in her driveway and rush out in time to take her hand as she gets out of her Jeep. She rolls her eyes because, yeah, I'm being a little corny about it now, but also, I just really want to give her all my attention.

Her dad, however, seems pretty tired of seeing me. I saw him shining his truck when we pulled in. He tosses the shammy into a bucket near his front passenger tire and heads our way.

"You're starting to seem like a stalker, Wyatt. You two dating or something?" There's no humor in his voice. He's dead serious, and I'm not sure how to answer him. Peyton seems uninterested in answering at all.

"I was just making sure she got home safe, Coach. Seemed like no one else was."

Fuck, that second part wasn't supposed to be out loud.

His short laugh isn't the amused kind. He's wearing boots, and for some reason it makes him feel even more dangerous. His belt buckle is a Super Bowl brag, probably a replica of his ring. His *first* ring.

"I'm going to his game Friday, Dad. If you want to come," Peyton offers.

What the hell? I didn't know he was part of the package.

I give her a sideways glance, and I swear she chuckles.

"You don't have to come, sir. I'm sure you have better things to do on a bye week, and I'm not even sure where we're playing yet, you know . . . with the field."

His eyes dim, and I'm not sure by his expression, but I don't think he's fully aware of what happened to our end zone. I'm sure Coach Watts didn't call him up and tell him, but given how many of our guys know the story, I figured one of his old players would have said something.

"Field's not playable, huh?" He studies me for a moment, then shifts his gaze to his daughter. "I thought we didn't know about a fire."

Shit. I hope I didn't make trouble for Peyton.

"We don't," she says, her tone clearly saying otherwise. Her dad's focus remains on her for a few seconds, and all the while he continues to chew at the inside of his cheek. But in a flash, his gaze is back to me.

"You'll use ours. I'll call Watts. It's settled." He heads back to his truck, and I can't help but feel like I lost something just now. I'm not sure what, and maybe it's simply the sense of home field advantage, but there's definitely a hole in my chest. The wind is blowing right through it.

"Guess that means it will be an easy trip to make," Peyton says, sliding her hand down my arm and circling my wrist.

A nervous titter vibrates from my mouth, which is still hanging open.

"Yeah, there's a silver lining. But maybe the sweatshirt thing isn't such a good idea." I squint, mentally replaying the possessive move those guys made in the diner.

"We'll see," she says.

My nervous laugh ticks up a notch. I'm about to remind her that she just invited her dad to watch the game with her when she moves her palm against my cheek and steps up on her toes. Her lips find mine, and my face goes numb. Suddenly, wearing my sweatshirt in front of her dad feels like a kindergarten move.

"*Mmm*," she hums as our lips part. My tongue slips through my lips, chasing the ghost of our kiss as she skips her way toward her front door.

I'm not sure what hits me first, the snapping sound of a plastic bucket bouncing along the driveway or the droplets that splatter across my calves after Reed literally throws in the towel on his truck cleaning. His engine roars to life a second later, and he's down his driveway before my stomach fully drops into my feet.

There goes my idol. Somehow, in five days, I need to have the game of my life in front of him. And he couldn't possibly hate me more.

Chapter Seventeen

Peyton

Bye weeks are a gift. Not for my dad or the guys, necessarily, but for the rest of us? Bye weeks bring a certain peacefulness.

There was no rush to whip up a dance for halftime this week, which means we spent every practice inside and on the mat. We tied for second at our first comp, but ties won't get me tryouts with some of the schools I'm looking at.

I need to show up with golds. With hardware. On top of stunts.

Today, we tumbled for an hour. Straight. My brain is scrambled and I'm not sure where north is, let alone the floor versus the ceiling, but we tumbled. And for an hour, I thought of nothing but my hands hitting right and my feet landing square.

"Great work this week, everyone," Coach says, clapping to draw us in for her after-practice meeting.

I snag my long-sleeved T-shirt from the corner and jog to join the group as I slip it on. I'm sweaty now, but five minutes of standing still in this practice gym will turn me into ice.

"Now, I know it's an off week for us, but that doesn't mean we're off completely. As you know, our biggest fundraiser of the year is the Home Town Fest and parade, and this year we're looking at twice as many floats, twice as many marching bands—"

"So, two? Instead of one, we'll have two, right?" Tasha's smart-ass contribution earns her a fast glare from our coach.

"Yes, Tasha. Our band and the new high school's band." Coach seems purposeful in not saying their name—Vista.

"Got it," my friend says, sticking with sarcasm all the way. I elbow her to stop, but she sticks her tongue out at me and laughs.

"Anyway, my point is we will all be fighting for shared donations. People are going to have twice as many places to drop cash, so, Peyton . . ." Her gaze lands on me. I straighten my spine and nod, not sure where this is going.

"Peyt, I know it's your senior year, and you were maybe counting on being the parade queen, but we really can't afford to lose you at our booth. You drive the donations every year, and if we want to make it to Florida, we need those dollars."

I have no idea what my face looks like. I know how it feels. It feels as if a pot of boiling water was just thrown in my face and lemons were squirted in my eyes. I know the idea of being a parade queen is really not important. Hell, our parade lasts a mile and it travels down a two-lane road in front of city hall. But as stupid as the role is, I was really looking forward to it. My mom never got to do it. She was always on the sidelines. And I kind of wanted to sit on that seat and float down the road atop our football team's float in that throne.

"Right," I utter, my voice cracking a little.

Damn it.

I cough, embarrassed, and swallow down my disappointment. "So, we're selling the ribbons again, right? For homecoming the next week?" I know we are. There are boxes of them in my family's dining room. My parents paid for them.

I wish the school would just let my dad write a check to cover our cost for Florida, but apparently, everything needs to be equal across all clubs. He started a shit storm when he funded the stadium construction, and there were lawsuits that set a state precedent.

"Yes, that's right," Coach says, her expression puzzling a bit, probably because I seem so confused about things I clearly know.

Her attention drifts to my right.

"Lexi, as soon as you're done on the float, you'll need to join us at the booth—"

"I'm sorry, but we're still putting someone on the float?" I hear my voice, but I swear this isn't me. Why am I questioning this? I know what's happening. Lexi is riding in my place. And this isn't about my business skills. It's about not wanting drama at the parade because I dare to like a boy in a different jersey.

Coach's tongue is caught between her teeth, and I glance at my friend, whose eyes are sloped and heavy with stress. Lexi didn't ask for this, I'm guessing.

"You know what, it's fine. Yes, Lexi, join us when you're done," I say, and my friend's eyes snap to mine.

"No," she whispers, but I nod *yes*.

"Eyes on the prize, right?" Fuck, I hate this feeling of wanting to cry.

"Right. Great! Okay, break us down, Peyton," Coach says, walking away as we huddle up.

I manage to dig up enough spirit to lead us through a short cheer. Everyone lingers for a few seconds after, and I feel their eyes on me so I wave them off and smile.

"Guys, really. It's fine," I say.

"Daddy can't get you everything, I guess," Stephanie says behind my back.

And suddenly, it's not fine.

It *would* have been. I would have managed. But now? Now, I'm going to make things a lot worse.

I spin around and step into her space, bumping chests. She stumbles back, clearly not expecting me to react. Of course she wasn't. I'm always so . . . *together*.

"What is your deal?" My eyes bore into hers.

"I don't have one," she says, but she doesn't apologize. And today? I want an apology.

"No, I think you do."

"Is there a problem here?" Coach hollers from her office doorway,

"I don't know. Ask Stephanie," I snap.

The young cheerleader I fought to keep shakes her head and rolls her eyes to the side, and my resolve disappears. My hand flies up before my brain can compute what it's doing, and I swear I feel the sting on my palm before I realize I've slapped my teammate across the face.

"Peyton Johnson, get your ass in here now!" Coach's voice echoes throughout the empty gym, and my slap seems to have stunned everyone else silent. It's eerily quiet, the only sound the gasp Stephanie makes as she holds her face, her eyes welled up with tears.

Regret fills my chest, and I take a deep breath, my lips parting as I utter, "I'm—" But I stop short. Because I'm not sorry. I hate that I caused a shitstorm for our coach. I hate that I probably made a nightmare for my dad to deal with. But that slap? I'm glad I did it.

I don't know what that says about me. Maybe all of those stories my mom told me about being bullied when she was in high school have finally had their just dues through this act. I'm taking out all bullies for the both of us. Okay, well . . . *one* bully.

My eyes meet Lexi's, then Tasha's, and my friends both look shocked. Funny, a part of me sort of expects Tasha to high five me, but she looks pretty freaked out.

Oh God! I've freaked out.

I pivot and march straight into Coach Nelson's office, where she slams the door shut behind me. I brace myself.

"What the fuck, Peyton?"

"I know, I know," I say, covering my face in my hands. I fall into a chair, tears sliding down my hot cheeks.

I hear her sigh so I pull my hands away to find her sitting on the edge of her desk, her arms crossed over her chest. Her head leans to one side, and she doesn't look mad. She's definitely not happy, though.

"I just couldn't take it. Sometimes, it's hard. Being me is hard," I admit.

She goes to speak but snaps her mouth shut and instead exhales. She reaches to her side and grabs a tissue for me. I take it and dry my face as best I can, then wad the tissue into a tight ball with my hands in my lap, staring at it.

"Everyone assumes I get to be on the float because my dad is Reed Johnson. I'm the captain because my dad is Reed Johnson. I won homecoming princess last year because . . ." I look up and meet her gaze, shrugging as I shake my head.

"So what?" she says.

A breathy laugh leaves my lips.

"I know sometimes that's true. My dad's influence opens doors. I know I'm privileged, and I appreciate it, even when I'm embarrassed by it. But sometimes . . . sometimes I really think I earn shit on my own, you know? Sorry for the *S* word."

She chuckles and moves to take the seat next to me.

"Tell me the truth," I say, looking her directly in the eyes. "Did Principal Erikson ask you to pull me from the float?"

She breathes in and leans back.

"I thought so—"

"Peyton, your dad actually asked us to. He was worried about you taking the heat of the rivalry, and—"

I stand up, my body struck with a new sensation. Is this poison? I think I feel poisoned. I step around her desk, the sudden urge to pace taking over my legs.

"Peyton, he was coming from a good place. And really, it's just a float. I agree that it's an unnecessary risk to you. I can't afford to lose you because some idiot decides to do something stupid."

I suck in my top lip and hold in the new round of betrayal boiling inside me. I nod, but all I want to do is get out of here. To run away.

"I'll apologize to Stephanie. And I'll sit out next week or take detention. Whatever it is—"

"Peyton, I have to suspend you," she says through a sigh.

I nod, the tears threatening to come again.

Fuck! Fuck! Fuck!

I nod and suck my lip in tighter.

"I don't want to. And I'm sure when I interview the girls and Jordan, Stephanie's role in this will be clear."

"Don't punish her," I say.

She sighs again.

"I have to," she says.

I nod again.

I'm still not sorry for what I did. But I don't want it exploding like this, turning into such a scar. And if I'm honest with myself, I don't want Stephanie to have another reason to hate me so much. I'm not sure what that says about my self-worth.

"Can I go home?"

Her expression has softened a lot, and I almost think when I leave her alone, she might cry on my behalf. And I hate that. I hate being a burden.

"Go on," she says. "I'll talk to your dad after his practice."

"Okay," I say, currently not wanting to talk to my dad ever again. That will pass. It always does. But how could he be so short-sighted? Good place or not, I should have been a part of this decision.

I gather my gym bag. The gym is empty, though I'm sure my teammates are all sitting in the locker room talking about whatever the fuck just happened. I can't go in there. Instead, I exit through the main door and leave my change of clothes in my locker for, well, whenever I'm allowed back in there.

I make it to the Jeep without catching anyone's attention. Practice is still going strong on the field and my teammates are just starting to exit the locker room. I check my phone, seeing a text from Lexi, asking if I'm okay, and write her back.

ME: *I'll be fine. I'm really happy that you get to be queen.*

I don't want my friend suffering with guilt she doesn't deserve, but that text is a lie. I'm not fine. And I'm not happy about it. I probably should be. A better person would be. But I wanted the moment. And now, it's gone.

I peel out of the parking lot, sure my dad heard the squeal of the familiar tires. I hope it sinks in and simmers for a while until practice is done and he talks with my coach. And maybe he'll head home and get some better advice from Mom.

I don't go home. I simply can't face it. More than anything, I need someone who is all in on me. I pull up Wyatt's driveway and kill the engine, shutting my phone off to avoid the texts coming in asking about my meltdown. I hug my knees to my chest and stare in the rearview mirror for the next hour until his headlights light up the inside of the Jeep.

I get out as he pulls into his driveway, and when my gaze finally hits his, I cry for the third fucking time today. And these tears? They aren't stopping for a while.

Wyatt rushes to me and scoops me up in his arms, carrying me through his garage, which he closes behind us, and down a dark hallway to what I presume is his room. He holds me in his lap even as he sits on his bed, and when my tear-stained strands of hair stick to my face, he pulls them away.

He doesn't say a word for an hour, and when he finally does, it's to ask me if I want to stay. There's nowhere else I'd rather be right now than in his strong, supportive arms. I turn my face and murmur into his neck.

"Yes."

Chapter Eighteen

Wyatt

For the last hour, we've done nothing but sit in my bed like this—my back against the wall, Peyton curled up between my legs, her body against my chest, head in the crook of my neck.

My mom is working the overnight shift at the hospital. She's an admin, so she has been taking on any overtime she can to get us caught up on bills. I wish I could work to help her. I've offered, but it only makes her mad when I bring it up. My football practice is the priority, she always says. It would kill me to quit, but I would if it ever came down to it. I told Peyton that, and she simply shook her head and said quitting would kill my mom, too. She's probably right.

I let Peyton talk about what happened when she was ready. And now she keeps apologizing as if she did something wrong. I'm the one fucking up her life . . . but I don't think I can walk away. My dad always said I would know when I met someone who made me want to be *all in*. I thought he was corny, but he swore the feeling is real. It's how he felt about mom the moment he met her.

You were right, Dad.

"I'm sorry about this." She keeps saying those same words.

"*Shh*," I hush, my mouth at her ear.

"Would it help if I said you could ride on our float with me? It's just a Ford F-450 with a bunch of hay stacked in the back and Christmas taped to the sides, but I think it's the tallest thing in the parade." I'd have to kick Whiskey off, but I bet he'd step down for Peyton.

Her head rolls against my chest as she gazes up at me.

"You think me riding on the rival float is going to cause less of a stir?"

I smirk and tuck a strand of hair behind her ear.

"Probably not."

She reaches up and places her palm along my jaw, then runs her thumb along the fresh scar on my upper lip. It's smaller than I thought it would be.

"I really think your dad is trying to protect you," I say, my mind immediately going to the two guys I had a run-in with at Jack's while she was working.

She exhales, her eyelashes flickering as she stares out into the center of my room. It's dim in here, the LED lava lamp I got for Christmas two years ago casting a purple glow. Lately, the low light helps me sleep.

"I know you're right. But still . . ."

I run my hand through her hair once, then tip her chin back up so I can look her in the eyes.

"You wish he asked you."

She nods at my response. I know that's the part that hurts the most.

She shifts against me, reaching across my body to her phone that I fetched from her Jeep an hour ago. She still hasn't turned it back on, so I hold my breath as she does now. It buzzes to life with dozens of notifications, but she ignores them all. Instead, she opens her music app and starts a playlist.

The first song is Whiskey's anthem, and we both laugh as she fumbles to pick her phone up again and skip ahead.

"Whiskey is not the mood I'm going for," she says, the next song still a bit country, but softer and maybe a little bluesy.

"I like this," I say, hugging her tighter and looking over her shoulder at the list of songs.

"Chris Stapleton. He's one of my favorites," she says, reaching back across me to set her phone on my nightstand.

"Ah, yeah. My dad listened to him a lot." My heart soothes with the sudden memory.

Peyton slides back into place but pivots to her hip, resting her hand on my chest so she can better look me in the eyes.

"Tell me about him."

I'm flooded with so many feelings all at once, and I'm

not sure where to start. But the mere thought of bragging about him to a girl I'm falling for feels really good.

"He taught me, basically, everything I know. How to fry an egg. How to throw a spiral. How to change the oil on that truck." I lean my head in the direction of the garage.

"He teach you how to talk to girls?" she asks with a soft laugh.

My smile goes crooked as I recall the times he tried.

"He did his best. But I wasn't exactly a good student. I'm kind of shy."

Peyton laughs out, pushing against my chest and shifting so she's on her knees, sitting in front of me.

"What?" I hold on to her wrists, her palms flat against my chest.

"I wouldn't classify you as shy, Wyatt Stone." She drops her chin and dims her eyes, her stare suspicious.

"Really? Because those first few times I talked to you scared the shit out of me," I laugh out.

Her head tilts and her eyes widen.

"No way! You didn't seem nervous."

"Well, I was. You're clearly the hottest girl in town, and here I am this nobody from the city coming in all broken and full of dreams and shit."

She bats her lashes and bites her bottom lip, then leans in, resting her forearms on my chest.

"Hottest girl in town?"

My lip tugs up, and she can't see my coloring thanks to the purple light, but I know my cheeks are red.

"Definitely," I say with a nod.

She leans in closer, her nose grazing mine, and I slide my hands up her body until they're both tangled in her hair. Our mouths hover an inch apart, and I nip at her bottom lip a few times, wanting more of it.

"Hey, Wyatt?" she whispers.

"*Hmm?*" I nip again, snagging her bottom lip between mine and sucking lightly before letting go.

"You aren't broken. And your dreams . . . you're going to reach them."

My right hand weaves deeper into her hair and I coax her head back just enough to meet her gaze. She has no idea how much her words just soothed me, how much she breathed life into me right now. I wish I had the right words in response, but all I can do is hold her gaze long enough that I hope she understands.

Unable to resist any longer, I sit up and pull her into me, my mouth crashing into hers with the hungry kiss I wanted to give her the first time we touched. Her hands shove my T-shirt up my chest and I pull it over my head, tossing it to the floor. I do the same with hers, and she wriggles out of her sports bra as soon as her shirt is gone. My palms slide along her smooth back as my tongue moves against hers, her nails digging into my shoulder blades.

I move my hands around her hips, lifting her and rolling on the bed so she's lying flat. I hold myself above her, my arms caging her as I kiss my way from her mouth down the curve of her neck to the ripe peaks of her breasts.

I flick her nipple with my tongue and she arches in response. The way I make her move, the way my touch seems to turn her on, makes me flex beneath my sweatpants. I've been hard most of the night, and I'm sure she felt it while I held her. But now, my dick aches.

My mouth trails down the center of her stomach to her navel, and I dare to slide the front of her shorts an inch lower to kiss her there. She lifts her hips, and I glance up to meet her eyes as she nods, her bottom lip caught in her teeth. I lower myself against her and brace my weight on my elbows so my fingers can hook into the band of her shorts. I roll them over her hips, then pull them from her legs. Her white panties are low on her hips, and the cotton narrows into a thin strip as it curves between her legs.

I lick my lips as I glance up her body to her face, her eyes closed and her arms resting above her head. She draws her knees up halfway, and I take the invitation to press my palms on the insides of her thighs, sliding them closer and closer to her center until my right index finger strokes her over the cotton.

"Ah," she gasps, arching her back again and tilting her head even farther back. I run my finger over her swollen middle again, and this time she hisses. Careful not to rush things, I tease her along the side of the cotton strip until finally getting the nerve to slip my finger underneath. Her sensitive skin is swollen and wet, and she rolls her hips as I tease her gently, drawing languid circles around her before slowly sinking one finger inside of her. She whimpers, and I begin to pull my finger back, but her hand quickly covers mine and urges me to touch her deeper.

Feeling all of her, I slide down slowly with my hand never once leaving her, until my mouth is inches away from kissing where she aches. Tugging the cotton to the side, I press my lips to her pink skin, then move my tongue along the same path my finger took before. Her legs pull in, squeezing around my head before she opens them wider, inviting me in.

I press my cock against the mattress to ease the ache and keep myself focused on her. My hands work her panties down her hips and she pulls one leg out at a time while my gaze remains fixed on her incredibly sexy body. The thin trail of light brown hair leads to my new favorite taste.

When her hands dive into my hair and grip strands, I let go of some restraint and lick her with more force, pressing my tongue into her center, dipping it inside and sucking her in. I devour her for several minutes, her breath now a steady pant and her whimpers coming out more often and louder.

"What do you want?" I ask her, kissing her abdomen just above her dusting of hair.

She lifts her head, her eyes heavy with want, her mouth in a constant state of open.

"I want you," she says, and my dick flexes again, so ready to give in.

"Are you sure?" I ask, already shifting to my knees. I grab myself over my sweatpants to satisfy my urgent need for relief. I'm not a fuck boy like a lot of the guys on our team—like Bryce Hampton. I'd like to make this last longer than ten seconds.

"Yes, Wyatt. I want to do this. So bad," she whines.

I stroke myself over my pants again and hold her gaze for another second—until she nods—before reaching into my night drawer and pulling out the small box of condoms I never really thought I'd need so soon but oh so desperately hoped I would with her. One day.

Tonight.

I pull out a foil and tear it open with my teeth as I pull myself out with my other hand. My eyes are on Peyton's, and I note every flicker of her eyes and dart of her tongue through her lips as she takes me in while I roll the condom down my shaft.

She stills herself as I adjust my position, moving until my tip kisses her center. The heat is instant, and I beg myself to take it slow. My cock in my hand, I paint her with it, stroking her center and coating myself in her wetness until I push halfway in.

"Oh, my God!" She arches her back as her hands fly to her sides and grip my blanket in her fists.

I pull back, not wanting to hurt her, then slide in again, deeper this time. Her whimper is soft. Sweet. I push in more, letting her adjust to me until I'm completely buried inside her. Rocking my hips, I slip out almost completely, before diving in again, this time faster—harder. And her whimper is louder.

Her knees lift, and as I rock in and out of her, she

eventually wraps one of her legs around me, pulling me into her with each thrust and coaxing me deeper. My pumps are soon met with thrusts of her own, her hips rising to meet me with each push. Her hands reach up to cup my face, and I hover above her, waiting as her eyes open on mine and the softest, sexiest smile curves her lips.

Her breasts bounce with each thrust, and I lower my mouth to suckle them as I thrust faster. When I bite one of the raw tips, Peyton cries out but holds my head to her breast, lifting her torso to meet me and make it easier to access her. Holding her leg at my hip, I sink into her, putting more force into each pump as I drop my mouth to hers. Her teeth cling to my lower lip, and as her tongue passes along my skin, I feel myself on the verge of losing control.

"Come for me, Peyton. I want to feel you." My voice is raw, my breathing ragged. I work my hips as hard and fast as I can, chasing each cry until she writhes beneath me, dropping her fist to her mouth, biting her knuckles with her teeth. Her entire body pulses around me and a second later, I fill the condom.

I push into her a few more times, wanting to be sure she feels every last thing. I want this to be what she dreams about tonight. I want to hold her until she falls asleep naked in my arms. I want to wake her with kisses at three a.m. and taste her until she comes again.

I want her to be happy. To never show up again with tears because of me. Though she says I'm not the cause, I know I am. But I want to be worth it. Worth the rumors and the shit-talking. Worth her giving up one of her favorite things, like riding on a float down Main Street. Because right now, I'd give it all up to make her happy.

I am all in.

Chapter Nineteen

Peyton

A small part of me wishes that I kept up with my messages last night. Ignoring them was good for my mental health at the time, but facing the reality of them right now feels like a major slide backward.

I rub my eyes as I sit up in Wyatt's bed, his comforter clutched to my chest while his back rises and falls with the rhythm of his breathing. I don't want to wake him. Not yet. He was everything I needed last night. And also, he made me feel things on my body that I didn't think were real.

What we did wasn't sex. It was love. The way he cared for me, put me first, and cherished me? I was beginning to believe those were fantasies in my romance novels. But they aren't. They are real when you find someone worthy. When you find the right person.

As blissful as the thought is of snuggling up next to

him and repeating everything from last night, I have to deal with the day ahead of me.

It's Friday, and I am pretty sure I'm not going to school. The CALL ME text from my mom is a pretty solid indicator that I might lose the keys to the Jeep too. I take care of my messages from Lexi and Tasha first, assuring them that I am all right and I'll update them when I find out what my punishment is. There's a voicemail from Coach Nelson too. But as for my dad, absolute radio silence.

"Hey." Wyatt's voice is groggy. He sits up next to me and kisses my bare shoulder.

"Sorry, I didn't mean to wake you." I kiss his lips but hold my lips closed, not sure what state my breath is in. He chuckles and slips out of the bed, his bare ass on full display.

"Oh, hey! It's daylight." I chuckle, covering my eyes with my hand but spreading my fingers apart for an easy peek.

He shoots me a grin over his shoulder before slipping on his sweatpants.

"You want something of mine?" he asks.

I shrug and scan the room for my discarded clothes. He picks them up and sets them on the foot of the bed, then grabs a very large Buffalo Bills sweatshirt from his closet.

"It was my dad's," he says, tossing it to me.

"Oh, I shouldn't take it, then," I say, feeling the warn cotton in my hands.

"It's fine. I have a lot of his things. And to be clear, I'm not giving that to you permanently," he says through laughter.

I smile and slip it over my body.

"Fair enough," I say.

I put on my shorts and wrap my bra and panties in my T-shirt before hunting down my shoes. I spot them near Wyatt's dresser, so I get up to shove my feet into them and run my fingers through what feels like pretty crazy hair. I manage to work it into a bun, taking a pen from on his desk to push through the center and hold it in place.

I'm listening to my message from my coach when Wyatt steps back into his room, showered and dressed for school. He waits while I finish, getting the gist of what she has to tell me. I'm suspended for two days, today and Monday. And cheering next Friday is up in the air. Also, my dad wants to talk to me.

"Great. That's settled," I say, clicking my phone screen off and tucking my phone into my side pocket.

"Mom? Dad? Or—"

"Coach," I say, filling in the third option. I suppose it could have been the dean or the athletic director, but given how close everyone is with my dad, I figured everyone would pretty much defer to him on this mess.

"How bad?" Wyatt asks.

"Not as bad as I expected," I admit. "No school today or Monday, though that doesn't mean I don't get all the work."

"Ha, yeah, that's not really a punishment. That's more of a vacation."

"*Hmm.*" I nod in agreement.

"Technically, even though my game is at *your* school tonight, it's not really your school's event, so does that mean . . . ?" His hopeful eyes, all wide and puppy-dogged, are irresistible. I step into his open arms and give in, letting him kiss me and my bad breath.

"I will be at your game even if I have to break out of prison to do it," I promise. I doubt that will be the case, though. I may, however, be stuck in awkward silence sitting next to my father. I really wish I didn't invite him now.

"I guess I should go ahead and break the news to you now, then," Wyatt says. I take a step back, a little nervous and also anticipating one of his usual jokes. I tilt my head and squint one eye.

"My mom's in the kitchen. She got off early, and she'd love to meet you. Odds are high we'll also get a lecture about safe sex, which will no doubt make both of us want to crawl into holes, but, well . . ."

"Oh . . . *wow.*" My mouth hangs open as I pace his room and stop at the foot of his bed so I can flop down before I pass out.

"Really, my mom is amazing. And this way you'll recognize her at the game tonight." He's trying so hard to spin this as a positive.

"This is *not* how I wanted to meet your mom, Wyatt. She's going to think—"

He steps in front of me and cups my chin, lifting my gaze to his.

"That you make me very happy. And that we are both eighteen and responsible young adults."

"Minus the fact that one of us is now a delinquent with a two-day suspension?" My pulse races from my anxiety. It's pushing against my eardrums and making it hard to focus.

Wyatt reaches for my hands, urging me to stand.

"When I tell her why you were suspended, I promise she'll want to buy you dinner and celebrate. Theresa Stone has zero tolerance for bullies." The serious look on his face sets me at ease, at least about my suspension. However, I'm still a ball of nerves about meeting his mom.

I blow out hard enough that a few stray hairs that were tickling my nose blast away from my face. I follow Wyatt out of his room, my keys, phone, and wallet clutched to my stomach, my body now sweating bullets under this Bills sweatshirt. The blunt smell of strong coffee hits my nose, but so does the alluring scent of bacon. My senses are definitely weakened, and then my gaze lands on the small woman with short dark brown hair and chocolate eyes.

"Breakfast?" She pushes a plate to the center of the table, then pulls her hands back to cradle her coffee mug in front of her. She arches a brow at Wyatt.

"Thanks, Mom," he says, doing his best to ignore her, I think. She reaches forward as he sits down, though, and shifts the plate in my direction.

"You can make your own plate. This is for our guest."

He laughs softly through his nose and shuts his eyes before moving into the kitchen and making himself a plate of bacon and what looks like quiche, I think.

"They're frozen, so don't feel guilty like I spent hours slaving in the kitchen," she says to me. She likely noticed the way I eyed the very nice meal with curiosity.

"Thank you," I cough out. I slide back the heavy wooden chair, squealing it along the tile. I wince and mouth, "Sorry," but take my seat and immediately spear the egg dish with my fork. It oozes cheese, and it smells incredible. I carve out a bite and blow on it to cool.

"So, Peyton, yes?"

"*Mmm hmm*," I say, nodding and glancing up as I eat my first bite. My hunch was right. This is *so good*.

"I've heard . . . a little about you. Though, I have to say, most of my conclusions are based on the fact when I grill my son for information, he turns bright red and runs away. But it's nice to meet you. You must be special to him."

I suck in my lips, my cheeks balling tightly with my desire to smile, but I also want to crawl under the table and hide. Hard to say which urge is winning.

"Thank you," I say, dropping my gaze back to my plate. *Thank you? Was that the right thing to say?*

"I assume you will not be moving in with us, and this was a . . . *rare* occurrence."

I choke on my bite, coughing as I bring my eyes up to hers. *Wyatt tried to warn me.*

"Yes. I mean . . . no? I don't know what the right answer is, but no, I'm not moving in. I had a terrible day yesterday, and—"

Wyatt's hand lands on my shoulder, shutting off my verbal spigot.

"She came over after practice. We know about being safe. I was a gentleman, and she needed someone to listen." His foot slides into mine under the table, and I have a feeling it's a warning for me not to question that *gentleman* part. Though, he was a gentleman. I wouldn't have felt the way I did if he weren't.

"Okay." His mom nods. She sips her coffee but eyes both of us over the rim. Her gaze dips briefly to the sweatshirt I'm wearing.

"She's coming to my game tonight," Wyatt says, pulling her attention back to him.

"Oh, yeah? Have you been before? To one of his games?"

I swallow hard, and I'm pretty sure I just heard Wyatt do the same.

"Not a Vista game. No. I'm usually busy. I cheer."

Her brow lifts in interest.

"At . . . Coolidge," I croak out.

Her brow lifts more and her gaze slides to Wyatt. He simply smiles and shovels food in his mouth.

"Oh, you go to Coolidge. Aren't they sort of—"

"Our rivals," Wyatt barks out, his mouth full. He's so comfortable with this.

"Ah, yeah. That's what I thought. You all don't have a game tonight, Peyton?"

"No, ma'am," I say, shaking my head. I probably shouldn't have called her *ma'am*. I know my mom hates that. But I'm petrified of fucking this up, and I want her to like me.

"They have a bye week. And we're using their field. It's . . . a long story," Wyatt says, somehow already scraping the last dregs of food from his plate.

I've barely nibbled at mine, so I try to catch up. I don't need them both watching me eat. I'm not even that hungry.

"Well, since you've probably seen a lot of football games, I'm guessing you won't be surprised when I stand up and yell in the bleachers. I can be kind of loud," she admits.

Wyatt gets up and moves behind her, placing his hands on her shoulders. She glances up with an adoring expression. My heart stretches at the sweet sight.

"She is downplaying that. She can be *very* loud. I could hear her over my dad sometimes. It's not even a competition," he says. His mom reaches up and pats his cheek.

"I won't be surprised. Believe me. I've seen it all." I instantly regret letting that slip. I pour my focus onto my plate, stuffing half of my quiche into my mouth, the tip of my tongue singed from the melted cheese.

"I bet you get a lot of flak as a cheerleader. I'm sure you've seen a lot," she says, and I relax into my seat, glad she drew her own conclusion. I'm pretty sure Wyatt hasn't discussed who my father is with her yet, given that she's been grilling him to no avail about most everything about me.

"We should head out. Save the dishes for me for tonight, Mom." He snags a backpack from one of the chairs and helps me scoot my chair back, leaving half of my breakfast still on the plate. Grandpa hates waste. I almost want to ask for a box, but I've done enough damage this morning.

"Thank you! It was really nice to meet you," I manage to get out before the door closes.

Wyatt walks me through his garage and to my Jeep, holding the door open for me and kissing me before stepping back and pushing it shut.

"So, are you heading home or . . ." He shrugs.

I chuckle, but inside, my chest lights up with nerves.

"I have to see my mom. That's first. And then I guess I'll go from there. I need to text my coach to see if I need to do anything or sign something. I don't know, Wyatt. I've never been suspended before. I suppose at some point, I'll need to see my dad. I'm kind of planning on going to your game about seven hours early and just sitting in the bleachers."

He laughs and drops his gaze to the ground, where he kicks his toe into the roadway.

"I'm really sorry you're going through this. Truly." His gaze lifts to mine, his eyes soft.

"I know. But I'll be fine. I'm Peyton Johnson. Grandpa built us strong." Of everyone in my family, my grandpa is actually the person I need most right now. He has a way of saying the perfect thing, of putting trouble in order and showing me the reason for it all. Some people have church. I have Buck Johnson.

Wyatt leans in to kiss me one last time before jogging up his driveway to his truck. I take off and am around the corner before he has a chance to catch up to me. I have to pull the Band-Aid off what's coming, and I need to start with Mom.

I send her a text from the stoplight about two miles away from home, and she tells me to come find her in the barn. She might have me shovel shit today, and I'd take the penance gladly. Anything not to have to talk about what set me off or to face my dad for a while. I'm still not sure I'm ready to face him. I'm still hurt.

My mom is saddling one of our oldest horses, Otis, when I reach the barn, and it looks as though the space has already been cleaned for the day, so no shovels for me. She has me wait by the door while she finishes up and walks Otis out toward the arena. She must have a new client today. Otis is gentle, and when someone hasn't ridden before, he's a good start.

"I'm guessing Coach called you?"

My mom nods. I try to read her face, and I can't tell whether I need to brace myself for crushing disappointment or one of those slow-to-boil rage-outs. She hasn't really yelled at me since I crashed the Jeep, but I think I prefer that to crushing disappointment.

"I let my emotions get to me, Mom, and I'm really sorry."

She halts us, Otis stomping to a stop in the dirt as he snorts and kicks up dust.

"Peyton, as a parent I should probably be angry and discipline you, and I still might, but not because you stood up for yourself. I would have given anything to be able to do that when I was your age. It took me years to find my self-confidence. To know my worth. So, yeah, you shouldn't hit people. But also . . ." Her lip raises on one side, and I match her half smile with my own.

She guides Otis forward again, and I trail along at his other side. I move ahead when we reach the arena, holding open the gate so she can bring him in and let him run a little. Running for Otis is more of a trot.

"You said I might still be in trouble?" I ask as I latch the gate behind me.

"*Hmm*, yeah. I get being hurt, Peyton. But when you don't come home, and you don't call, I get really worried. If it weren't for Lexi picking up and letting me know you stayed at her house, I might have called the sheriff."

She gives me side eyes in warning, and I'm not sure what to react to first—the amazing lie my friend told for me or the fact the sheriff could have been cruising around town with a spotlight in search of me.

"I understand," I say.

She holds my gaze for a few paces, then turns her focus back to Otis, running her palm along his neck. I've always loved the way his gray color reflects the sun. He's my favorite.

"Coach Nelson said to call her during her prep hour. She'll make sure you get your assignments. You won't have to miss next Friday's game, and let's just call that a gift from your mom, who can be quite convincing when she wants to be."

My lungs open up, a weight falling away from my

shoulders. I didn't realize how badly I wanted to join my squad.

"Thank you."

My mom nods, but she keeps her gaze fixed on Otis.

"I am sorry," I say, my chest tightening. I need her to look at me, I think. She pauses after a few seconds and finally levels me with a heavy look, her eyes slightly red, like she's been crying. The invisible rope around my chest pulls.

"Mom?" I step into her and she pulls me to her chest, hugging me tight. Her hand cups the back of my head, and her body quivers but only for a second. She sniffles before letting go.

"I know it's hard to live with this last name. Your dad meant well." So she knows the full story. That's . . . good, I guess. It saves me from having to tattle on my father.

"It's fine," I say, that word I keep trying to sell still not coming out true.

She shakes her head.

"It's not, and I know it won't be until that parade is well in the past. But I'm asking you to give your dad some grace when you see him. I want you to give him grace, but be honest. He says he'll see you at the game, whatever that means."

I shake, partly in fear of having hard conversations but mostly because I want to hug my dad, too. I'm so mad at him, but I love him.

"I will. I'll give him grace. I promise."

Chapter Twenty

Wyatt

We may not be playing these guys this week, but being here—in their house—sure makes it feel like we are.

Nothing about this situation feels like a home game. Our boosters did their best; there's a banner hung on the back of the home stands with our logo, a Mustang, bold and center. But the small showing of black and maroon is surrounded by all the Coolidge gold and blue. It's practically swallowed by it.

Coach Watts is standing at the front of the bus, the doors not yet open to spill out the team. Hands on his hips, he seems to be scouting our borrowed landscape the same way he does mid-game. I know I am. The lot is full of student cars since school is still in session, but nobody seems to be out yet. A few trucks are parked near the home stands, all hitched to flat trailers pulling what looks like floats for the parade.

"All right, gentleman. Remember, we are guests. Treat this place with respect." Coach turns to look us in the eyes after his ominous warning.

"We didn't light their field on fire," Jody finally says, breaking the silence. I look down, wishing he hadn't.

He's sitting directly in front of me, so it feels as if everyone's eyes are on me, which normally I love. I respect the leadership role with my whole heart. But I feel as though I'm navigating a bus filled with ticking time bombs.

"And we won't," I utter, sticking with Coach's message and reminding my brothers that we're better than that.

I get up from my seat and step into the aisle, the players in seats in front of me shifting to look my direction. My palms land on the seat backs on either side of me and I squeeze them as I look down at the rubber flooring filled with dirt and gravel from our shoes. We get here in a regular bus, but Coolidge travels in a coach. The thought makes me chuckle as I kick at a dirt spot right in front of me.

"We don't need fire to change this field. We need to show it how football *should* be played. That's not the easy way, where teams come in here and are awed by the greatness of the facility, by the slickness of the turf, the bright lights of that big-ass scoreboard out there." I gesture out the right side windows toward the field, and a few of the guys chuckle, others begin to clap loudly.

"We are going to intimidate this team from West Ridge by scoring on our opening drive. And they'll remember us because of the way our defense forces them to go three and out. And when that scoreboard hits numbers it's never shown before, that's how we'll make our presence known. They may be playing in Coolidge's house tonight, but they're playing *our* game. And there ain't *nobody* who plays our game better! Nobody!"

My hand slaps down on the seat to my right, and the guys pound their fists into theirs, slapping the vinyl and howling like rabid dogs ready to sink their teeth into fresh meat. Coach Watts meets my gaze over our now riled-up team, and he gives me a faint smirk and a nod. This team is fully mine now. And that record Reed Johnson holds? I'm taking it here—tonight. I not only have to, but I also *want* to.

It takes us several minutes to clear out from the bus. Most of our gear is housed underneath, with the rest of it in the booster trailer parked beside us. We were able to get two of our student team managers out of class early, but it's still too much for just two of them to carry out to the field alone, so I whistle to get Whiskey and Jody's attention and wave them over to the trailer to help me carry the rest of our gear to the sidelines.

The cameras and closed circuit equipment are the most important, and I let Whiskey handle the large screen our offensive coach uses on the sidelines to walk us through the last set of downs. Jody joins our two managers at the top of the bleachers, leaving them to set up the cameras on top of the press box while Whiskey and I get the electricity run across the track to power up the screen.

"I don't know if we can leave this out here like this, man," Whiskey says once we finish plugging everything in.

I glance around the empty field, both sides set up with water and the training tables. We'll be out here running drills and warmups before the other team shows up, but it's not them he's worried about.

Pulling my phone from the pocket of my joggers, I check the time just as the bell dings across campus, alerting students to switch classes. I glance up to meet Whiskey's stare, and he lifts a brow.

"You really think they'd mess with our shit?" I ask, scanning the campus beyond the field, hundreds of students spilling out from doors and into hallways. A few Coolidge jerseys stand out amongst the crowd. I wonder if they'll show up to the game tonight and sit on the West Ridge side?

"I'll hang out here. You go on and get dressed out. Your arm is more important than my legs anyway. Let's get you warm and used to this field." Whiskey sits on the tabletop, next to our monitor, and I immediately inspect the structural integrity of the folding table legs.

"I'm not *that* heavy, fuck shit," he says, pushing me back a few steps with a palm to my chest.

I chuckle and shake my head, eyes still on the flimsy metal legs that seem to be sinking into the turf.

"I don't know, man. If things start to go, you save that TV." I point to our monitor.

"I'll save my dick," he throws back, grabbing his crotch,

then flipping me off before laughing like some wild beast in an Irish pub.

I roll my eyes and wave him off as I head across the track to meet Jody. At least he's hyped for this game.

Jody and I jog toward the practice gym, where the Coolidge athletic director is holding a door open for us to their spare locker room area. This space is used for tournaments as well as the dance students for their fall and spring showcases; at least, that's what Peyton told me. It's a pretty blank canvas inside, but that's better than having to walk into a space dominated by Coolidge trophies and state championship banners. The only thing ready to greet us in here is a rolling whiteboard that looks like it was borrowed from a science class. There are faint chemical formulas scribbled in the center, the board used so much it no longer handles being erased. Good thing Coach Watts isn't big on drawing plays. He trained us to visualize during camp.

I find my gear bag parked on a bench at the end of the first row of lockers. It's not a very team-oriented space, the rows close together with narrow benches. I change out of my travel clothes and am squeezing my way into my pads when Whiskey finally comes in. He plops down on the bench, taking up most of it, which is fine since I'm just trying to get my shoulder pads on right now.

"Hey, can you shove the right shoulder pad in?" I take a knee next to him as he slowly rotates to face me. He's barely halfway around when enough of his face comes into view.

"Whisk, what the fuck?" I jump to my feet, his entire

right side covered in thick, blue paint. It's dripping from his hair, down his shaggy beard, and into the collar of his black practice shirt. His maroon pants are splattered.

"I'm gonna need a minute," he says, his voice menacingly low.

"I gotta tell Coach," I say, gritting my teeth and moving past him. He snags the back of my jersey before I can get away, though, and I fall back a step, crashing into the empty locker next to him.

His eyes drill into mine, the white part red with hate. His jaw cracks as he shifts his bottom teeth from one side to the other, as if he's sharpening his molars while at the same time breaking them on one another.

"Whisk, we can't let this go. We gotta tell Coach."

His gaze drops, but only an inch or two.

"This ain't about school rules and shit, Wyatt. That fucker was my friend. I did him favors. I kept him from getting his ass flattened. I kept my mouth shut when he stepped out on Peyt." He glances up at me, his eyes even redder now.

"Bryce do this to you?"

My chest is growing hot, and my pulse has been racing since we got off the bus. But to hear Whiskey admit to covering up for that asshole when he was unfaithful to Peyton shifts my rage into a new gear.

The clomp of cleats on concrete filters behind me, and I shift my body, leaning one arm on the locker while resting my foot on the bench in an effort to shield Whiskey's appearance from the others.

"Yo, you comin' Wyatt?" I hear Anthony ask.

"Yeah, be right out!" I hold still, waiting for the sound of the door closing. There are a few more bodies shuffling around the space, and I haven't seen Coach walk by yet, so I'm sure he's still talking with the assistants in the guest office.

"Don't do anything stupid," I say to my friend. Knowing full well that *I* am on the verge of doing very stupid things.

He lifts his chin so we're staring eye to eye as he draws in a long, full breath.

"I won't fuck this win up for us, but what he just did? That shit was personal. I cannot pretend it was anything but that."

I suck in my lips and hold his stare for a beat before nodding. I don't know where it happened, but judging by the way the paint covers him, I'd guess it was a face-to-face interaction. Pretty bold move to throw paint on a guy twice your size.

"All right, as long as you do not fuck up your season. My season. *Our* season. You deal with this shit away from the team, and *legally*." I can't believe I have to fucking say that.

More cleats rush by, so I adjust my posture again, sliding my right foot over to cover a paint drop on the ground.

"You're literally soaking in this crap, Whisk. You gotta get that shirt off, at least. Here . . ."

I move to my locker while he pulls the shirt up over his

head, smearing the blue paint across the side of his face and in his hair. It's going to be a bitch when that stuff dries. I pull the small nylon bag from my bigger duffle. I usually put my cleats in it to cut down on the smell, but it has another purpose today. Probably its final purpose before the trash.

I open it wide and Whiskey shoves the paint-soiled shirt inside, then marches into the bathroom, somehow not drawing attention from the coaches. By the time he gets back, there's a blue tint to his cheek and a few splotches on his pants that are probably permanent, but other than his blue-ish tinted wet hair, he's typical Whiskey.

I wait for him to suit up before heading out to the field. We cross part of the parking lot, and it's impossible not to see the enormous patch of blue splattered near the student exit. I study Whiskey's expression as we trounce over it, but his eyes remain fixed straight ahead, on the field.

The paint trails thin out in the direction of the parade floats, and the one made to look like the CHS field is covered in a fresh coat of blue and yellow. Maybe there were students I didn't see out working on it when we pulled up. Or perhaps one of them was taking a break, off to get a fresh bucket of paint.

The scene is writing itself for me, though I'm sure Whiskey will tell me when he's ready. Or I'll read it in the paper after he lands his ass in jail. Regardless, my guess is Bryce and some of his minions were working on that float for the mere purpose of waiting for our arrival. And when

Whiskey and he crossed paths, Bryce's self-control failed him.

I just hope my best protection out on that field can keep his emotions in check for the next few hours. It's too much to ask him to hold on to his grudge without acting for the next few weeks, but after we win tonight, I sure like hell am going to try.

If Bryce Hampton crosses either of us again, though? All bets are off.

Chapter Twenty-One

Peyton

It's been a while since I watched a high school football game from the stands. I kind of miss it. Though, it would be nice to have more than just two girls my age sitting with me in what feels like hostile territory.

"They're all looking at me," I grumble to Tasha. She plops down on the metal bleacher next to me and glances across my chest, then cranes her neck to look behind her.

"Literally *nobody* is looking at you," she says, tearing her straw wrapper away with her teeth and pushing it into her foam cup.

"Please say you did not spike that." I arch a brow and eye her as her lips wrap around it slowly.

She shakes her head as she takes a drink, but as soon as she's done says, "You probably wouldn't like it, though, so we shouldn't share."

I roll my eyes and glance to my right, where the Vista band is filing into the stands.

"Is your dad coming?" Lexi asks as she takes a seat in front of Tasha and me, straddling the metal bench and offering up her bag of kettle corn. I scoop out a handful before letting her down with my response.

"He said he is, but I doubt he'll be sitting by me."

My friends give me instant pity faces.

"It's fine. You don't have to look at me that way." I reach forward to scoop more popcorn from Lexi's bag. My friends are up to speed on what led to me getting the boot from the parade. I don't need them to revisit the topic tonight. It's bad enough I had to wait for them to get out of practice to head to the game. I should have been there. We're working on a new stunt, and it's not like I'm the linchpin for it, but I'm definitely stronger than any of the girls who sub in my place.

"Wyatt might break my dad's passing record tonight," I say, shifting to a topic that gives me a little more pleasure. Maybe I should feel guilty for rooting for my dad's record to fall, but there's something poetic about it happening tonight. Maybe a little passive aggressive, too.

"Wow, that's a big deal. How short is he?"

"He needs to throw for a hundred thirty yards, which is basically nothing for him this season," I brag. I catch my tone but not before Tasha puckers her lips into a knowing smile.

"What?" I say, feeling the heat crawl up my neck.

"You're in love," she teases in a sing-songy voice.

I roll my eyes and reach for more popcorn. Not that I

want it, but because I'm suddenly so nervous that I need to do something—*anything*—with my hands.

"He's a good guy, Peyton. And you spent a lot of time with a pretty shitty one," Tasha adds.

I glance up and meet Lexi's eyes, and though my friend has always thought Bryce was the hottest thing on Earth, she relents a half smile and a shrug before nodding in agreement at Tasha's assessment.

"This whole rivalry thing is pretty bad, though. Spending time with him feels—"

"Amazing," Tasha pipes in.

I roll my head to the side to gaze at her.

"It does, yes. And it should. But I also feel guilty, somehow. Like I'm letting down the family brand or something." It doesn't help that every time we're in public together, someone on my dad's team sees us and turns it into an act of war.

"Fuck that," Tasha says. "You deserve to be happy."

I loop my arm through hers and hug her bicep, then take a drink from her soda, my tongue hit with a dose of . . . *rum, I think?*

"Oh, wow!" I cough out.

"I told you it wasn't your kind of drink." She snickers.

I look around us, relieved nobody is in our immediate area yet. But before I can warn her to be careful, she takes a big drink through her straw and meets my gaze.

"Don't worry, Peyton. This ain't my first rodeo."

Her lopsided smirk makes me wonder how often her

water bottle is spiked with something other than Gatorade at our home games. I also think my friend maybe needs to work through her issues before she gets to college. I worry about her if we end up at different schools, which it's looking like we might. She wants to stay here. I've been dreaming of leaving since I was old enough to know I could. Lately, though, I've been less excited about taking off on my own. I've also been afraid to ask Wyatt when he plans to commit. And those two emotions together have made me confused.

The Vista band sounds off with the Mustang fight song, so my friends and I get to our feet, joining the hundred or so parents who came to watch their boys take the field. Their record is the same as ours, but they don't seem to have the same following that we do. Or maybe our massive stands have a way of making a modest crowd look small. I probably could have gotten away with wearing Wyatt's team shirt tonight, but I opted instead for the oversized Bills sweatshirt and black leggings. The desert nights are finally starting to cool, so I thought the extra layer would be nice. Plus, it still smells like his bedroom. And when I close my eyes, it almost feels like his arms around me.

Wyatt is the first to burst through the banner held by their cheer squad, and he races toward the center of the field with the school flag hoisted over his shoulder as he runs.

"I like their uniforms better," Lexi says through a mouthful of popcorn. "They look tougher."

"*Hmm*, yeah. And maybe . . . hotter, too. Can you get me an intro with that one right there?" Tasha points to the growing crowd on the sidelines and I squint ,attempting to guess who she means.

"Which number?" I ask.

"Oh, any of them. I meant that one as in . . ." She draws an air circle around the team, and Lexi and I both slap our palms over our faces with laughter.

We all stand for the national anthem, then stay on our feet to wait for the kickoff. I use the opportunity to scope out the crowd, and I meet Wyatt's mom's eyes across the stands. She raises her hand and I do the same. She's not alone, which makes me feel better about not sitting next to her. It's going to take me a while to recover from walking straight out of Wyatt's bedroom to breakfast with her.

A few Vista students trickle in, and the away stands are filling in more as well. It's nothing compared to our home crowds, but at least it feels respectable now. I catch myself ogling Wyatt as he strides out to the center of the field for the coin toss, his right hand clutched in Whiskey's. There's something comforting in their friendship. I'm glad they have each other. Glad Wyatt has someone like him to keep him safe. I'm sure Bryce misses him, though his ego would never allow him to admit it.

"You think your dad made them all show up?" Tasha says, nudging my side with her elbow.

I follow her sightline to the fence behind the north end zone, where the sea of gold and blue jerseys are all lined up. I spot Bryce's favorite white and gold hat immediately, and my stomach tightens. Not that he could do anything, or would, to ruin Wyatt's game, but I can't help but think his reason for being here is to root against him and his run on my dad's record.

"Not sure, but I am sure he didn't ask the media to be here."

I point to the small set of stands on the field behind the north field goal. It's where family members sit for our home games, a special tradition that was carried over from the old stadium. The only people there now are a few news cameras and my dad.

"You think this is about the record?" Lexi asks.

"Definitely," I hum, my focus locked on my dad despite the kickoff happening on the field in front of me. I feel a slight pinch in my chest; maybe a part of me is sad for him.

Any empathy floating around my chest is immediately overshadowed the second Wyatt takes his first snap on the field. He's unlike anything I've ever seen, sidestepping a sack and rolling to his right to somehow find a receiver thirty yards down the field. The precision reminds me of watching my dad during his last pro years. He wasn't the rough-and-tumble guy he was when he was young, so he had to learn to be exact. He was a surgeon with the ball, just as Wyatt is now. His receiver gets pushed out of bounds midfield, and just like that, Wyatt is a single digit away from making my dad number two in Arizona's high school record books.

As if automatic, my gaze crosses the field to see if my dad is watching, knowing he is. The reporter off to the side, my dad is standing in the middle of the VIP bleachers, his arms crossed over his chest. Part of him might be proud.

But I know there's a part of him that hurts. I know it because as angry as I am with my dad, we're still connected in our hearts. There's an invisible thread that's been between us since my first word, which happened to be *Daddy*. And for right now, this small moment, I wish I was sitting down there with him instead.

It takes Wyatt five passes to drive the ball down the field and cut the distance between him and my dad's record in half. The crowd gasps every time a pass is caught, and a few times the band breaks out with the fight song too early, probably miscounting the yards. He owns the record by halftime, though, carving into new territory in the second half to the point where my dad's incredible numbers will likely be seen as the old guard. Bryce will likely pass my father's record this year too, at least in passing. But he won't catch Wyatt, who is well on his way to setting scoring records—and rushing records too—by the end of the season.

With twenty seconds left, Wyatt takes a knee at the forty-yard line to let the clock run out, and my friends and I shout at the top of our lungs while we jump up and down on a middle-row of the home stands.

"Oh, my God, why do we cheer again? This is so much more fun," Tasha jokes.

I sling my arm around her while Lexi manages to do a standing pike on her bleacher seat.

"Maybe we can talk Coach into letting us cheer from up here," I laugh out, doing my best to mimic my friend's jump. She's far nimbler than I am, so I'm sure to onlookers my jump looked more like a blip, but it was fun. All of this —watching Wyatt, rooting for him to take the record, for the Mustangs to win their home game on an away field—is the most fun I've had with football in ages. Since I sat on my grandpa's shoulders for my dad's first playoff game in San Diego fifteen years ago. And all I have of that memory is the box of photos my mom had printed at Walgreens from her phone. This memory, it lives inside my chest. And it stars the boy on the field whose eyes are set on me as Whiskey hoists him in the air and rushes toward the sideline.

"Hey, we should probably scoot," Lexi says, pulling my attention back to Earth, where my dad's team is clustered around the main gates as Vista families exit.

"They're stirring shit up," I mutter.

"Probably," Tasha sighs out.

We can't hear them from this far away, but it's obvious in their posture and the way they walk closely behind people as they exit, then turn around and laugh. They're being dicks, because that's the culture Bryce has instilled in them. And heart tugs or not, my dad has let it fester.

Grandpa would be disappointed.

I hover near the bottom row for a few seconds while the bleachers clear out, hoping to catch Wyatt's attention, but his coach has called the team into a circle, and everyone has taken a knee. I don't want to distract him, and he promised to come over after the game, so I catch up to my friends, who are waiting near the concession stand. I make one last attempt to catch Wyatt's attention, stepping up on the first iron bar along the exit gate, but his back is to me. One of the local news outlets stuck around, too, and my dad is standing with the reporter and a camera guy, probably waiting to capture some disingenuous passing of the torch when he shakes Wyatt's hand or something.

"We can stay if you want," Lexi offers, but it's late, and I'm sure there's a party brewing in the desert that they want to get to. Even though it wasn't *our* game night, it's a Friday in the fall. Coolidge Bears will drink and be stupid.

A few of the pickup trucks I recognize as belonging to our guys speed out of the lot, one of them fishtailing in the dirt road that heads the opposite direction from town. A part of me wishes the truck would tip over, but I dash that thought because of the bad luck that likely comes with being petty like that.

"Hey, uh, Peyt? We have a problem," Tasha says while I'm busy clearing my head of being vindictive.

"Yeah, uh? Sorry, what's wrong?" I ask, my stomach twisting as soon as I see her eyes drawn in and mouth pulled tight. I spin around to where her focus is fixed and suddenly take back all of the mental halts I put into the universe over wishing that truck tipped. I want them all to tip now. One truck in particular—Bryce's.

"Fuck!" My hands move to my head, fingers threading together on top as I march toward the two completely flat driver's side tires on my Jeep. My *dad's* Jeep.

"Someone slashed them," Lexi says, kneeling and running her finger along the massive gash on the sidewall of the front tire.

"You all right, Peyton?"

I turn around, all wild-eyed and stressed, to come face-to-face with Wyatt's mom. Her gaze darts from me to the tire where Lexi is standing, dusting her hands off on her jeans.

"Oh, damn. Do you girls need a ride home? Is there someone you can call?" His mom dives right into solution mode, which is actually really kind, and I would be so grateful if this weren't such a political nightmare.

"It's okay. We'll be fine. I'm sure it was just . . . an accident. Probably ran over something," I say excitedly, trying to sell it. I sound more manic than anything, and her face puzzles as she gives me a sideways glance.

The clatter of cleats on concrete grows louder and on top of things, the Vista bus parked close enough to me that there's no way to hide this shit show from Wyatt.

"Peyton, it looks like your car was vandalized. I don't think a curb caused this," his mom says, her voice full of suspicion.

"Peyt! What's wrong?" My dad's voice pulls me in the other direction, and I spin around to see him marching my way. His strides are long and fast, and there are too many variables in the air to stop the chaotic storm I'm about to find myself in.

"Someone slashed her tires, Mr. Johnson," Lexi answers for me. Sweet Lexi, it's probably best the news came from her. I'm somewhere between panicked and pissed. No panic in my dad's face, though. He's full-on lit.

"Let me see!" he growls, stepping around me and taking Lexi's position by the tire.

Wyatt's mom takes a step or two back, a flash of recognition on her face. I can tell when someone knows who my dad is, and I know she's a football fan. Plus, Wyatt has mentioned how much his dad liked mine as a player. The way her gaze now shifts between me and my dad pretty much seals it for me—I'm sure she knows exactly who I am now. Just as quickly, though, she seems to put the new information away, insisting she helps.

Wyatt and Whiskey are headed this way, ignoring their coach's shouts asking where the hell they're going. The only person missing is Bryce, whose truck I still see, so it's likely just a matter of time.

"Dammit!" My dad abruptly stands, hands on his hips,` as his furrowed eyes stare lasers into the front busted tire.

"It's fine, Dad. It's nothing." If I could gobble my words before they reached his ears, I would. I'd do it right now. That would be my superpower. But that's not a real thing, and sometimes I talk before I think. My dad is in my face in about a half second flat, finger pointing at me and face red.

"No, Peyton! It's not *nothing!* This shit ends now!"

My dad storms across the parking lot toward Bryce's truck, which is parked next to two others. Some of his players are sitting in the back of one, and as my dad approaches they stand and hop out of the truck bed. I wouldn't be shocked if they sprinted into the desert.

"Was this Bryce?" Wyatt says, his tone not far removed from my father's. I turn to face him, his eyes wild and his stare set on the back gash.

"I don't think he would do this," I say, knowing that even if it wasn't him, it was with his blessing. Maybe even his direction.

"I don't think we know Bryce at all anymore," Whiskey says over Wyatt's shoulder. His eyes are steely, his mouth set in a hard line.

My spine shrinks, my body sinking into the ground beneath me with the weight of it all.

"This is so stupid. It's just football. It's *football!*" I reach my hands up to the heavens and stare at the black sky. Wyatt's hand reaches around my waist and he pulls me into him. I move reluctantly at first, but when he has me in a full embrace, I flatten my cheek against his chest and watch my dad wave his hands with his words while his players, which now include Bryce, shrink where they stand next to their pickups.

"Can I do something? I really don't mind giving you ladies a ride," Wyatt's mom suggests again.

"Mom, Peyton's dad will handle it. I'll fill you in at home," Wyatt says, stepping away from me and reaching out a hand for his mom. She eyes her son silently, then shifts her gaze to the scene behind him. Her mouth hardens while at the same time her eyes soften.

"Okay," she finally relents, and I think she's pieced together enough to know this is a battle of male egos on full display.

"Peyton, I'm really sorry," she says to me, her expression weighed down, full of sympathy. She pulls her son in for a quick hug, her hand patting his back before she spins and heads to an old Camaro parked in the very center of the now-empty lot.

"You should walk her to her car. Then maybe fill your coach in," I suggest, nodding toward the Vista bus, where Coach Watts is now standing with a handful of players watching my dad read their rights to their rivals.

Wyatt breathes out a short, annoyed laugh before stepping into me and pressing his lips to mine as his hands cup my cheeks.

"Easier said than done," he says, glancing to Whiskey before taking off to walk his mom to her car.

"What did he do to you?" I utter at Whiskey's side, not making eye contact.

"He ended our friendship for good," he says before putting his palm on my shoulder and squeezing me gently. He heads toward his bus without another word.

My dad's voice is loud enough that a few key words cut through the night—*sick of this* and *time to grow up*—before he's on a hot path back to me and my friends.

"Girls, get in my truck. Peyton, toss me your keys." He holds his hand up and catches them in the air when I throw them. He steps into the driver's seat, throwing the keys on the dash and scanning the inside for evidence, I'm guessing.

He slams the door shut when he's done and waves for

me to follow him to his truck while he presses his phone to his ear.

"Jared, it's Reed. Hey, I need you to come grab the Jeep. It's in the back lot at the school. Someone cut the tires. Yeah, keys are in it." He shoves his phone into his back pocket, and his stride practically doubles. I'm jogging to keep up.

"Tasha, I'll drop you off first," he barks, pressing his key fob. My friends climb into the back seat of his crew cab and I slide into the passenger seat. The Jeep sits broken by itself in the side mirror when I close the door.

"That was some game, huh, Mr. Johnson," Lexi says, her voice timid.

My dad's gaze flicks up to the rearview mirror and his nostrils flare. He doesn't open his mouth, and behind me Tasha whispers, "Not now," to our friend.

We drop them off within minutes, and for the first ten minutes of the drive home alone with my father, it's eerily silent. The air isn't on in the truck. The radio is off. Somehow, the bumpy road seems smooth all of a sudden. Maybe neither of us knows how to begin. We're both angry and not fully with each other, but there's this new wall we've started to build, and the bricks feel heavy.

We're halfway down the dark desert road that leads to our ranch when my dad hits the brakes. I fling forward, my hands wrapping around the seat belt where it slices across my chest. My dad punches the steering wheel twice, then flicks the hazards on before slowly pulling to the side of the road.

My heart is racing as my eyes move from him to the dark night and disappearing road in front of us. The last of Coolidge's farms are to my right, the fall crops just peeking through the soil. It smells like manure out here, even with the truck's vents off. The headlights make the haze in the air glow like a stale green potion that clings to the dry desert like a fungus. *How does anything grow out here at all?*

The windows begin to fog, I think from the hot air the two of us are puffing out like dragons. One of us needs to be first, and if there is one thing I've learned from my mom it's that sometimes, Dad needs a push.

"You should have asked me," I say.

I feel him shift to look at me, but I keep my eyes on the opaque glass, the view on the other side growing less clear with every breath I take. When he doesn't respond after nearly a minute, I give in and meet his stare. I drop my gaze and huff out a short laugh.

"I thought maybe you didn't know what I was talking about. But I can see in your eyes that you do." My dad doesn't have much of a poker face. His eyes are sloped at the corners, the corners of his mouth weighing down his chin. He knows.

"I was trying to protect you."

"Ha!" I laugh out for real this time and look at the dash again. I pull the sleeve of Wyatt's sweatshirt over my palm and lean forward, rubbing a circle on the glass so I can see through it again. The heat and the chill mix out here in the night, and it's somehow never hot or cold this time of year. It feels like . . . nothing. How appropriate.

"I should have talked to you about it first, I know."

"You should have."

I pivot and meet his eyes. He mashes his lips and shakes his head slowly.

"Would you have agreed with me, though?"

"That me being the parade queen would have been a distraction for everyone and for once taken the focus off football?" I quirk a brow, and his head tilts to the side.

"Peyt, that's not why I didn't think it was a good idea. And you know that."

I chew at the inside of my cheek and shift my gaze just to the side of his face. I give it the thought it deserves, and after a few seconds, nod. He's right. I do know that. But damn, sometimes it feels like that's how rules go for me. *Football first.*

"This whole rivalry thing was getting out of hand. And the fire—"

My gaze flickers back to meet his.

We haven't talked about the fire, me and him. I know how things go in the football world out here. A whole lot of discussions happen off the books, with handshakes at the bar over a game of pool, and in after-practice meetings somewhere between the field and the parking lot. I'm sure he and Coach Watts let the inner circle know things were heating up. Boosters out here aren't just for fundraising. Messages get sent, unwritten contracts negotiated. It's how players get transferred without penalty in a system where coaches aren't supposed to recruit. Everyone knows it's all a sham.

"I didn't want you to be a target at the parade," he says.

I shake my head and laugh.

"Turns out I didn't need a parade to be a target. All I had to do was watch a boy I like play a stupid game."

His mouth straightens and he swallows hard, and the air inside thins.

"You like him, huh?" His eyes somehow hold sorrow, but not the way I thought. He doesn't care that it's not Bryce. He cares that it's something real.

"I like him enough to think about staying in state for college after all," I admit with a shrug.

His lip ticks up on the right and he turns to face the steering wheel again, laying his wrist over the top.

"Staying home, huh?"

"I said in-state. I did not say *home*."

"Same thing," he says, that lip quirk now a full-on smirk. He shifts the truck into drive and presses the hazard light button off.

"Definitely not the same thing, Dad," I repeat.

It's still quiet and remains so for most of the way home, but the air is lighter now. Not fully clear, and there are apologies left to be said, but the doors are open.

My dad turns the truck into our drive, and there's a familiar red truck parked next to my mom's SUV.

"Uncle Jason is here?" I sit up on my palms, anxious to see his new baby and my Aunt Sarah. She and my mom have been best friends since grade school, the original *ride-or-dies*. My dad chuckles when the front door to the house opens, his brother standing in the doorway and tapping on his watch.

"I forgot that was tonight. They're staying through next Sunday, you know, for the . . ."

"Parade," I finish.

My Aunt Sarah got to be the parade queen. She was the first one, in fact. My mom says she basically created the role, making her own crown and wearing it while marching to the front of the parade and shooting confetti cannons along Main Street. She was a menace. A bold, loud, amazing menace, and my mom's voice when she needed to borrow one. That's Tasha for me. My confetti cannon.

"I know you were looking forward to it, and I'm really sorry. It wasn't that I didn't want to see you shine, or to put the spotlight on you and brag to the town that you're my kid. I live for that," my dad says, rolling his head against his seat back until our eyes meet. "But the spotlight feels more like a searchlight this year. I was worried someone would do something like they did tonight, only *to you*. And let's face it, your mother would lose her mind."

We both break into a short laugh, adding on jokes about how high the bail would be set to get my mom out of jail, and then the headlines in the tabloids about Former NFL Housewives Behaving Badly. My dad's O-line doesn't have a chance against Nolan Johnson when she's angry and defending her family.

"I'm going to bench Bryce," my dad says suddenly.

My laughter dies and I swallow the instant rock in my

throat. I hold his gaze for a few seconds and let the words sink in.

"You think that's a good idea?"

He breathes in through his nose and hikes his shoulders.

"I have no clue. But I have to do something. It's our side that is starting this, and Bryce has a future in this game. He needs to learn how to lead. The hard way, apparently. Not just when he's winning, but when things aren't going perfectly. The guy doesn't know what messy is."

"He kinda does now," I say, squinting my right eye and twisting my mouth.

"Yeah, and he has no idea how to navigate it."

My dad's right. He doesn't. Bryce has never really had adversity. He got forgiveness when he acted out as a freshman—from me *and* my dad. And maybe that's on us. Some people take second chances and they grow. Others think they've dodged a bullet.

"The alumni around here will protest. They'll come for your job," I say.

My dad chuckles and pushes open the driver's door.

"Let 'em try. I'm Reed fucking Johnson."

Chapter Twenty-Two

Wyatt

Everyone in this damn town drives a truck nicer than mine. It isn't hard, I suppose; mine's sixteen years old, and it needs parts that require special ordering because nobody keeps them on hand. Not in a town this size, at least.

I'm not sure whose red Ford is parked in Peyton's driveway tonight, but I'm pretty sure I can match every Coolidge coach with what they drive, and this truck . . . it's not a coach's.

I stuff my hands into the front of my hoodie. My hair is still wet from my shower, and this beanie isn't doing much to keep the chill at bay. It's finally fall in the desert. Or maybe it's because it's midnight. Either way, I'm cold. But I have plans tonight, and no matter how cold Peyton might say she is, she's going to have to tough this out. A lot of work went into this surprise.

I send her a text to let her know I'm waiting in the

driveway, then promptly shove my phone and hands back into my front pocket, blowing out to test whether I can see my breath yet. Nothing there. All right, maybe I'm being dramatic. But sixty degrees out here feels different. There's nothing but stark desert in all directions, a massive field of barley down the road. The wind cuts.

"I'm pretty sure that was you who broke Dad's MVP trophy! Besides, we both know you threw the ball in the house a lot more than I did." The guy shouting over his shoulder as he steps through the front door with a bag of trash pauses on the stone step, his mouth hung open and head askew.

I raise a hand.

"Hi. I'm here for Peyton."

His spine straightens, and he pulls the front door shut behind him, wrapping the band for the trash bag around his wrist and taking deliberate steps toward me. The thought that he might swing that thing and knock me out with it crosses my mind. More than once.

"You must be the boy," he says, jutting his palm out but not quite smiling.

"Boy, uh . . . yeah, I suppose I'm the boy," I say, smart enough to know this guy can call me whatever he wants. He looks a lot like Reed. I'm pretty sure they're related.

"Boy, you got a name?" His brow quirks, our hands still gripped, his hold tighter.

"Wyatt, sir. I'm friends with—"

"Ah ah, don't do that," he says, finally letting my hand

go. I flex my fingers because *fuck!* He waggles a finger at me.

"I'm sorry. What was I doing?" I shove my hands back into my pocket, mostly to hide that I'm working feeling back into my right one.

"You were lying. You aren't friends. I know my niece, and she was telling me and my wife Sarah about how you broke my brother's record tonight, and she had that thing. You know, the thing?" He whirls his finger around the front of his face.

I shake my head in a quick, tiny burst. I have no idea what *thing* he's talking about.

He snaps his fingers, then looks over his shoulder at the woman who just opened the door.

"Babe, what's the thing Peyt had when she was talking about this fool? You know, like her face? Glow! That's it; she was glowing." He turns back to face me, pointing and smiling a bit more, though I think only because he remembered a four-letter word.

"Ugh, I'm sorry for this. They've been drinking, and they're in their forties now. One of us is getting *up* there," she says, weaving her fingers into his free hand.

"It's fine. I'm just waiting for Peyton. I'm—"

"Oh, we know. You're Wyatt. The boy," the woman says, her half smirk pushing a dent into her right cheek. *Boy. I'm still the boy.*

"I'm Sarah, and this is my dumbass husband, Jason. Peyton's on her way out. She had to grab a jacket. She thinks it's cold." Sarah rolls her eyes. I don't dare mention

I'm a little chilly too. I don't know why I feel everyone in Peyton's family can kick my ass, but I do. I believe there's fact woven in that theory.

"Nice to meet you," I say, nodding but keeping my hand right where it is. I don't trust her grip, either. Not on my throwing hand.

"Uncle Jason, are you trying to ruin my love life?" Peyton says, pushing through the door as she zips up a light pink jacket and pulls the hood up over her hair.

"Of course I am. It's my job. And you're too young to have a love life," Jason says, slinging the trash bag over his shoulder. Bottles clank inside.

"You ready?" I say through a toothy, freaked-out grin.

"We can't leave fast enough," Peyton says, her expression much the same. She skips down the stone porch and takes my hand, leaning in to kiss me. My eyes remain on her uncle the entire time, and I swear he's making threats without speaking.

I lead her to my truck, opening the passenger door and blocking her view of what's in the back. I fumble my keys and drop them on the ground outside my door, and by the time I get situated in the driver's seat, Peyton is having a good laugh at my expense.

"What? The men in your family are intimidating! I thought your dad put me on edge. Your uncle is just plain direct," I laugh out, checking my mirrors and half expecting him to pop up in one of them.

"Wait until you get to know my grandpa," she warns.

I adjust the rearview mirror, then glance at her profile.

Her lashes are like butterfly wings batting wildly with her laughter, her smile, the way she fidgets with my vents to adjust the heat, then sits on her hands to keep them warm.

"I'd like to get to know your grandpa," I say, my eyes on her. She sneaks a short glance my way and a faint smile puckers her lips.

"He's going to love you," she says, and for some reason, that little tip of confidence is enough to get me to go full out tonight and be the corny romantic my dad always said I'd be one day. When I knew. When I met that person who was . . . *different*.

I let Peyton pick the music as I drive us to the main square in Old Town. I promised her hot chocolate at the late-night coffee shop, but we have a little pit stop to make first—the *real* reason I'm dragging her out at midnight.

The downtown area is basically rolled up for bed when I stop in front of the library, the storefronts all dark, small parking lots empty, and the blue glow of security lights shining on the front book displays of the library. The statue of an old man feeding birds is just where Jeff, my dad's old captain, told me I'd find it, so I shift into park but leave the motor running as I dash around the front of my truck while Peyton eyes me suspiciously.

"Give me one second. I promise it will be worth it," I shout over the grind of my engine.

Her brows lift, and she mouths, "Okay."

I dip behind the statue and feel around the base for the electric panel Jeff said would be there. His cousin is a captain with the Coolidge Fire Department, and he called in a favor for me when I came up with this crazy idea at about eight o'clock this morning. I guess that's yesterday by this point. I only wanted Jeff to hook me up with a little ride-along, but once his cousin Dale got involved, he wanted to do things up right. Because, as it turns out, Dale happens to be a big Reed Johnson fan. Doing a solid for his daughter? No brainer.

Does this guy have any haters?

I pull my phone out to text Jeff and Dale that I'm in position, and then I shine my phone's light on the panel so I can type in the twelve digits that Dale sent me earlier tonight. In a blink, the sleeping downtown turns into a winter wonderland of sparkling trees and candy cane light poles. It's still months until the holiday season, but instead of paying to put lights up every year, Coolidge invested in a sort of permanent installation that they can use year round for events like, well, parades.

"Wyatt? How—?" Peyton's gotten out of the truck, so I jog around to kill the engine. I only wanted to keep it running to keep her warm.

I step up behind her, my hands at her hips while she spins in a slow circle, taking in the trees I'm sure she's seen many times. I hope they look different tonight, though. I hope they look like a surprise, like a stupid boy in love. Because that's what they are. A really cheesy gesture that maybe will make all the shit she's put up with for me worthwhile.

"Your chariot, my queen," I say, nudging her to turn to

her right, where the fire truck is pulling around the corner and driving our way.

"Wyatt? What did you do?" Her skeptical tone is also flush with giddiness, so I reach into the back of my truck for the crown, robe, and scepter that I borrowed from the Vista theater department.

"I officially ordain you this year's pre-fall festival parade queen. Your crown," I say, taking a knee and holding the plastic gold headpiece in my palms.

"Are you serious right now?" She giggles and takes her crown from my hands, placing it on her head as I stand and unfurl her robe. I swing it around her shoulders, my eyes meeting hers as I tie the purple ribbon below her chin.

"I'm very serious, Peyton. You are not missing out on being someone's queen." My hands drop to my sides, and I take a step back. She sucks in her bottom lip, and I nearly tell her I'm falling in love when the oh-so-romantic sound of air brakes spoils the moment.

"Your scepter," I say instead, handing her the brass pole with what looks like a glass curtain rod finial on the end.

Drawing it to her chest, she lowers her chin and hits me with a serious stare.

"Sir Stone, I hereby knight thee," she says, tapping each of my shoulders with the prop.

"I think I'm supposed to kneel for that," I whisper in her ear as I lead her toward the truck.

"It's okay because this is pretend. You aren't really a knight," she teases.

"Hey, Wyatt. I'm Dale," a towering man says as he climbs out of the passenger side of the fire truck and heads toward me. His handlebar mustache is thicker than Jeff's, but the roundness of their faces and the red cheeks are family traits.

"Thank you so much for doing this," I say, shaking his hand. He covers the back of my palm with his other hand.

"Absolutely, man. Your dad was an amazing guy. He and I went through the academy together. You ever need anything, we've got you, son."

A flame fires in my chest, but it doesn't burn. It warms me to my core, leaving behind a lightness in my heart, a strong beat in my chest as if my life was somehow renewed through this small degree of separation.

"I appreciate that, Dale. Thank you," I say, glancing to Peyton. Her soft smile twitches, and she gives me a tiny nod.

Dale introduces us to DJ, his engineer, then leads us to the back of the truck, where a built-in ladder leads to the top. We sit in the hose bed and promise not to move while they steer the truck slowly around the town square.

"Cross our hearts," Peyton says, gripping my hand when Dale climbs down and leaves us up top alone.

"Is the queen afraid of heights?" I tease.

"I never said I was a flyer in cheer. To be honest, I don't *love* heights," she admits, a small tremble in her hand when the brakes release and the truck begins to roll.

"You should try climbing up a roof with Whiskey," I laugh out.

"Just so we're clear, I am never agreeing to an idea

Whiskey has—ever." She's making a joke, but her nerves make her voice come out wavery and serious.

"Okay." I chuckle, putting an arm around her and holding her tight against my side.

By the first turn, her body relaxes against me and her eyes light up. The canopy of white lights strung throughout the trees casts a warm glow on her face, her lashes like flecks of gold, her lips like candy. An older couple pulls their car over across from the town park, getting out to take photos amidst the lights.

"Happy pre-fall festival to you!" Peyton shouts from above. The couple waves as Peyton blows kisses, throwing them into the air as if she's the goddess of rain.

"You're really something, you know that?"

She sinks down, nestling close to me again, and resting her head on my shoulder.

"You're the one who's something, Wyatt Stone."

I rub my palm along her arm, keeping her warm as we finish the last quarter turn, and I brace her for the stop.

Her smile beams all the way to my truck, where I lift her just outside the passenger door, swinging her around and holding her up so she can fly among the lights one last time before turning them off. I set her in the passenger seat as the fire truck pulls away, our hands tangled and, I think, both of us anxious to touch one another.

"Hi," she whispers, a nervous tilt to her mouth.

"Hi," I reply, my eyes locked on hers while our fingers slip in and out of one another's.

She scoots to the edge of the seat, her legs wrapping

around my thighs and her feet hooking behind my legs to pull me closer. I run my palms up her cheeks, then straighten her crown, my gaze drifting to hers, and then to her mouth.

"Kiss your queen," she says, her tone teasingly demanding. It's sexy.

"As you wish," I say, my smile hovering over her mouth for a few extra seconds, long enough to let my gaze roam from her mouth to her chin and then the place where her legs have spread around me.

My mouth drops to hers and my hand curves around her hip to her ass, pulling her against me so she can feel what her teasing does. She unties the royal robe's ribbon from under her neck as she slowly leans back. Her palms grasp the dash and the back of the seat for support and I follow, leaning over her as my teeth graze her bottom lip before breaking our kiss.

"Do you know how fucking hot you are?" I say, looking down at her, my flexed arms holding my weight up just enough.

A coy grin paints her lips as her right hand lets go of its grip on the seat, her back fully arched over my console now. She grabs the golden pull tab of her jacket zipper and drags it down the middle of her chest, stopping between her breasts when it becomes obvious that she did not wear anything underneath.

"Well, fuck me," I groan.

"Okay," she says through a playful smirk, her voice soft and full of want.

My eyes flash to hers to gauge the seriousness of her tease. She scoots back a little more and her legs widen as I step out of the truck to scan the quiet empty streets one more time to make sure we're alone.

Satisfied enough, I unzip my jeans to give my cock relief, stroking myself a few times before resting my right knee on the edge of the passenger seat to hold myself over her. She pulls her jacket zipper down completely, her nipples barely hidden by the jagged edges.

"My queen," I say, drawing a soft laugh from her before I lean forward and drag her jacket edges open to expose her breasts to the cool night air. I suck the hard pink tips and she arches more over the console, her body scooting back a few more inches to lift her breasts higher, pushing them into my mouth. My tongue swirls one then the other, her hips writhing beneath me.

I step back to pull her leggings and panties down her hips and over her knees, leaving them around her ankles so she has to spread her knees apart for me to take her. Gripping myself with one hand, I reach into my jean pocket with my other in search of my wallet. I hand it to her and she pulls out the foil packet, tearing it open with her teeth before handing me the condom to slip on.

Gliding over her in the tight, cramped space, I brace myself with one foot on the passenger floor. Peyton lifts her hips and I support her with my hand under her ass as I guide my tip between her legs. She scoots down a few inches, enough that I can enter her, and the moment we connect, her head falls back as she lets out a moan that makes my cock flex inside of her.

My hips thrust, pushing into her, pressing her into my palm, into the truck seat, her breasts shaking with every push of my body into hers. I pull her into me, my hand digging into her soft, round ass cheek with every pump, and my mouth drops to her raw, pink nipple again to give it the attention it needs. My tongue flicks the tip as I hold it between my teeth and Peyton's hands grip my back, holding on through every thrust. She begins to whimper under my weight, so I move in and out of her faster, drawing out her orgasm just as I fall over the edge with her.

We cling to each other for several quiet minutes, our out-of-breath laughter filling the cab of my truck as we make jokes about the older couple driving by and seeing the windows fogged up now that I've pulled the door shut behind me.

"You really need a bigger truck," she jokes as I fumble with the zipper of her jacket.

"Ha! Or maybe you spend more nights at my house since your dad scares the shit out of me," I laugh out.

The condom disposed of in a nearby trash, Peyton runs her fingers through her hair and straightens her clothes and crown, pulling her royal robe back over her shoulders as I climb back into the driver's side and crank the engine.

It's nearly one by the time I get her back home, and it's the end of a painfully long week. I walk her to her front door, laughter bellowing from the other side, and I can't help but laugh softly along with them even though I didn't hear the joke.

"You should come in," she says.

"Ah, I don't know," I say, my heart wanting to, desperately. To spend more time with her, but also to soak up the sound of family.

"Really, it's okay. My mom gave me permission to be out tonight, not that I need to ask for it—"

"But I like that you do," I say, kissing her nose as she steps into me and stuffs her hands into my hoodie pocket.

"I'm not sure I'm your dad's favorite person," I lament.

"Why? Because you broke his record?" She snorts out a short laugh but I wince.

"I actually hadn't thought of that yet. The interview was . . . awkward. Your dad had a prepared monologue for me, and he patted my shoulder with the stiffness of a Ken doll." I can feel the tapping sensation on my shoulder simply thinking of it.

"Don't let that stop you from coming in. Honestly, you're kind of my uncle's favorite person right now because it gives him something to give my dad shit about."

"Ha, sure. I doubt that," I say with wide eyes. "I'm pretty sure if your aunt didn't come out to save me, your uncle was figuring out a way to stuff me into the trash, too."

"*Pfft*, no way," she says, tugging my sweatshirt toward her, her hands now clutching mine inside the pocket.

"Your dad doesn't really seem too hip on me, Peyton,

and while I'm willing to work to win him over, I just don't know—"

"Please," she says, her hands giving mine a gentle squeeze as she looks at me through her lashes.

I think this may just be one of those moments for me, one that I'll etch deep inside and hold on to forever. This is when I learn that I will never be able to say no to Peyton Johnson.

"Okay," I say, watching in wonder as her smile spreads across her face.

She bursts through the door before I have a chance to change my mind, her family all gathered around a large wooden table covered in cards and cash. Her mom is sitting on her dad's lap, and her aunt is filling a glass with wine.

"Hey, it's the new state passing record holder," her uncle proclaims, standing from his chair and approaching me as if he's about to bow.

"I don't think you need to—"

I stop talking when he drops to a knee in front of Peyton, and she promptly knights him just as she did me. Her uncle winks at me as he stands, then slaps my bicep with a heavy palm. My body quakes from the swift force. I thought I had put on enough weight, but these Johnson men are making me question that.

"Relax, *boyfriend*. We're all drunk, and I've come around to liking you. My brother will get over it eventually." He rushes over to Reed and play-punches his shoulder several times.

While everyone else seems loose and relaxed, Reed still

has an edge. And as Peyton leads me to a giant sectional in the family room just beyond the table, his eyes follow me like one of those creepy paintings in a haunted house.

I think it's Peyton's plan to have me sleep here. *Right* here, on this couch. She's pulling out extra blankets from a trunk and fluffing a pillow for me to lie down. Thankfully, she puts a movie on while her family starts a new round of whatever weird version of poker they're playing. But she lays her head on my thigh, and every time I glance over my shoulder, Reed's glare is there waiting for me. I leave my arms up on the sofa back and guard my expression for the next two hours until Peyton's fallen asleep next to me and Reed and Nolan are cleaning up the mess left on the table.

When the lights switch off behind me, I exhale. There's no way I'm sleeping a wink here. But maybe now I'll be able to breathe. And I can watch Peyton. I'd fight off a dozen sleepless nights to watch the way her top lip curls up when she's like this.

"Hey." The whisper from behind me jacks my heart rate up about a thousand, and for a moment, I think I might throw up.

I crane my neck and spot Reed standing near a small light he's left on behind a massive kitchen island. He calls me over with his hand, and I slowly slip out from under Peyton's head, resting it on one of the pillows.

All the way to the kitchen I pray for aliens to abduct me, and when that doesn't happen, I brace myself with one hand on the counter as I stand about two feet away from my idol.

Then Reed holds out his hand, his gaze fixed on mine, his eyes pretty clear for a guy who had several beers. I take his palm and wait for the vice grip I got from his brother, but that's not what he gives me at all. His shake is firm, brief, and seemingly tinged with respect. I'm so on edge that I half expect it to be followed up with a punch to the face. But it isn't. Instead, he pulls a stool out and takes a seat, then gestures for me to do the same.

"You like cookies?" He quirks a brow.

"I . . . are you tricking me?"

He chuckles softly, his whisper more like a growl thanks to the alcohol and the fact he's the manliest man I've met other than my dad. He gets up and snags a container sitting next to the fridge, then slides it on the counter between us, pulling the lid off to reveal about a dozen massive chocolate chip cookies.

"My stepmother bakes all damn day. She loves to cook, but she's going to make me fat. Eat up," he says, nudging the container closer to me. I take one out and break off a piece, the chocolate literally melting with the butter the second it hits my tongue.

"Oh, my God," I praise.

He laughs silently and breaks off half a cookie for himself.

"Right? Now you see my problem."

Reed leaves me with the cookies while he fills two glasses with milk and sets them next to the decadent treats. For a few seconds, we gush over the cookies and enjoy a few bites in uncomfortable silence. The television is a low hum with some afterhours B movie playing that I hope like hell doesn't have a sex scene right now.

He takes a big swig of his milk, then runs his hand across his mouth, erasing any hint of a 'stache. Then he says, "Congratulations."

I blink a few times while I swallow my last bite.

"Thank you, Coach," I basically croak.

A breathy laugh slips out, and he smirks on one side.

"You know, if you're going to date my daughter, you should probably start calling me Reed." He lowers his chin and gives me a direct stare.

"I'm going to try, Coach. But you have no idea," I say through nervous laughter. I take a drink of milk to coat my suddenly dry mouth, then rub the chill from my palms after setting it down.

"Try me," Reed says.

I look back toward the TV, checking to make sure Peyton is still asleep.

"She's fine. Girl slept through a hurricane once in Florida. Like, the whole-ass hurricane. For thirty hours straight."

I nod, impressed.

"Okay, well, I'm not sure how much you know about me, but—"

"I could probably tell you every play you're going to try against us in two weeks. And how fast your forty is. The launch angle of your throw, and which side is your weakest per quarter." He squints when he's done, and I get the distinct impression that this man keeps a database in his head.

"Yeah, that's . . . flattering?"

We both laugh softly.

"I mean more of my story. Like, how I got here, why football, all that?"

His mouth tightens, and he crosses his arms while leaning back, seeming to ready himself for it. I'm sure he knows my dad died. Those stories were in the regional papers, and if he kept tabs on my stats, surely he made a note of my dad.

"My dad died of cancer in January," I begin, waiting while he shifts his weight and drops his gaze. I've gotten good at this part. *What a terrible thing to be good at.*

"I'm sorry," he utters.

"Thank you, yeah. It was . . . it *is* pretty shitty." I shrug, no other way to put it. "My dad taught me everything. I mean, yeah, I've had coaches refine things here and there, and I put in a ton of work with strength and conditioning, but the foundation? That's all him. I get up at five every morning to run. I eat so much protein I actually don't like steak anymore. I study film on my own and try to mimic the greats. I watch you."

He leans back and lifts his brows, and I can tell he thinks I'm just kissing ass, so I solidify it for him.

"No, I'm serious. You can tell me all those things about me, but I can probably do the same with you. I know every game. Every playoff comeback. The passes that missed and sent you throwing your helmet at the bench?"

His head tilts a notch.

"I know those too. And I read your thoughts on what you think went wrong. Mr. Johnson, you were literally my idol. My dad had your jersey. Hell, I bet my mom kept it. When she realizes I'm dating your daughter, puts it all together, she's going to flip her lid. And my mom, Mr. Johnson? She's one cool character. She can handle a lot. Nothing rattles her. Life has tried its damnedest.

"But our lives somehow weaving into yours? You're the guy my dad respected most in this game. The coach he always wanted me to play against just so he could show me off. The guy whose record my dad and I talked about beating, even weeks before he died. I'm sorry if I struggle to call you Reed.

"But also, you need to know that I had no idea who your daughter was when I met her. And she pretty much had me from the first breath she took in my presence."

"You know, for a minute there, I thought you were going to quote that Tom Cruise movie," he says, holding a serious face for about a second before laughing and flattening a palm on the countertop between us.

"I'm not that cheesy," I reply.

"Nah, you are. You're that cheesy, Wyatt," he says, and I sink into my stool a little. "But you're also that good. And I don't just mean at the game, which you are really fucking good at."

"Thank you," I croak, my heart beating so fast from hearing such a massive compliment I feel like I might throw up.

"But you're better at being a man. That's where you excel. That's the stuff that's going to get you through this season, through some really hard years ahead. Your character is exactly why I'm actually relieved you're the one my daughter seems to have fallen for. Just don't fuck it up."

He slides his palm an inch or two toward me and holds my stare for a beat before nodding as if the silent contract is done. He pats the granite surface twice, then stands from his seat, taking the container of cookies, slipping out the half he left behind before putting the lid on and placing it back in the corner by the fridge.

"Good night, Wyatt," he says, turning the soft light off from under the upper cabinets. "And by the way, your bed? It's down that hall, through the double doors. The sofa in the den pulls out. You'll be way more comfortable there. And I'll be way more comfortable with . . . this." He circles his finger in the air between me and the couch where his daughter is fast asleep.

"Understood," I say. And just to prove to him that I can, I add, "Good night, Reed," before he heads up the stairs.

Chapter Twenty-Three

Peyton

Since I missed school Monday for my suspension, and we had gym time all week to practice for our next competition, Coach decided to push our team meeting for the fall fundraiser to today. She says she wanted my input and ideas, but I think she wanted to orchestrate this moment, where we are all forced to sit on the gym floor in a circle and stare at one another.

Thursdays are now my least favorite day of the week. At least, *this* Thursday is.

I've been able to skip over all the awkwardness and confrontation thanks to getting right to work every time I stepped foot in this gym. But now, I'm sitting directly across from Stephanie, our circle seemingly divided into two sides. The younger members are all around her, while the seniors and a few of the juniors are near me. I'm tempted to say something about being divided by maturity, but that really wouldn't be very mature of me.

"Okay, ladies . . . and Jordan. I mentioned this in my text to you all, but it looks like our usual candy products are off the table this year. A Vista club already contracted with the vendor, so we are going to have to come up with a new idea, preferably one as profitable since those sales have easily pulled in a few thousand for us in the past. Anyone want to go first?"

Coach scans the circle, her gaze pausing on me for a few seconds before moving on to Tasha, then Lexi.

"I know this isn't really the topic we're on, Coach, but now that we aren't selling the candy, can't Peyton take over on the float again?" Lexi suggests.

My chest tightens, and my stomach feels like it's full of rocks.

"We'll be selling something, so no, I should stay with the booth," I say, meeting my friend's eyes with a brief warning in my gaze.

"Actually, I'm glad you brought this up, Lexi. And thank you, Peyton, for your willingness to put the team first. I know that was hard for you," our coach says.

I nod and give her a tight-lipped smile, but given she's sitting closer to Stephanie, it's impossible not to see her reaction to our conversation. Her gaze up and to the side, she shakes her head and huffs audibly.

"And Stephanie," I say, deciding I can't let this fester. Coach is right. I need to put the team first. And if Stephanie's opinion truly doesn't matter to me, then I shouldn't give it weight.

"Yeah," she says, her tone flat.

"I'm sorry I took my hurt ego out on you. That wasn't fair." The bullshit coming out of my mouth makes me a little sick, but I swallow it down.

"Gee, thank you, Peyton . . . for being so selfless."

I lock on to Stephanie's stare, my mouth fighting to stay shut while everything I probably should say boils up my throat. Finally, I end it, and simply say, "You're welcome."

A few of the younger girls snicker, maybe understanding the sarcastic undertone in my response. It seems to be enough to end this war for now as my new nemesis has nothing else to say. There won't be any love lost between me and Stephanie. But I can share a mat with her for six more weeks. If she thinks I'm putting her on the squad for basketball games, she's delusional.

Coach urges us to focus on our fundraiser, and after a few product sales ideas that get lukewarm receptions, I throw the idea of hosting a dunk tank into the mix.

"Look, I bet I can get my dad to take a turn, and if we all take turns sitting in the hot seat, I think we could raise a ton of money," I argue.

"Yeah, people would pay huge money to dunk your ass," Tasha teases, nudging me and glancing toward Stephanie. I level her with the same warning look I gave Lexi, but Tasha is immune to my scolding.

"We could sell it as *dunking daddy's girl,*" she says, laughing out hard and fast.

"Tasha . . ." Coach admonishes her, but then I decide

she might be on to something, and wave my hand in the air to cut her off.

"No, wait. Actually, that's a really good idea. I know Tasha is joking, but seriously, why not? I don't care what people say about me. At least, not for this. And if it taps into some itch people need to scratch, and we can sell them three softball tosses for twenty bucks? Call me daddy's girl all you want. I am. I'm a daddy's girl. Kinda proud of it." I meet Stephanie's eyes again, a renewed confidence lifting me up, making me sit a little taller.

"Yeah, and Stephanie can be the bi—"

"No," I stop Tasha, squinting my eyes and holding my breath.

But suddenly, the strangest thing happens. Stephanie's lip inches up, and her gaze moves to the center of our circle while she seems to be playing that concept out in her head.

"I'll be the bitch," she finally says.

"Really?" I ask.

She lifts her gaze, and for a blip, I think maybe there's an apology buried in there.

"Yeah, I can play that role." She shrugs.

"Great!" I say, clapping my hands together, holding in my urge to snarkily add, *It's not a role as much as a character trait.*

"I guess I'm the bully," Tasha laughs out.

"Yeah, you are," Lexi teases, and the entire squad laughs.

"This is good," Coach says, building on the idea with ways we can spin it to talk about ditching those stereotypes and embracing positivity. It's a stretch, but I get that she needs the school board to sign off on it. I say we go for it and ask for forgiveness after. It's not like the school board has given a damn about bullying in the past, so why give them credit now.

After an hour of planning, Coach manages to make a few calls to secure two donated dunking booths for us, and we've managed to make up nicknames for every member of our team, saving Lexi, *the Queen,* for last. The coldness between Stephanie and me is still there, but it's definitely melted a tad. I don't expect much more.

I break us down, just as I have every day except for Monday when Tasha took the lead. Everyone piles into the locker room to change out from our spankies and into our Coolidge Bears sweats and hoodies. I'm thankful for the shift to a real, actual fall. But I'm more thankful for these new team sweats now that I'll be sticking around for football practice to end so I can ride home with my dad.

We should get the Jeep back this weekend. My dad opted to have his restoration guy do some extra work on it to make it safer for me to take to whatever school I decide on for next year. It's pretty clear, though, where his hopes lie as he keeps mentioning how tuning up the rear-wheel differential and replacing the shocks will make it easy for me to navigate some of the off-road trails in Tucson. Where he went.

Where Wyatt is probably going to go.

I wait for Tasha and Lexi to finish changing, and the three of us walk out together. I hug my friends good-bye near

Tasha's car, then shuffle my way toward the stadium, the lights humming as the sun sets and they warm up. My backpack slung around to my front, I'm digging inside, attempting to fish out my headphones so I can wrap up some homework during the final hour of practice, when Bryce stops me behind the concession building on his way to the field.

"You know I didn't do that to your tires, right?"

He isn't dressed in pads. Only the guys taking the field wear pads for Thursday practice, and my dad benched him. I never influenced my dad either way, and I'm still not sure that all of this—the elevated rivalry, the fire, my tires—is totally on his shoulders and his alone. But my dad has a point. Leaders should lead. And Bryce isn't exactly trying to stop any of it.

"I never thought you did," I say, sighing as he has me stopped in my tracks. He's not blocking my way completely, but his stance is dominating. And it makes me uneasy, the way his body is just a little too close.

"You did. You blame me. Your dad does, too."

"Whatever my dad's issue is with you is between coach and player. I have homework to do, so if you don't mind," I say, taking a wide berth to walk around him.

He trails just behind my left shoulder, and I consider throwing a fist back to catch him in the nuts.

"Your dad have the same kind of talk with your new boyfriend? Because this is as much his fault as mine."

I don't stop, but my eyes flutter as I walk and chuckle to myself.

"Wyatt is nothing like you, Bryce. Nothing."

His footsteps mirror mine, and by the time I reach the bleachers, we're shoulder to shoulder. I'm thankful that I'm in everyone's view. I don't *think* Bryce would be physical with me, but his actions lately have been so erratic. And when I look back at his pattern of behavior from the moment we met, he's never actually been nice. He's been calculated. And selfish. A good time.

I climb up a few rows and plop my bag in front of me so I can pull my laptop out to finish working on a paper I need to write. When I open the screen, though, Bryce gently shuts it.

"Okay, Bryce. You have my attention. What else do you have to say? Say it so we can be done with this and I can get back to what I need to do."

I flatten my palms on top of my computer and breathe in deeply, trying to keep myself calm. I catch my dad's gaze from the field, and he takes a few steps in our direction. I shake my head, alerting him that I don't need rescuing, and Bryce follows my sightline.

"See, that's what I mean, Peyton. Your dad thinks he needs to rescue you from me. What the hell? Why would he think I'm that kind of person? Wyatt poisoned him against me. And he has you thinking I'm some sort of—"

"Selfish prick?" I finish for him. I can't take it anymore, and my words stun him.

"What? Peyt, I have always put you first; you are liter-ally the girl of my dreams. I—"

I laugh out hard, breaking up his string of lies. God, I used to think he was so smooth.

"I know what you do when you go to camp, Bryce. And no, Whiskey never had to tell on you. You were bad at hiding things. And honestly? By the end, I didn't even care. I think I was just looking for a reason to let myself fall out of love with you. And it turns out, I never really was. I was infatuated. I was a freshman when we met. And I grew up. You? You're still picking fights at bonfires and whining that some other quarterback is better than you."

"Wyatt Stone is not better than me. He got lucky. He's played shit teams for most of his high school career. When we get to college and he's fighting not to get cut, I'm going to have people talking Heisman. That's not whining, Peyton. That's fact."

He stands and steps down two rows before turning to face me. I shake my head, the corners of my mouth pinched into a pity grin.

"He's the one with the record, Bryce. You're chasing *him*."

"Not for long," he says.

I breathe in and will myself to just let him have those last words. They're meaningless anyway. But Bryce, he can't stop himself. He leans forward, sliding my bag out of his way so he can rest one foot in front of me to break into my personal space.

"When we lose tomorrow night, that's on you, Peyton."

He hovers a few inches from my face, and I swear I get a whiff of alcohol. He puckers his lips and blows an air kiss at me that turns my stomach, but he steps back and turns to head back to the sidelines. I wait until his feet hit the track.

"You're wrong, Bryce!" I make sure he can hear me, and though he keeps walking, I know he can. "If we lose, that's on you. Because you're the one who got yourself benched. Guess that means Wyatt will be one more game up on you, too. Good luck chasing."

His stride slows for a few steps, and his left hand draws into a tight fist at his side, but he keeps going. And he never looks my way again.

Chapter Twenty-Four

Wyatt

It's nice being back on our home field. For the first few weeks of practice and the first couple of games, this place still felt impersonal. It's new, so the personality of Vista isn't really baked in yet.

But something about having our field branded by the old guard in town did something to the place, something all the banners and paint in the world couldn't.

"This is our house!" Whiskey shouts as he struts—shirtless, but thankfully in pants—around the locker room.

For whatever reason, our team has taken up barking. It doesn't make sense because we're the Mustangs, but Whiskey started calling this the dog house, and then Jody started barking. It took about two minutes for it to solidify into a tradition. It's pretty cool that we get to start it.

"Gentleman!" Coach claps his hand against the back of his clipboard as he steps up on one of the benches.

I whistle with my fingers in my mouth—one of the best things my dad taught me—and everyone settles down to give Coach their attention.

Coach pulls his reading glasses from his pocket and slides them on his face as he peers at his phone. He glances around the room then back to his screen, lifting his chin as if he needs to adjust his focus on something.

"St. Mary's, sixteen!" He's telling us the Coolidge score. Everyone hushes, and the room gets even more silent, though only briefly.

"Someone got a safety!" Whiskey shouts.

The locker room booms with our laughter. St. Mary's probably kicked three field goals to get to that score, but it's a whole lot sweeter to imagine Coolidge getting sacked in their end zone.

"Coolidge High Bears!" Coach's volume quiets us back down.

He draws out the tension, studying his phone screen, then making random eye contact with one of us. I smirk at him when his gaze lands on me, and he instantly glances back at his screen.

"Seven," he finally announces.

We literally erupt.

"That's what I'm talking about!" Jody bellows, now matching Whiskey stomp for stomp as the two of them pound on their chests as they howl, faces up at the ceiling.

The vibe is infectious. And it's impossible not to feel the electricity, most of us branded with smiles that stretch ear to ear. You'd think we were in the playoffs already and waiting for opponents to get knocked out, but it's this rivalry that has fueled that. And that can be good. But we have a whole lot more to do, and while I love to see the guys celebrate getting a game up on them, I don't want them getting complacent.

My gaze meets Coach's, and he nods for me to step into his office. I hug Jody as he passes me and slap hands with a few of the other guys before slipping through his door and leaving it open a crack.

"Next week is going to be the real deal," Coach says, eluding to the hometown rivalry that threatens to erupt on the field. "They're going to be coming for us."

"I know." I think he can tell from my serious tone that I'm not under any false pretenses about how next Friday night is going to go. Coolidge likely lost tonight because Bryce was benched. I may hate the guy, but he's a strong quarterback, and the backup is a sophomore. It's actually pretty telling that the game was as close as it was with a young arm slinging for them.

"This week is going to require spectacular focus," he says.

I nod.

"I agree."

He sits in his chair and leans back with his eyes on me, every second uncomfortable. My gut is trying to prepare me, but in the back of my mind, I'm holding out hope that this meeting isn't about what I think it is.

"You think right now is a good time for you to be hanging out with Reed Johnson's daughter?"

Fuck.

I twist my lips, mostly to keep myself from telling him to do something to himself that will likely get *me* benched. Coach Watts holds respect over winning. Hell, that rule is posted above his office door.

Respect Comes First. Winning Comes Second.

"Do you think there is a problem with that?"

He laughs under his breath and moves his hands behind his head as he studies me. He twists side to side in his chair, almost like he's waiting me out. But if Reed himself couldn't get me to leave his daughter alone, there's no way Coach Watts is.

"You're probably going to break another record next Friday," he says, switching topics. Kind of.

I breathe in slowly through my nose.

"I know." I've been dreading it, though I should be excited. I'm one touchdown away from tying Reed's record for TDs by a quarterback in Arizona. If I carry it in twice, that record is mine. I've honestly been thinking about only passing and handing off when we're in the red zone, but I keep coming back to how unfair that would be to the team.

"If you need to, can you do what needs to be done?" Seems Coach has been reading my thoughts.

I nod.

He holds my gaze for a few more silent seconds, the locker room clearing out behind me.

"Okay," he finally says.

He stands and holds out his hand. I shake it.

"Good win. Let's get one more."

"Yes, sir," I answer, leaving his office with a new mountain of pressure on my shoulders, the kind that won't be easy to explain but that I'm hoping Peyton can help me parse out tonight.

Whiskey found a new spot near the dry riverbed, and it's become the party place of choice. Most of the guys are heading there, and I'm sure they will wake up with the sun, massively hungover and regretting that they have to drag their asses in for film. If we get a playoff win in a few weeks, that's when I'll go. But until then, my mind and my heart are better served somewhere in the middle of the desert at the end of a ridiculously long driveway.

I make it to the ranch twenty minutes later and text Peyton from her driveway. The heart-to-heart with Reed went a long way in making me feel less like the enemy when I'm at her house. But I've got a long way to go before I can just barge through her front door and make myself at home.

My phone buzzes in my palm as I hover on the stoop.

PEYTON: Vanilla or chocolate?

My face puzzles.

ME: Is this a trick question?

The door opens a second later, and she's standing there in my Bills sweatshirt and super baggy sweatpants, her hair pulled into a braid. She giggles as I step inside.

"Not a trick question. Grandpa is making sundaes to celebrate."

I pause a few steps in front of her, all of that comfort her dad built erased with one word—grandpa. I'm almost more afraid of meeting him. Then another thing about what she said hits me.

"Celebrating? But didn't you guys lose?" I noticed her dad's truck wasn't in the driveway. I'm guessing he's with his staff, probably working out how they're going to take Bryce off the bench but still teach him a lesson. Good luck with that. I think there are some things that dude can't be taught. Right and wrong are at the top of that list.

"We did," she says, stepping around me and moving her arms around my neck.

"We're celebrating your win."

Her hands are cold against my skin, but it feels nice. Besides, her lips warm me a second later. Of course, when I hear an older man clear his throat just beyond her shoulder and I pop one eye open to see her grandfather giving me an evil stare, all of that warmth turns into a sudden need to vomit.

I pull my lips away, but Peyton holds on to my bottom lip with her teeth, somehow making the whole scene feel even more inappropriate.

"You Wyatt?" the man snarls.

I fucking suck at first impressions.

"Yes, sir. I am. You must be Mr. Johnson." My mouth feels like a desert. And my tongue feels fat. Yet, somehow I push forward and shake his hand. He leans forward as he laughs, but doesn't leave what looks like a mobility chair. There's an oxygen tank fixed to the side, but the cannula isn't on his face.

"My son said he tried to break you of that Mr. Johnson bull crap. I'm Buck. Everybody calls me Buck. You go around trying to get my attention with the *mister* business, I'll never turn around. You got it?"

He drops my hand and laughs again.

I think he means to set me at ease, but my muscles are cramping from shoulder to toe, I'm so tense.

"Vanilla or chocolate, Wyatt?" he says. His chair is pushed up to the table and two giant tubs of ice cream sit in the middle along with various toppings and whipped cream cans. Clearly, he isn't worried about overdoing the sweets.

"Can I have both?" I say.

He pauses with the scoop over the chocolate and gives me a wink before looking at Peyton.

"I like this kid. Good choice," he says.

And finally, I breathe.

The next hour is passed with too much ice cream and stories about Coolidge High's greatest team of all time, which—despite what history says—is actually Buck's senior year, when the school was a hundred and forty students strong. I don't dare challenge him. And frankly, after learning the details of just how crappy the playing conditions were and how lax the safety rules were, I think he might be right. His team was certainly the toughest.

Peyton's gaze bounces between the two of us while we

swap tales of our favorite moments from his son's career, and I think I score a few points by being able to rattle off his Super Bowl stats from the top of my head.

By the end of the evening, which borders on turning into the next day, I earn a hug from Buck Johnson. And I call him Buck twice, to his face. Peeling myself away is hard, but I can tell he's getting tired. Plus, the front windows of Peyton's house are lighting up with headlights, which probably means Reed is home.

"You better skedaddle. He won't want you making a habit of spending the night here. Now, what goes on in college . . ." He quirks a brow and my face heats up. Peyton is practically cherry red.

"Oh, my God! Grandpa!" She covers her face with both hands.

As embarrassed as I am discussing anything having to do with me, Peyton, and sleeping—which really means *not* sleeping—in front of Buck, the idea that we might be in the same place next year makes my heart kick extra hard.

"Thank you for the amazing calories," I say, rubbing my stomach with one hand and taking Peyton's in the other.

She grins at her grandpa, then twists her head to gaze up at me and mouths, "You did great."

She walks me to the door, and I'm about to ask her if she'll walk me out to my truck so I can kiss her like I really want to when Reed flings the door open. His eyes are wide, his jaw flexed, and his mouth is set in a hard line. My stomach drops in an instant.

"Good. I'm glad you're here and not out in the river

bottom with the rest of those jackholes!" He stomps through the house, answering a call on his cell phone as he digs through a kitchen drawer.

My eyes flash to Peyton's, and she shrugs before following after her dad.

"What's going on?" she asks. He holds up a finger, answering whoever is on the other line first.

"That's right. Tell them I said their asses better be running up and down the home stands when I get there." He pulls out a crinkled notepad and flips through a few pages, seeming to find the one he needs and folding the pages back.

"Yeah, and if Watts's guys are there, tell them they can run too. Their coach said so. I'm over this shit."

Reed flattens his phone on the counter and rests his palms on either side. His chin drops into his chest as he mutters a few choice words, then pops his gaze up to meet mine.

I shake my head, the ominous feeling growing in my belly like a bad bowl of chili.

"I'm about out of favors with the Sherriff's Department. We're lucky the guys who pulled up on them tonight were former teammates of mine and they called me instead. But someone at the district found out about this shit. And now I have to call the superintendent at . . ." He flips his phone over and huffs out a laugh. "One in the morning. *God dammit!*"

"What *shit* did the district find out about?" I swear, if Whiskey was playing with matches . . .

Reed's eyes flutter slowly, either from exhaustion or frustration. Probably a little of both.

"Apparently, our teams decided it was a good idea to settle their differences by playing chicken in the river bottom. Whiskey's mom is going to lock that boy in their basement when she sees what he did to his car, which now has a fucking cactus wedged into the front fender."

My eyes shut lazily the same way Reed's did.

"Bryce flipped his truck on its side. I guess it's a blessing the two of them didn't ram each other head-on. I mean, of course it is, but *what the hell?* What is wrong with these stupid numb nuts?"

"Reed?" Nolan peeks around the corner, her eyes swollen from the rude awakening. Her husband was far from quiet.

He moves over to her and wraps his arms around her, holding her against him as he kisses the top of her head, his rage level instantly softening from a ten to maybe a four. His head is still sunk in his shoulders, and his hands . . . still fists.

"Boys being boys. Well, more like boys being idiots. But I'm gonna be out all night. I need to nip this now before someone gets killed."

Nolan steps back a hair and looks up at him with concern, her eyes suddenly more awake.

"Nobody got hurt. Miraculously," Reed says. "I'll fill you in tomorrow. Get some sleep."

She slides a palm along his cheek and holds his gaze for a few seconds, seeming to right his mood with just a look.

He waits until she heads back upstairs before turning to me.

"You should probably be a part of this. I need someone your age to have their head on straight."

"I'll come too," Peyton says, instantly rushing to the door where her fuzzy boots lay on their sides.

"Peyt, I love that you want to help, honey, but—"

She drops her shoe back to the floor, seeming to understand her dad's concern. Her mouth pulls up on one side.

"You got a whole town of adolescent males fighting over you," I tease, trying to make her feel better. As much as some of Bryce's beef with me is centered on her, though, she's not the root of what's going on. Testosterone is. And ego.

All thanks to a bunch of board members who got together when Vista opened and decided to carve the town's beloved football team in half.

"I'll follow you," I say to her dad. He grabs the notebook, and from a quick glance at it I see what looks to be a phone number. I'm guessing he's calling the superintendent during his drive.

"Call me when you're done?" Peyton says, squeezing me tight and kissing my cheek.

"It's probably going to be well into the morning," I warn her.

"I don't care. I'll be up."

I nod and agree. She's probably right. This isn't the kind of thing you forget about and fall blissfully asleep.

There's a line of traffic waiting to get into the parking

lot when we pull up near the school. I recognize a few of the cars as my teammates', and I also recognize some of their parents behind the wheels.

One of Reed's assistant coaches finally gets the gate open, and the vehicles file into the lot. I park a few spots away from Reed and wait in my truck for a moment so it doesn't look like I'm walking in with him. Given the climate that led to this, the last thing we need is to show up together.

I spot Whiskey after about a minute, so with Reed already heading toward the home stands, I jog over to give my friend some words of my own. I'm not sure how he got here, given his car is probably totaled.

"What the hell, man!"

Whiskey turns around to face me when I shout at him. There's dried blood on his nose and visible bruising under one eye. I step up so our chests touch and breathe hard through my nose, my molars grinding together.

"I fucked up, man. I know it. I fucked up. I let him get to me, and I just—"

I push his chest, somehow moving this massive man back a step. He lets me because if he wanted to, he could flatten me on my ass. It's how I know he's reached regret.

"Fuck, Whisk," I mutter, pinching the bridge of my nose and pacing a few steps ahead of him before spinning around again.

"Are you sober?" *Please at least be sober.*

He nods.

"We started messaging about racing the minute I left

the locker room. I never even made it to the party. Nobody did. Shit, Anthony has a truckload of beer ain't nobody drank."

I hold his stare for a beat, then urge him to walk with me again.

"Good. No more partying this season. If we still have one," I mutter, just loud enough to perk his ears.

"Fuck, Wyatt. I'm sorry."

I nod as we walk and finally utter, "I know."

Bryce is sitting in the front row when Whiskey and I step up, and I make sure he feels the heat coming off my glare. His hands stuffed in his pockets and hoodie pulled over his head, his lip snarls as he leans forward and spits on the footing in front of him.

"Come on," I say to Whiskey, nudging him to keep moving with me to the other end.

It takes about ten minutes for everyone to pile onto the bleachers, nearly two teams' worth of us packed in tight in the cold air. The lights were shut off hours ago, but Reed had his grounds crew guy turn one on. It makes the world seem dim, which is fitting. Because right now? It is.

Coach Watts steps up after a few minutes and shakes Reed's hand before walking over to stand in front of Whiskey and me. Our eyes meet for a breath, and all I can do is grimace and shake my head. Surely, he knows I wasn't involved in this after that talk in his office; after he suggested I cool things off with Peyton.

There are a few guys not here, mostly the younger players and the ones who don't really get into the after-game scene. *The smart ones.* They might just be all that's left when this meeting is done. Football in this town might be done.

Reed leans his back against the railing and crosses his arms over his chest, his black polo shirt pulled tight across his muscled torso. His forehead wrinkles are heavier than normal, and I bet if we were in a silent room we'd all be able to hear his teeth grinding. His posture manages to quiet everyone, and after a few long seconds of nobody saying a word, his head pops up and his gaze lands right on his prized quarterback.

"Standing out here at two in the fucking morning is not something I ever expected I'd be doing, I've gotta tell you," he says, an irritated chuckle sliding out.

"Never expected to be standing in front of you gentlemen with this much disappointment in my heart. And I mean that for all of you. Both schools. Because I know most of you well. I know your families. I've watched you grow up. I coached most of you at some point. And I gotta say, standing up here right now and looking many of your parents in the eyes, I'm pretty sure my disappointment is shared with them. Racing? In a river bottom?"

His head falls back and he stares at the sky, his Adam's apple bobbing as he swallows down anger.

"I know not everyone here was directly involved. Believe me, I know *everything*." His gaze moves to Whiskey, and my friend drops his chin to his chest and wrings his hands together. At least this speech is getting through to someone.

"I don't know what to do. I knew this season would be hard. I knew there would be bumps in the road. Some hurt feelings. And a lot of the usual bullshit that comes with good, clean competition. But boys, you've taken things way past shit talking. You're flirting with getting someone killed with what you're doing. Makes me want to quit. Makes me want to sell my home and move my family out of this place I love. Makes me ashamed.

"I don't want to feel ashamed. I'm proud of this town, of where I came from. I don't care what color your jersey is, we're all Coolidge. This place means something in our world. When you're in football circles and you tell folks this is where you play, this is where you come from? Ears perk up, boys. Coaches write down names. Colleges open up checkbooks and start doling out scholarships. And that . . . *that* is what this should be about. That's winning at life.

"Getting butt-hurt because someone broke a record you wanted? That's childish."

Most of our eyes are on Bryce at this point, and my stomach clenches with a touch of sympathy for the guy, though I doubt he deserves it. Reed isn't pulling any punches. He's laying this on him, and it should only be on him.

"We need to do better," I say, standing up with my words and meeting Reed's wide eyes. I glance to my coach, and he nods, urging me to keep going.

I step up on the first-row bench and scan the stands. There are at least a hundred and fifty people out here, half of them the parents who look exhausted and sad. The other half? Fuming.

"I know you said we aren't all involved, Coach, but I have to disagree," I say. I glance down at Whiskey, his neck craned as he looks up at me.

"We're a team. Two teams, but like Coach said, one town. We should be holding each other accountable. I take full responsibility for not speaking up sooner, for not making it clear the standard I set for myself and expect of you guys. And Bryce . . ."

I stare at him, waiting for him to lift his head and meet my eyes, but his stare remains fixed straight ahead. Still posturing, putting up his tough-guy front. I don't know how to help him.

"You gotta do better, too. You're a hell of a quarterback, dude."

"Yeah, I am," he mutters, his words just loud enough that I mostly make them out. If anything, I get the gist.

I hop down from the bleacher and walk over to him, and a few players shift, some starting to get up. I hold out my palm to urge them to relax. I'm not going in to start something. I'm trying to lead.

Stepping into his sightline, I leave him with no choice but to look me in the eyes. He sits up tall and rolls his shoulders back, his lips pursed and his head tilted with disrespect. It's fine. I don't need his respect. I need to give him mine where I can.

"You are," I repeat.

He blinks, but his posture remains stiff.

"Fuck, dude. When I found out we were moving out here and I'd be facing off with you at some point, I got excited. Like, heart pounding, lightning running through my legs, can't sleep, night-before-Christmas excited. You know why?"

He tips his chin, barely.

"Because facing you will make me better. Holding myself up to you puts my goals in focus. It's like a barometer for how hard I'm working, where I need to improve to get where I wanna be. Where I know you want to be."

He shrugs and his eyes flutter as if my words are no big deal, but I know he's glowing a little inside. Bryce soaks up compliments like a hungry kid with a cookie jar. He should have a tummy ache with everything I just said.

"I can't wait to play you Friday. Assuming . . . we still have a game next Friday?" I turn to meet Reed's eyes.

"Working on it. Some of you are going to get tickets for tonight. And some of your parents might think it's time for you to quit the team and focus on learning how to be a man. At least one of you is getting a job on my ranch where you will be shoveling shit for my wife until you leave for college next year. And you won't complain a lick. Because you are going to pay your mom back for the insurance claim she's going to need to file for wrapping her damn car around a saguaro, am I clear?"

"Yes, Coach," Whiskey says, his voice bold and loud. His eyes are heavy with regret, his mouth a hard line. And as much as I want to kick his ass for all of this, I'm proud of him for owning his mistake.

"I heard Coach Johnson say something about running bleachers tonight. And I think that's a good idea. I think we all should. Every last one of us. I mean, not you, Mrs. Olsen. Or you, Mr. Hampton. But us. I'm holding myself accountable starting right now. Starting right now, everything I do will have purpose. And I expect the same of my teammates."

My gaze lingers on Bryce for a few seconds, but when it's clear he's not going to soften in front of others and give in to me, I move back to Whiskey and hold out my hand. He grasps mine as I pull him to stand with me.

"You ready?" My head leans to the right, to empty rows behind me that are about to be pounded with feet for at least an hour.

"Yeah, I'm ready," he says.

Whiskey and I are the first to take the bleachers a row at a time. It's a steady pace, nothing fast but not lazy. I wish I were dressed differently, not in the jeans I put on after the game and headed to Peyton's house. But it is what it is, and if I want to really make a difference tonight, I have to see this through.

By the time Whiskey and I are heading back down the fifty or so rows, more players have joined us. Bryce finally starts his jog after my second full trip. The thunder of shoes stomping up and down is almost deafening. Both Reed and Coach Watts have moved the parents together on the other end to talk through whatever is going to happen next.

I meant what I said. I'm looking forward to next Friday. And I hope like hell we get to have our game. All of this rivalry stuff is pointless anywhere but the field. That's where I'll make my statement. Bryce can show up or shut up. But I sure as hell hope he shows. Because if we do it right, this game is going to be one for the ages. The tone-setter for every future town rivalry game to come. We get one shot. And I know how I want Vista to be talked about over ice cream at the kitchen table.

Chapter Twenty-Five

Peyton

The sun is cresting over the San Tan mountains to the east, the sky that soft shade of purplish pink that announces morning has arrived.

When my dad didn't come home for several hours, I figured there was a reason Wyatt hadn't called or texted yet either, so I drove here to wait for him. I spoke to his mom as she rolled in from the night shift about an hour ago and filled her in on most of the drama. Naturally, none of it surprised her. She's been around the high school football scene long enough to get the politics and the stupid choices often made by players and coaches alike. I think what put her at ease was that her son was the one trying to fix things.

"Just like his dad," she said before hugging me in the middle of her driveway.

She invited me inside, but I said I wanted to wait here. I need to see his truck head toward me; to get the first glimpse that whatever needed to happen last night is done.

I've been waiting for hours, and his mom has been sleeping inside, catching up before another night shift. I couldn't help but recall the word her son used to describe her when we first met—*resilient*.

Wyatt's headlights finally appear just as the pink in the sky is getting brighter. I step out of my Jeep and wait for him in his driveway, and when he parks and practically tumbles out of his truck, I wrap my arms around him and hold up his weight.

"Rough night?" I ask, a whisper of a laugh at his ear.

His chin tucks into my neck as he nods and chuckles softly.

"Yeah, but it was necessary," he hums.

I rub my palms up his back, his shirt damp and cold from sweat.

"Let's get you inside."

We walk toward his house, my arm around his back, his over my shoulder, keeping me close. He punches in a code on the garage to open the door and we slip inside quietly, shutting it behind us.

"I saw your mom. We talked," I tell him. He nods, his gaze flitting to mine as we quietly make our way down the hall toward his room.

"Was she angry?" he asks once inside his room.

I shake my head and lean against the door jamb as he pushes his shoes off with his toes.

"Not even close." He lifts his head to meet my eyes, his brow drawn in a hint with perhaps concern or confusion.

I step toward him and help lift his shirt up over his

head. My fingertips paint down the center of his chest and I press my palm over his heart.

"She was proud of you," I say, moving my hand back up to his jawline. "She said your dad would be, too."

His slow blink is followed by a soft sniffle before he runs the butt of his palm under his eyes.

"Thank you for talking to her," he utters.

I nod, reaching up to smooth back his wild hair.

"You need a shower," I say with a smirk.

He drops his chin and squints his eyes closed as he smiles.

"That bad?" He cracks one eye open.

"Worse," I joke. Sort of.

Wyatt steps forward, and I take one back, maintaining the few inches between us as he shuffles us from his bedroom, through the hallway, and into his bathroom across the way.

"Your mom is home," I whisper.

"And she's asleep all the way over there," he says, leaning his head to the side as our eyes meet.

I bite my bottom lip, and he pushes the door closed behind him.

"Plus, this thing locks," he says, the soft click filling me with a little more courage.

My ass against the sink counter, Wyatt moves into me, his hands reaching for the bottom of the Bills sweatshirt I've come to love. He begins to pull it up my stomach, and I help him along the way, pulling it over my head and tossing it by the sink. His hands fall to the countertop on either side of me, caging me, as his mouth drops to my neck. His kiss is hot against my skin, and as his right hand glides up my arm and over my shoulder to my bra strap, I drop my hands to the button and zipper for his jeans.

He slips the strap over my shoulder as I push his jeans down his hips, and my hand sinks into his boxers. He reaches behind me to unclasp the white lace demi-cup bra so it can fall between us.

My hand finds him hard, and I grasp his length, stroking him slowly as he sinks his teeth into my shoulder to muffle his growl. His hands slide to my hips, hooking into the band of my sweats and panties, pushing them down my body. He moves back and steps out of his jeans and boxers before turning to the glass shower door. Once inside, he turns the water on and turns to face me as the water cascades down his hard chest and flattens his hair over his eyes. He pushes it back, his gaze no longer as tired as it is hungry, and he bends his finger, urging me under the water with him.

I step through the door and latch it behind me before holding out a palm to feel the water's temperature. It's still cool, but it's warming quickly—as am I. Wyatt gently tugs my wrist, drawing me into him, and once I'm in his arms, he slides his palm up my spine and into my hair as his mouth covers mine.

The water rains down on us as our fingers roam each other's curves. His hard-on is hot against my thigh, and a few times I move to let it slide between my legs. Each time his tip grazes along my swollen skin, I nearly come undone.

Wyatt must sense it because eventually his hand trails down my stomach and between my legs where he sinks a finger inside.

My face rests against his chest, my mouth open as the water cascades over my face. I take his cock in my hand and stroke him long and slow, running my thumb gently over the tip when I feel him swell under my touch. We touch each other with heat and urgency, stealing kisses between breaths as our hands work one another until I'm grinding against his palm with shudders as he comes against my thigh.

His hand remains between my legs, even after I let go of him, and he turns me so my back is against his body while he continues to kiss my neck. He rubs me in small circles, bringing me to the brink again, and when my knees threaten to give out, he holds me tighter against his body, his other hand clutching my breast while I endure wave after wave.

Finally, my head slung forward, he removes his hand from my lower body and urges me to face him again. He pours a small dab of body wash into his palm to lather my body while I stare at his beautiful face. His dark lashes blink as they are flecked with small droplets of water, and his full lips rest in this barely there smile that looks both guilty and satisfied. Unable to resist, I step up on my toes and cup his face in my palms, forcing him to blink his eyes open on mine.

"Give me some of that," I say, glancing to the body wash on the shelf. "You need it more than I do."

His lip curls on one side as he tries to hold in his laughter, and he hands me the soap. I pour a generous amount into my palm and glide my hands over the ridges along his stomach and chest, then up his neck and into his hair. Touching him like this somehow feels more intimate.

The water cools, so Wyatt twists it off and opens the glass door to snag a towel from the nearby hook. He holds it out for me, wrapping it around my torso as I step onto the soft blue rug in the middle of the bathroom. He wraps a second towel around himself before gathering up our discarded clothes and unlocking the door. He scans the hallway before ushering me back into his room, dressing me back in my clothes and kissing my lips raw before forcing himself to get ready to head to Vista to watch film.

Chapter Twenty-Six

Peyton

Football is my life. It's been my life from the moment I was born. I expect it will be a part of my life for the foreseeable future.

Of course, cheering in college means I'll be bound to football in an auxiliary sort of way; it's always in the background of this sport I love. Stunts and tumbling. Choreography with strength. A sense of team that I can call my own. But maybe I care about the game a little more than I used to. Perhaps there's something else I love about it, beyond just a setting for me to cheer.

I think I love the boy. And nobody is more surprised by that than I am.

The air is thick with the scent of grilled turkey legs, kettle corn, hot dogs, and sugar. It's a fall Friday night in Coolidge, Arizona, and this stadium was built for this. I've been shaking my hands with glittery blue poms for the last hour as the marching band plays the fight song on constant repeat. My cheeks hurt from smiling. I'm pretty sure the entire town shut down for this game. And the news trucks parked behind the south end zone lead me to believe there are people from outside our boundaries here tonight, too.

"You ready?" I say to my dad as he passes behind our cheer line. We've greeted every guest on their way into the stadium, Vista Mustang and Coolidge Bear fan alike.

"Born ready, sweetheart," he says, kissing my cheek as I jut it toward him.

My father jogs toward the locker room while I continue the stomping and spinning, pom poms glittering at my sides to the rhythm of the drumline.

"One more time," our drum major shouts, his finger spinning in the air to repeat the fight song again.

"Jesus," Tasha mutters at my side.

I laugh, but as painful as the smile on my face is, I can't help it. I'm happy to be here. To have this. Because, unlike my best friends, I know how close it all was to falling apart.

There are some things I can't talk about outside the family—football business I'm privy to—though I told Wyatt everything. Some of the shadiness that happens behind the scenes makes me uncomfortable because there are always politics involved. If we were in the Valley, part of a bigger school system, or in a big city, both of our seasons would have been wiped away this week. We'd maybe have gotten to play this game, but most of the players would have been suspended. And the game wouldn't have counted for shit.

My dad got the superintendent on his side with a lot of

assurances that things like fires and desert parties would stop. I have my doubts about the partying part. I don't think adults can control that, and given the stories I've heard my father tell—and my grandpa, for that matter—about post-game desert parties out here, that tradition is pretty entrenched.

This is our time to be young and stupid, as my mom always says. Just maybe a touch less stupid.

Moving forward, I think a standard of conduct might have been set that night my dad called everyone to the home stands. Wyatt didn't tell me the details. He said he didn't want me to stress out and called himself a corny optimist. But my dad told me enough. Apparently, Wyatt made a grand speech, and the fact my dad said he was proud of him feels like a miracle. When I tell my dad I've decided to go to Arizona in Tucson, that should enshrine Wyatt in his eyes for a lifetime.

I'm not doing it solely to follow a boy to college. If anything, I like to think Wyatt is going to commit to Arizona for me. Two more D1 offers rolled in for him this week, both impressive schools in the Midwest. Powerhouses. But something about the way this season has unfolded—the way it changed this town and changed me, has tethered me to it—and I want to remain close.

The shrinking time I have left with my grandpa has something to do with it, too. He isn't the healthiest fool on the planet, though he keeps defying odds—and strokes. But I'd miss the ability to drive home after a bad day and sit on the porch with him. There are benefits to living ninety minutes from home. To attending yet another school where the Johnson name carries weight.

I want to learn more from my mom, too, and maybe build on her dream with one of my own. I have no desire to shovel shit as much as she does, but the way she helps families with children on the autism spectrum navigate a complicated system intrigues me. It seems rewarding, yes, but also so damn necessary. That's what I want out of life—to matter beyond myself.

And if a certain boy happens to be in the place where I do that, well . . .

The pre-game clock behind me is now under three minutes. The band wraps the final run-through of the fight song—*for now*—and we all get a short break before locking in for the first high school game I remember actually being nervous for.

"Is it bad that I'm rooting for your boyfriend's team?" Tasha says, her hand on my shoulder as we weave our way through the crowd to make one last stop in the restroom.

As soon as we duck through the ladies' room door, I glance around to make sure we're semi-alone, then lift the bottom of my form-fitted Bears sweater to show off the maroon Vista practice jersey I stole from Wyatt.

"You rebel," Tasha teases.

When the bathroom door opens, I shift quickly and stuff my sweater back into my waistband. It's only a group of younger classmen trying to sneak quick puffs off the same vape pen. I'm about to lecture them when Tasha asks for a hit, too, so instead, I roll my eyes and tell my friend I'll meet her outside.

The thunder of the drumline reverberates off the building and the nearby stands, so I push up on my toes and scan the dark open space between the locker room and the field where the players are piling up. When Tasha comes out, I tug her sleeve and urge her to jog back to the track with me so we can grab our poms and head out to the field. It's all starting to hit me how few of these moments we have left, and while I spent so many games complaining about forming a tunnel for the team to run through, it turns out I'm going to miss it. Sure, they do the same at the university, but that's the thing—it's at a university. The smallness will be gone. The personal touch. The hometown flavor of things that are not quite perfect, which somehow makes everything even more so, like the crooked letters someone painted on the paper spelling out CHS Bears, or the way our cheer squad is uneven in height and numbers, so we can never hold the banner up quite right.

These imperfect perfects. Three more games, then play-offs, and that's it for me. All the more reason to stay close. To come back.

Lexi sits on my shoulders while a younger cheerleader, McKenna, balances on Tasha's, and we help steady the banner as the drumline approaches. Our home stands are overcrowded, fans standing along the fence line and on top of trucks and cars across the street just to get a glimpse of kickoff. Everyone's eyes are on us, and this hand-drawn banner and the team pooling up on the other side about to break through.

But not me. My attention is across the field, on the six-foot-plus dark-haired dream throwing passes along the sideline to keep his arm warm. His helmet by his feet, he barely strides as he slings ball after ball to his assistant coach. His focus is unwavering, and his body is ready for every hurdle and hit coming for him. He promised it was.

Our team bursts through the tunnel, Bryce and a few of the other seniors racing across the field with the large flags spelling out CHS. One of the booster parents takes them over and plants them into the stands near the end of the home bleachers, and my dad jogs along the field behind his team. *How many times has he run that same path? Sure, it's different grass. But the spot is the same.*

Within seconds, the crowd falls silent as our band plays the national anthem and we all face the bright new flag that hangs just to the right of the scoreboard. The flag was a gift from the class the year before, our previous one retired and donated to the local veterans' retirement home where it is on display behind glass.

"I'm nervous," Tasha says, briefly linking our arms.

"I want to vomit," I laugh out. I'm not sure which I'm more anxious over, Wyatt doing well or my dad getting a win. I wish ties were a thing out here. Never have been in this town, though, so I'm going to have to find a way to survive the next two and a half hours.

My poms are up for kickoff, and one of the Vista players manages to run the ball back to the fifty-yard line. I start to jump in place but quickly quiet my heels, not wanting to show my true feelings on the wrong side of the stadium.

Any hope I had for a Vista blowout is dashed within minutes as Wyatt is able to get the ball fifteen yards before running out of downs and our guys force a kick. The play goes on like this for the entire first quarter, the score by the second three to three. Our kickers are the only stars on the field it seems. Well, and both of our defenses, I suppose.

With thirty seconds on the clock before the half, Vista gets the ball back on a fumble, and Wyatt rushes onto the field, putting his helmet on as his team huddles around him. They break fast, and I'm sure I imagine it, but I swear Wyatt looks right at me as he moves into position.

"I love you," I say silently, not wanting to be heard by my friends—by anyone. I just wanted to put it into the universe, to feel how the words felt on my lips. I smile because they felt nice.

"Blue, thirty-three, blue, thirty-three!" Wyatt backs up to take the ball from the shotgun, and it zings into his hands a heartbeat later.

His feet work to find the pocket, the Coolidge offense coming for him like rabid animals out for blood, and eventually, he has to spin out and rush to the sideline. He's able to pick up seven yards and get out of bounds, but now he's left with twenty seconds to make it down the field.

"Let's get some defense, guys," Coach Nelson shouts through her bullhorn, snapping my mind back to reality.

I count down for our cheer, and we begin shouting

words I don't feel in my gut at all. I don't want the defense to succeed. I don't want anyone to "push them back," especially not "*wayyyyy* back." Turns out Wyatt doesn't want that either, finding an open receiver about twenty yards down the field and putting the ball right in his hands. That guy manages to get out of bounds with twelve seconds left. Meanwhile, my body sways side to side, poms banging on my hips then clapping above my head as we lead the crowd into chants of defense. The play goes off behind me, and I crane my neck to see, but there are too many players and fellow cheerleaders in my way. When the Vista band sounds off with their fight song, I know in my gut that Wyatt found a way in, and it's confirmed when the scoreboard clock runs down to zero and the score changes to ten to three.

I rush over to the small bench where we keep our gear and water bottles to get myself a drink. It takes me a few seconds to realize that the Vista band has stopped playing. And when the quiet sweeping across our fans in the stands washes past me, my heart sinks into my gut.

"What's wrong?" I step up on the bench to look out on the field.

Somehow, before I see it, I know. The way my mom always knew when my dad was flat on his back on the field, even when she refused to watch the TV.

Wyatt is surrounded by the training staff, his coach, my dad, and several players. I drop my poms to the ground and sprint from the bench onto the field, pushing through the line of our players who have all taken a knee. My heart is pounding so hard I can feel it in my head as I race toward my dad, Wyatt's mom rushing in from the other side.

"Give him room, guys, give him room," our trainer says. When Wyatt sits up on his own, my body deflates of all strength and energy like a power surge that leaves me utterly deflated. My legs grow numb so I sink down and sit back on my heels while my arms wrap around my stomach.

"Peyt. You have to get out of here." A voice breaks into the steel dome that's shrouded my head.

"Peyt, come on," the voice says, a little clear now.

I shake my head and look up as Tasha tugs under my arms. I glance back to Wyatt, his gaze fuzzy but on my face. His helmet is off and his coach is kneeling next to him, speaking at his side. Wyatt nods as his gaze seems to come even more into focus on me. And then his lip pulls up on one side, and that asshole actually winks.

"Damn you, Wyatt Stone," I mutter, my voice only loud enough that Tasha can hear me. I jog back to our side with her, my cheeks now burning with embarrassment. I can't believe I reacted that way. I've watched Bryce get knocked out cold before, and I stood on the sideline holding hands with my teammates the entire time. Was I worried then? I pretended to be, I suppose. I certainly told myself I was. But I never felt anything like that. The fear. The rush of adrenaline.

The love.

I take some ribbing from a few of the players as we pass through our sideline. I purposely avoid eye contact with Bryce. But I do glance into the stands to the spot where my mom usually sits with my sister. Grandpa gets to sit on the field behind the end zone, but Ellie is too adventurous. She's apt to race out onto the field in the middle of a play just to get to her daddy. Or to get the ball. She's destined for women's rugby, I swear.

My brow lifts high when my eyes meet my mom's, and she rests her hand on her chest, patting it a few times as her way of telling me to relax. I nod and turn my attention to my squad, but the last five minutes have changed me. I watched my mom worry, and I always knew it was hard. I worried, too. My dad getting hurt was scary. But nothing has ever hit me quite like seeing Wyatt not look invincible. Scary as it feels, I never want to miss watching him on the field. Because if there ever comes a day—a play—when he doesn't sit up on his own, I want to be there to help him. Whether I'm supposed to run out on the damn field or not.

Halftime and the second half seem to fly by. Or perhaps I've become a zombie. I know I've cheered. My shoulders still hurt from the spot where Lexy climbed to a stand on them. And my throat is hoarse from screaming for the last hour. Still, I would swear that Wyatt was on his back only a second ago.

The game ends with a Coolidge win, twenty to seventeen, thanks to one hell of a field goal from our kicker. Vista scored two touchdowns, both taken in by Wyatt, which means he's now erased another of my father's records. That feat won't be celebrated out loud on this field, but my dad knew it was coming. And Grandpa made sure to lay in extra ice cream for a celebration later tonight. As proud as Grandpa Buck is of my dad, I think he also enjoys ribbing him about getting old.

Knowing my dad will be in his office for the next hour or two rehashing every play—each weakness and opportunity missed—with his staff, I send him a text to let him know we'll save him some ice cream, then wander to the opposite end of the parking lot where the Vista players are slowly making their way to their bus from the away locker room.

"Hey, doc!" Whiskey says as he walks across the small grass hill and onto the pavement, coming toward me.

"Nice game, Jack Olsen," I say, rubbing in his real name because I can. "Why am I doc?"

He swallows me in a sweaty hug and laughs.

"I figured you were one now, or an EMT or something. You know, the way you sprinted out there to give Wyatt mouth-to-mouth."

I shove him in the center of his chest and he laughs out the last few words.

"Really, though. It was sweet. You two are sweet. I like him for you."

"Thanks," I say through a crooked grin, my eyes dimmed a hint. "Not that I need your stamp of approval, but I'll take it."

"Hey, if you see Bryce, tell him I said he played a good game. I'd like us to be okay. Not friends or nothin'. Probably never friends. But okay. You know. Civil and shit," Whiskey says.

I nod, but we both know I probably won't be talking to Bryce anytime soon if I can help it.

"I'm gone for like five minutes, and look at that, Mr. Smooth Moves tries to horn in on my girl," Wyatt's voice utters behind me.

I flip around and land with my hands on his chest. He clutches them around the wrists and looks at Whiskey over my shoulder.

"Just keeping her warm for you, son," Whiskey says.

"Eww! He was not," I say, shooting a scowl at him over my shoulder.

Whiskey chuckles as he leaves us alone and climbs onto the bus. I step up on Wyatt's feet and let him walk me backward a few steps away from the bus entrance, though to not nearly as private a place as I'd like.

"You know, I'm going to get the wind knocked out of me sometimes," he says, his annoying smirk also adorable. The damn dimple helps.

"I know," I say, dropping my forehead into his chest. He wraps his arms around my head and kisses the top of it.

"It's okay. It was sweet."

I shift so my chin is in his chest and I'm looking up into his eyes. I squint so one of mine is smaller than the other.

"Was it? Sweet, I mean?"

He nods, then drops his mouth down to mine for a chaste kiss.

"I guess I'll need to get used to seeing that stuff," I

continue, my mouth brushing against his as I talk with our mouths close.

"Oh, yeah?" he utters against me.

"*Mmm hmm,*" I say, nipping at his bottom lip before pulling back enough to gaze at him again. "Since I'll be on your sideline next year. And the year after. And—"

"What? For real?" His hands move to my face, palms on my cheeks as he looks at me with wide eyes.

I giggle and nod.

"I maybe decided to go to Arizona. But it's not for you. It's for me," I say, as he's already swinging me in circles and holding me to his chest.

"Yeah, yeah. I don't care. You're going? To U of A?"

I nod and laugh.

"Damn, if only we had won, this would be the best day of my life!" He sets my feet back on the ground and kisses me so hard that our lips smack when we part.

"But it's for me. Because I want to be there," I reiterate, not wanting to add layers of pressure on what I already know is hard. Taking a relationship from high school to college comes with challenges. I never want either of us giving up parts of ourselves just to fit the other. I think it's why we work so well. We are strong on our own. And because of that, we can be strong for each other.

"So, not even a tiny bit?" He holds up pinched fingers and squints. I push his thumb and index finger closer together.

"Maybe that much for you," I joke.

He widens the gap and I quickly shrink it again.

"I mean, of course I love you and all, though," I let slip out, and my heart stops as I realize those words were out loud.

My wide eyes are glued to the pinched fingers Wyatt is still holding up in front of my face, and I blink, wondering if I broke him with that confession. He's not moving. A quick glance at his chest doesn't seem to show any signs of breath. I pull his finger and thumb apart more, then look up at him, his eyes on mine, waiting. The grin on his face stretches from ear to ear, and my pulse rockets in my body.

"You love me that much?" he asks.

I glance at his finger and thumb again, then back to his face.

"Eh, that might not be to scale," I tease, my voice wavering with nerves.

He moves his hands back to my face and rests his forehead against mine, the tips of our noses touching as his lashes kiss the ends of mine.

"I love you more, Peyton Johnson. So much fucking more." His mouth crashes over mine before I can take a breath, and his kiss nearly leaves me faint.

When the bus honks, we both jump and look up, spotting a laughing Whiskey in the driver's seat. It takes about fifteen seconds for the actual driver to climb on board and shoo him away.

But it's obvious that other than the coaching staff, Wyatt is the only one not on board.

"So, I can expect you in an hour for ice cream?" I remind him as our hands slip apart. He takes the first step.

"Forty-five minutes, tops," he says, his grin still etched on his face.

The Vista coaches have made it to the parking lot and are headed toward me, so I let Wyatt climb the rest of the way up the steps and walk along the side of his bus, ignoring the smooching sounds Whiskey and a few of his other teammates make through open windows. He takes a seat near the back and pushes his window open, resting his arms on the edge so he can peer down at me.

"Hey, so do I get to call you Bub now?" I ask, harkening back to when we met that older man Terry in the hot tub.

Wyatt's gaze lingers on me for several seconds, a knowing smirk playing at his lips when he finally utters, "Depends."

"On what?" I shout back, the sudden rumble of the bus making it hard for either of us to hear.

Wyatt's smile still firmly in place, his eyes dazzle against the football lights.

"You'll see," he says, winking and falling back into his seat and out of my clear view.

I squint at his window, my lips puckered with fake frustration and, somehow, even more love. I walk away, repeating his words under my breath—*you'll see*—and wondering what they mean. He can be so cryptic.

When I reach my Jeep, I gaze across the grass hill to the propped-open home locker room door. My mom is kissing my dad good-bye for the night as my sister tugs at the back of my mom's shirt. They laugh, I assume about how hard it is to do something as simple as kiss each other sometimes, and I'm suddenly hit with a glimpse of my future.

"I'll see," I say to myself as I climb into the Jeep and stare at the taillights of Wyatt's bus as it pulls away. My mouth hangs open, a smile teasing the corners as I let myself imagine. As scary as the thought is of a future far from now—one where I'm in my mom's shoes, Wyatt in my dad's—it's also strangely comforting. It makes me hopeful. Happy.

And whether it comes true, well, I guess I'll just have to wait and see.

Epilogue

Wyatt

Peyton has been a good sport today. I know it stung a little not being the one to ride the one-mile stretch down Main Street for the Fall Festival. But she's been rocking the fundraising part to the point that she's blown past being named royalty. She's a tycoon.

"What's the grand total so far?" I ask her as she takes the towel from my hands on her way out of the dunk tank. Every cheer member did fifteen minutes in the hotseat, and last I checked, they were up to six grand. Peyton had a hell of a line waiting to send her to the cold water. She even let Bryce pay for a round but charged him double.

It took every ounce of self-control in my body to sit back and let him throw at the target like that. Unlike the rest of her customers, she didn't even have to heckle him to get him going. He's still working through his bruised ego. At least my girl got forty bucks out of him.

"Tash, where are we at after my turn?" Peyton steps

behind her friend as she counts cash, then adds the newest round of bills to a deposit bag and tally spreadsheet.

"Sixty-eight hundred. You pulled in eight on your own. Damn, girl. People love to hate on you!"

They high five, but when Tasha goes back to managing the booth, I make sure to square Peyton's shoulders with mine and look her in the eyes.

"Nobody hates you," I say, not wanting anything negative to ever tear her down.

Her head tilts to the side and she glances up through her batting lashes.

"*Pshh*, I know. I'm awesome," she says, laughing before finishing her brag.

She glances over my shoulder, her smile falling a tad. Bryce is lifting another Coolidge cheerleader over his shoulder and carrying her to the Ferris wheel.

"Is that hard to see?" I ask, that jealous itch in my belly needing a scratch. I look back to Peyton. She shrugs.

"Not at all. I'm just not sure who I feel worse for in that duo—Stephanie or Bryce. Maybe they deserve each other."

I nudge her chin toward me and tickle her lips with mine, closing my eyes as I hum.

"I don't deserve you," I say.

She lifts up on her toes and deepens the kiss, suckling on my bottom lip, which is maybe my favorite thing in the world.

"You don't just deserve me, you're stuck with me," she says, falling back on her heels and patting the center of my chest. "So, are you going to suck it up and come to my homecoming with me next weekend or not?" She gives me a coy look, but I decided the second she told me she got permission from the school for me to attend that there was zero chance I'd miss out on being her plus-one. Apparently, Coolidge homecoming is a big deal. And it's in her family's barn. I don't think I could avoid the event if I wanted to.

"I am. But I should probably ask your dad's permission. You know, sort of a classic gentleman move."

She smirks, and I tilt my head and suck in my lips, curious—and very cautious.

"That look means something," I say.

"No, it doesn't. Oh, and are you going to donate to our booth? You promised." She holds out a flat open palm.

My head falls back as I chuckle and reach for my wallet.

"Ah, I see. This is all to get twenty bucks out of me," I joke.

She rips the bill from my fingers as soon as it's out of my wallet and immediately hands it to Tasha at the booth behind her.

"Thank you very much, Mr. Stone. Here are your three softballs, and *there*"—she spins me around to face my idol, now perched on the dunk tank hot seat—"Is your chance to ask my dad for permission."

"That was not nice, Peyton," I laugh out.

"What's this I hear about homecoming?" her dad shouts at me, clearly in on it.

"Uh," I stammer.

"What's wrong, big fancy record-breaker? Cat got your

tongue?" Reed is piling it on, and his voice booms so there's now a bit of a crowd. Coach Watts has even stepped up behind me to throw his weight in my corner.

"Don't fuck this up, Stone," he taunts. *Okay, so maybe not quite in my corner.*

I toss the ball in my hand a few times, then let it fly at the target, missing by a few inches. Reed's laugh breaks through the area like a sharp thunder roll. Soon, others are laughing with him. This is fun for him; I can tell. And I get it. I'm the young punk who broke his records. And I'm in love with his daughter. But I'm gonna hit that target with one of these.

"Guess my accuracy record isn't in trouble," he barks out.

I scowl jokingly.

"That's not even a thing," I yell, letting the next ball rip. It misses but comes closer.

"Good thing, because you'd never make the list!"

Shit. Now I really want to dunk him. But I'm also still a little afraid of him. And literally half the town is here watching. I glance up and catch the Ferris wheel cart that Bryce is in, and it's hard to tell from here, but I'm pretty sure he's watching too. I bet if it weren't so loud out here with music and the crowd, I could hear him razzing me from up above.

"Come on, Wyatt. You wanna take me to hoco, don't you?" Peyton says at my ear, her teasing voice definitely not appropriate for her father to hear. I swallow hard and block out the distractions, my focus on the black and white target about thirty feet away.

"All I'm saying is I would have done it on the first toss. So maybe you're not the hotshot they say you are," Reed says, and before he can finish his taunt, I sail the ball at the target, nailing it dead center and sending him plummeting into the frigid tank.

"Yes!" Peyton shouts, rushing at me and leaping into my arms, her legs wrapping around my waist as her wet hair chills my cheeks and neck. She kisses me as I swing her around, and when I put her back on the ground, she rushes to her dad with a towel. He's climbed out of the booth.

"Did you seriously get in that thing just to harass me?"

He chuckles and runs the towel over his head, his CHS coaching shirt glued to his body. Dude looks like Jack Reacher.

He walks past me, still laughing, and his massive hand slaps me on the back twice.

"I sure did, kid. I sure did."

I turn slowly as he walks over to a picnic table where Nolan is waiting for him with a dry shirt. She holds up a hand in a wave, her smirk matching the same one her daughter flashes.

"You were all in on that, weren't you?" I piece it together as the words leave my mouth.

"Maybe," Peyton hums, circling her arms around my waist and resting her head on my chest. "Welcome to the family, Wyatt Stone."

I keep my eyes on her parents and baby sister while I bend my head down and to the side to kiss the top of her head. I manage to keep my breath steady, but I don't know what my heart is doing. I don't want to freak her out with how much her words just hit me, and I definitely don't want to cry in public right now with so many eyes on me. But that one word—*family*—is big. It's maybe even bigger than love. Or maybe it *is* love. My tiny family has had a really hard year, though. And the fact hers just opened their arms—that Peyton gifted this to me—means more than any stupid record in the books. It's everything. And so is she.

Second Epilogue

Peyton

The campus feels even bigger now that I'm grown. I've been coming to games at this university for most of my life. My dad has had so many alumni events here, been honored on the field during halftimes, and spoken to the sports management program students for graduations.

Of course, he's never carried a plastic bin full of fuzzy blankets up three sets of stairs. A first time for everything, I suppose.

"You know they have rooms on the first floor," he gripes. He's secretly loving this, and I know it. He's gushed about how proud he is that I'm now a Wildcat no less than a hundred times since I made the decision.

"Yeah, but Wyatt's room is on the first floor. I thought—"

"Never mind. I love stairs. All the stairs. In fact, let's get you moved to the roof. Or across campus. Or, how about you commute?" He's kidding. Sort of.

"You could also try the elevator," I tease. He waves me off, though, probably because he can't stand waiting in lines and the line for the elevator is pretty chaotic.

My mom and sister are busy loading my clothes into my closet as my dad and I walk in with the final load from the car. My mom keeps hugging every sweater, T-shirt, and dress she pulls out of the garment bag. Ellie keeps trying my clothes on.

"Need any help here?"

Wyatt knocks on the open door as he enters, and my dad instantly scowls at his feet. I think he's steamed at the fact he walked in so easily.

"He's not a vampire, Dad," I say.

"Hmm, so you think," my dad grumbles.

My dad turns his attention to setting up the loft system for my bed as Wyatt and I make eyes at one another. I move into him, my hands finding their favorite place along his sides, my cheek flattening over his heart.

"He loves you," I say.

"You keep saying that," Wyatt says with a soft, playful laugh.

Truth is, my dad truly does. He's even come to terms with losing all of his records to Wyatt, as well as the playoff game that sent Vista into the state championship game—which they ultimately won.

"Hey, Wy? Give me a hand." My dad waves Wyatt over, and I step back to watch them hold up my bed frame, aligning the brackets for my loft so I can somehow turn a ten-by-ten space into something bigger.

Tasha is in the adjoining room, which makes my mom nervous. Between her and Wyatt living in the same structure as me for the next several months, I won't be surprised if my parents up and buy property by campus just to pop in randomly and regularly.

I am looking forward to this little dose of freedom. It's such a huge step. Grown-up practice. Semi-adulting. I know that things are going to be a challenge for Wyatt and me, too. He'll have practice. I'll have practice. But every Saturday in the fall, and a few random Friday nights, we will be together under the lights. That connection has only grown stronger.

The rivalry between him and Bryce has grown stronger too. A part of me wonders if Bryce committed to Arizona State just to fuel things. Maybe he needs the co-dependent relationship of having me and Wyatt close by, but at his nemesis school. It gives him something to hate, and for whatever reason, Bryce is at his best on the field when he is filled with jealousy and rage.

My mom noticed it toward the end of the season. My dad did too. And we're all a little worried that he's going to burn out by going so hard and fast. He got hurt in our playoff game, trying to do it all himself. One major concussion took him out right after halftime. Head injuries are something this family takes seriously, and my dad forced Bryce to watch the video of the play that got him hurt over and over until he admitted to dropping his head and driving for a touchdown. I fear Bryce thinks it was worth it, though. I know I shouldn't worry about him. But I do. It would be cold of me not to.

But I don't love him. And now that I know what real love is, I'm certain I never really did. I liked the attention. The status. When it was good. But so often, it wasn't. He had the power to make me feel so small. I never want to feel that way again, to give someone that power again. And I don't think Wyatt is capable of doing anything but lifting me up.

"There. All done," my dad proclaims, slapping his palm on top of the mattress, which is now lifted several feet above my desk.

"Uh," I stammer. My mom looks on from the closet and echoes me.

"What?" My dad's brow pulls in as Wyatt steps back and checks things out from my view.

"Oh, yeah. We built a slide," Wyatt jokes.

I grimace but move into my dad and hug him anyway for helping. My bed is about six inches higher at the top, and my dad tries to convince us all that he did it on purpose so Wyatt won't ever be comfortable in it or will slide right out. But I think my dad is simply distracted by the fact this change—his little girl going to college—is happening.

He and I got close when I was in high school because he was finally home. He won't say it out loud, but I think a part of him feels like he missed out on daddy-daughter time because of the game. I don't see it that way, though.

This game . . . it's defined his lifetime. Grandpa's lifetime.

It's ours.

Mine.

And it's the glue for my most important relationships.

Including the one with the boy with dark blue eyes, who's staring at me right now.

Our game is just getting started.

THE END

GO BACK TO THE VERY BEGINNING

Waiting on the Sidelines was my very first book, and it will always be incredibly special to me. If you haven't experienced the lifelong journey of Nolan and Reed, you can see where this love story began with The Waiting Series.

Find them here: books2read.com/WaitingSeries

Ginger Scott

The boy.
His game.
Her whole entire heart.
Who says high school sweethearts can't be forever?
The Waiting Series follows high school sweethearts Reed
Johnson and Nolan Lennox through football, life, love and
everything messy that goes along with it. The series begins
with Waiting on the Sidelines and Going Long. Book 3,
The Hail Mary, is for more mature readers and deals with
adult themes.

"If you haven't started reading this series yet, I've never
been more adamant about a recommendation than I am
in this moment. This series gives you EVERYTHING."
-- Jessica Sotelo (Angie & Jessica's Dreamy Reads)

If you enjoyed this book, you might also like:

The Varsity Series

A New Adult Sports Romance Series

Begin Your Binge with Varsity Heartbreaker

Lucas Fuller is a lot of things.

He's the boy next door.

He's the first crush I ever had.

He was my first kiss.

He's also the only person who has ever broken my heart.

For two years, I've wondered what happened to the us I used to know.

We were best friends, and then suddenly…we weren't.

I tried to run away from it. I even changed schools just to make the hurt disappear.

But no matter how hard I tried to not think about Lucas, I just couldn't stay away from the high school quarterback with perfect blue eyes and so many secrets.

I'm back. We're seniors now. We've grown—all of us. And Lucas Fuller might be different, but I'm different too.

This is my time to take risks, to experience life and to fall in love for real.

I want Lucas Fuller to be a part of my story, but I know for that to happen, I need to know the truth about our past.

Acknowledgments

Well this book sure was a surprise. For you? Probably. For me? Definitely. I never planned on this. If you've read The Waiting Series, you probably know how deeply special that series is to me. The first two books, in fact, were supposed to be it. And then about seven years after they published, I got this nagging idea that wouldn't leave me alone. Nolan and Reed were married, and they had a daughter. That life needed its story to be told.

Turns out that first daughter of theirs needed her story told too. Peyton's story hit me like a bolt of lightning out of the blue. I was plotting an entirely different series in fact and then *bam!* There it was, a town divided. A new quarterback. A good guy, but a little moody. A story of his own.

These two had to meet.

And I know better than to rule out following these two to college. I probably will because this world—these characters—they will not shut up! I don't have any solid plans, so make sure you follow me in all of the usual spaces or sign up for my newsletter. When the lightning strikes, I'll let you know first. ;-)

Now, to Home Game. I have so many to thank. First and foremost, those readers who found Waiting on The

Sidelines more than a decade ago and lifted it up. You are the reason I kept going, the reason I get to do my dream job, the reason I write. For you. And every reader along the way. Thank you for taking a chance on my books and for sharing your love for them. It means everything to me.

Special thanks to Autumn, Wordsmith Publicity, who has been with me from the near very beginning, and who has never stopped whispering "Peyton" in my ears. Y'all should thank her, too. She's relentless LOL. But seriously, Autumn, what you do for me can't even be put into words. When I feel flat as a pancake you flip me over and remind me what I'm capable of. You champion my work with the ferocity of Bryce Harper in the playoffs. I love you.

Brenda, you are patient, and supportive, and so freaking smart. Thank you for giving me the comfort in knowing that the words I get on the page will be taken care of. Your editing goes beyond. And your support is everything.

Mom, you are the bomb. Period. I say it with every book, and I mean it every time. My mom reads every word I write. She's also a pretty damn good beta and proofreader. She's one hell of a cheerleader. And I bet she'd be a damn good quarterback, too.

And my boys—who answer my random questions as I write, such as, where would people sit on top of the fire truck? I love you so much. You are my life.

This book was such a joy. Being in this world was incredible. I'll be back. Probably sooner rather than later. Hell, I may never leave.

If you enjoyed Home Game, please consider leaving a review. Those little blurbs make all the difference in whether a book is seen or not seen. I'd be forever grateful. Heck, I'll even make you the fall parade queen.

Until next time,

XO,

Ginger

About the Author

Ginger Scott is a *USA Today, Wall Street Journal* and Amazon-bestselling author from Peoria, Arizona. She has also been nominated for the Goodreads Choice and RWA Rita Awards. She is the author of several young and new adult romances, including bestsellers Waiting on the Sidelines, The Hard Count, A Boy Like You, This Is Falling and Wild Reckless.

A sucker for a good romance, Ginger's other passion is sports, and she often blends the two in her stories. When she's not writing, the odds are high that she's somewhere near a baseball diamond, either watching her son swing for the fences or cheering on her favorite baseball team, the Arizona Diamondbacks. Ginger lives in Arizona and is married to her college sweetheart whom she met at ASU (fork 'em, Devils).

FIND GINGER ONLINE: www.littlemisswrite.com

facebook.com/GingerScottAuthor

instagram.com/authorgingerscott

tiktok.com/@authorgingerscott

Also By Ginger Scott

Final Score Series

The Tomboy & The Captain

The Wallflower & The Running Back

The Best Friend & The Short Stop

The Boys of Welles

Loner

Rebel

Habit

The Fuel Series

Shift

Wreck

Burn

The Varsity Series

Varsity Heartbreaker

Varsity Tiebreaker

Varsity Rule breaker

Varsity Captain

The Waiting Series

Waiting on the Sidelines

Going Long

The Hail Mary

The Waiting Series - Next Generation

Home Game

Like Us Duet

A Boy Like You

A Girl Like Me

The Falling Series

This Is Falling

You And Everything After

The Girl I Was Before

In Your Dreams

The Harper Boys

Wild Reckless

Wicked Restless

Standalone Reads

The Moon and Back

Southpaw

Candy Colored Sky

Cowboy Villain Damsel Duel

Drummer Girl

BRED

The Hard Count

Memphis

Hold My Breath

Blindness

How We Deal With Gravity